Ridgway Library District

3 9107 00015 1206

D0583238

OCT 3 1 2013

apostoloff

THE GERMAN LIST

SIBYLLE LEWITSCHAROFF

apostoloff

TRANSLATED BY KATY DERBYSHIRE

LONDON NEW YORK CALCUTTA

This publication was supported by a grant
from the Goethe-Institut India

Seagull Books, 2013

Sibylle Lewitscharoff, *Apostoloff* © Suhrkamp Verlag, Berlin, 2010
English Translation © Katy Derbyshire, 2013

ISBN   978 0 8574 2 088 6

British Library Cataloguing-in-Publication Data
A catalogue record for this book is available from the British Library

Typeset in Arno Pro by Seagull Books, Calcutta, India
Printed and bound by Maple Press, York, Pennsylvania, USA

For Lulin Danailoff

Contents

We came out of it relatively unscathed, I say to my sister. My sister is sitting in the front on the passenger seat and doesn't reply. Only a tiny inclination of her head towards the window indicates that she's understood me. She's used to my opening gambits and knows what I mean.

Gone, finito, The End, I say. A father who puts an end to it all before he wears down the whole family deserves more praise than damnation.

An end—it's as clear as day, surely? Someone's looking for admiration, at the end of the day. The be-all and end-all, dead end, end of story. I try to end the thought with a punch at the headrest, but everything stays hanging in mid-air, and my hand's back on my knee faster than I can lift it. Silly? Oh yes, plenty of things I do are silly, but there's no clever cure for that yet. My sister doesn't hear me or see me at that moment, since she's smiling at Rumen and since the noise of the car swallows up the subtler sounds.

Sometimes speaking to my sister is like talking into the wind. She knows the run-ups from my side, in which our father rarely comes off well, in fact usually comes off badly. We veil our mother in an iron silence. The enchanting thing about my sister is that she doesn't take me seriously and she forgives me everything. She's an exemplary older sister, treating her younger sibling with infinite patience. Although we're middle-aged by now, my sister, with her not quite two years' seniority, thinks she's dealing with an innocent child, my strange quirks giving rise to slight frowns, in good faith that I'll grow out of them.

Rumen Apostoloff is not used to us—his hair stands to attention up to its tips. He is shocked by my speeches and worships my sister. His hearing is excellent; he almost always understands what we're saying. Only when we deliberately slip into our broad Swabian dialect do his linguistic detection skills encounter problems with the soft, slurred sounds.

Rumen is our Hermes. He carries the languages to and fro, drives and finds the way as he's driving. One of those frantic Bulgarian drivers who have no eye for all the things dying wretched deaths by the edge of the road as they flit past. Our nervous devotee, he drives us across his frantic country, which is even more frantic by night.

We can't complain, I say to my sister. We had food on the table, we weren't beaten and we got our long educations paid for, and there was even enough left over in the end for a modest inheritance. What more can you ask?

I find my joylessly sensible words repulsive, prompting me to keep my mouth shut for a while. My sister is often silent anyway, and Rumen doesn't dare get mixed up in a speech set up to continue.

We roll along the well-kept road to Veliko Tarnovo, having just left Sofia behind us. On our left are ailing industrial buildings, hoisting reddish-yellow flags of smoke towards the sky. The entire left side is swathed in a red-and-yellow veil, its particles glinting poisonously in the sunlight. It stinks. There's a long row of trucks in front of us. Rumen Apostoloff adjusts his torso in his seat and grabs the steering wheel with determination, ahead of him the tough business of overtaking, on the backseat a woman he can't tolerate.

The wind rose of patriphobia swirls up many a spark of patriphilia, I say inaudibly to my sister, as we leave behind us the red dust clouds of the Kremikovski metallurgy combine, once a child of Bulgarian–Soviet friendship. We two are children of Bulgarian–German friendship, a friendship just as dubious as the Bulgarian–Soviet affection. A friendship built of lies, iron and tin, of which little remains but scrapped army tanks and piles of corpses, long since putrefied. Our father putrefied under a smaller, separate pile—a late corpse rather than a war corpse.

Let him show himself, that father, if he can!

Nada. The time's not yet ripe to knock out a portrait of our father with delicate blows of the hammer. Kristo—that was his pervasively symbolic name. Not an elastic, benevolent name that helps a boy find his way in the world. What an iron wreath of meanings burdens that cruciferous name. That Kristo-father, not yet our father back then, of course, but only a son, is said to have learnt to write quickly, but it took him a long time, we're told, before he could write his name without pause for thought. As an adult, a doctor, his handwriting was a disgrace, an imposition for every apothecary who had to decipher his prescriptions. His name itself was absolutely illegible. Oh yes, just as with the rest of us, our father's name, too, formed the core of his personality. An absolutely disgraceful personality, I say to my sister, and I think I hear her sighing—no doubt at my talk, at the inscrutable temperaments it follows.

A personality with no voice and no weight, at least for his daughters, should he even crop up in their minds, I say in triumph. But, oh yes, he crops up. He pops up with a whoosh as it pleases him, that zombie of a father!

It's the dreams begun by night and embellished by day in which our father regularly returns to life.

As my sister is persistently silent and Rumen only groans and punches the steering wheel when he believes a full-blown idiot is preventing him from driving at full-blown speed, I'm speaking on my sister's behalf here—although she usually denies that fathers appear in dreams, and denies our disgraceful father's appearance with some persistence.

The night before we flew to Sofia, he was sitting in my room. His presence was as unremarkable as in a Murakami short story, for instance, in which we learn—*Katagiri found a giant frog waiting for him in his apartment.*

I found not an outsized amphibian; only our father. He behaved more discreetly than Murakami's frog, holding his tongue. Why strain his vocal chords? There's nothing for us to talk about. He stood up, slowly, and walked through the wall. Once he had vanished, the end of his noose dragged along the floor until it too gradually vanished. My father usually has his noose with him—that's nothing new by any means.

Our Rumen is a hectic driver. He keeps tearing me away from my thoughts. Every time he overtakes, one instinctively asks oneself—Will he make it or won't he? He has just left a juggernaut behind him, loaded with tree trunks with a red pennant fluttering from the longest log. We got away with it this time.

Rumen Apostoloff wants to show us Bulgaria's treasures. My sister and I know better—these treasures exist only in the Bulgarians' minds. We're convinced Bulgaria is a ghastly country—no, not as dramatic as that: a ridiculous and bad country. Its regions? Sea, forests, mountains, meadows? The country may well have its hidden charms. But we're not ornithologists, and we're not up for bear hunts. We're not interested in the picturesque gorges of the Rhodopes, hammer blows in Rhodopian valleys can't shake us, chiming bells don't invite us into churches. Rose fields are rose fields are rose fields for us and not much else, rose fields don't make our hearts surge. Simply because you point to a blood-red field, we don't start acting like star-crossed lovers, nor does our blood run quicker. There's an art to staying sober. We practise that art adamantly, as soon as we catch a whiff of Bulgarian air, as soon as we take our first careful steps on Bulgarian ground.

And otherwise? Are the Bulgarian choirs something to be sniffed at? *Le Mystère des voix bulgares*, as they put it so classily? Doesn't it sound as if sung from on high in the firmament and echoing down from the mountains? Doesn't it make us ponder when we think of Orpheus, who sang so purely and enchantingly in the Rhodopes, striking his famous lyre, making rocks and trees gather round him, so that all the wild beasts lowered their horns, stags and does fell to their knees in rapture, fur on fur, fur on clothes of the hunted and the hunters lying down together on the soft moss, and peace and integrity abounded among all beings that have ears and in whose chests a heart beats, for all was only listening, a strange kind of listening, an excess of listening with stone hearts feeling and stone ears captivating, a listening not even known by the Bible?

Hmm, we say, that's as may be, but you've forgotten your great-great-great-grandmothers, those slavering maenads, those raucous bitches, vengeful, bloodthirsty and evil. They blew their horns and screeched and made such a racket that Orpheus' song cut no more ice and they could slay the singer. And then the marble-white pieces of his body floated on the Maritsa, Orpheus' head, still singing, floated past beeches and willows, past hazel bushes and poplars, the fair head floating and floating seawards and away. Away from this maleficent land, then still called Thrace. No treasure of intellectual comfort is concealed in your Rhodopes. It's not Orpheus sounding out of your choirs, it's the maenads, or at least their descendants. And that would solve the puzzle of why the larynxes are so unnaturally squashed in Bulgarian choirs.

He sang so beautifully, our good old gynaecologist, sighs the choir of patriphiliacs, all of them former patients who longed to hear their exotic Orpheus singing at the window, at his desk, tapping a fingernail against a hypodermic needle, bent over his medical instruments or elsewhere. Until he finally sang his own death ditty, a dying *kr-kr* graduating into a death rattle, embellished a little by our father's once extremely melodious voice, for as long as the last puff of air in his throat sufficed for embellishment.

Yet his head, oh that fatherly head, was covered in an abundance of black and already noosed into death.

Let's read on, I say, on and away into the Bulgarian mishap that this zombie of a father heaped upon his daughters' heads and hearts. Thank goodness, I don't happen to speak out loud as I usually do but so quietly that Rumen can't possibly hear me, even though I don't know whether he couldn't after all, his security-service hearing being so sharpened that it perceives sounds not yet on the air, still forming as tickles on the tongue.

Rumen, poor Rumen, have we talked about the Bulgarian ceramics yet that you so like to show us? About the peacock-eye decorations, the flowing pattern on all the brown jugs, bowls, plates, ashtrays and coffee cups, once popular souvenirs for holidaymakers from East Germany, now more appreciated by the English? The plates, cups and mugs look clumsy to us. Unpleasantly bulbous children's pottery. Aside from that, the stuff is not recommended for eating from—the burnt-in cobalt blue penetrates the glaze and is poisonous.

And what about the Black Sea coast? The Black Sea coast, that sounds like the plashing of waves, gulls, dunes, beachside cafes, boats bobbing on the tide, the clicking of yacht masts. It sounds rather further away, not in Bulgaria any more—like Ovid? But oh, no. Built up, messed up, silted up. The ash-grey sea—all fished out. Bulgarian cuisine? Sludge drenched in bad oil. The fish? A charred joke. Bulgarian art in the twentieth century? Hideous, without a single exception. The architecture, aside from monasteries, mosques and trading houses from the nineteenth century? A crime!

My sister shakes her head. Not in contradiction— she didn't hear me after all—only to get rid of a mosquito that's flown into her hair and got caught up in it.

As ever, her objection comes at the right moment.

Oh, I know! Secretly, I do know better, but I can't hold myself back. The very word Bulgaria suffices, a stimulus to prompt an attack, and that sweeps away all reason in that very second. Patriphobia and patriophobia are amalgamated and kept stubbornly on the boil. Bulgaria? Father? A snap mechanism. All the individual delicate-minded Bulgarians we've come across are of no use. Barely have I sighted them than I fly towards them with an almost insane euphoria. But the childish bookkeeper within me doesn't assign such people to the Bulgarians. They've settled on nation-free territory, where all my favourites settle.

Whatever Rumen shows us, my sister acknowledges with a sweet smile. I know that smile very well. My sister puts it on when she's bored to tears deep down inside. It's a smile to assure the world of her sweetness, which withholds all comment and takes no interest. The desiccated version of her smile, petrified in sugar. In secret, she too is glad whenever she gets a chance to note how brutish Bulgaria is. I know that very well, although my sister is far too polite, far too cautious to give free rein to her aversion. This ridiculous country proves that it wasn't a valuable father who died on us, only a silly old Bulgarian. We didn't suffer a loss; on the contrary, we were fortunate that his time was too short to infect us with his Bulgarian hocus-pocus. The only difference—my sister locks this thought up inside her and smiles, keeps on smiling, while I wind up Rumen by plucking apart the Bulgarian mishap with my torrent of words.

We've had enough of Bulgaria before we even get to know it properly. Sad but true: we consider the Bulgarian language the most ghastly in the world. Such a wimpish, crudely onward-plopping language, labial firecrackers that don't want to go off. Not a hint of bite in the consonants. Simply to annoy Rumen, I like to use the trick of praising the neighbouring Romanians. How pleasant Romanian sounds to the ear! How darkly heavy and lost to the world. Ah yes, the Romanians had the great advantage that their Slavic dialect pined for the Romance languages. And how attractive they look! Oh yes, they sometimes look like ancient Romans all grown up. And what wonderful black-magical literature they have! Of course, they played host to Ovid, they had significant dissidents and none of them were such toadies to the Soviets as the Bulgarians. The few Bulgarians that weren't were done away with in the quarries at Lovech or the Belene labour camp, that is.

The instant he hears the word Romania from my lips, Rumen pulls a face as if he had a toothache. I suspect he murders me in his dreams night after night, then grabs my sister and drags her off behind a Bulgarian hill.

I've gone too far a few times. Rumen's learnt now how to keep me in check. He perks up when I praise the Romanians. What, the Romanians, civilized? Pah! counters Rumen. Their favourite sport was locking Jews in pigsties and burning them alive. And they regret nothing, nothing at all, your magnificent Romanians, he shouts, his voice trembling with resentment and indignation.

Dusk has drawn in and the traffic thins out. We glide through a sparsely populated area. Do people live here at all, we wonder, having driven through hilly land for a quarter of an hour, and not a single settlement far and wide. Only the gypsies' carts drawn by donkeys and horses, trotting along the edge of the road now and then, reveal that there must be people living somewhere behind the hills, in some kind of thrown-together settlements with shabby shops nailed together provisionally out of boards, if there are any shops at all behind the hills. Nothing to stimulate wanderlust, to revive the fairy tale of the Balkan adventure. Poor old nags, the misery drawn into their coats with a hard pencil, amble along with the whip, their foreheads decorated with red pompoms.

This burdensome dusk is an outpost of the Bulgarian night. By night the Bulgarian mountains sleep like huge black beasts, dots of light only emanating here and there from crumbling houses. Now that he has fewer races to run with trucks, Rumen is slouching, relaxed in his seat, a lit cigarette in the corner of his mouth.

I'm in a better mood today—being chauffeured around does me good. And I'm happy to put up with the backseat, as I prefer to slip my poison in from behind. Aside from that, it would annoy Rumen even more if I were sitting next to him. And he's such a bad driver that it might put us at serious risk.

DO EXCUSE ME, PLEASE

Do excuse me, please, says our father. A surging wave of father floods the car interior, a temperamental grand *jeté* that sends the roof flying off and leaves us driving along in the open air for a moment or two.

He's never before said, do excuse me, please. Never before have we lost him so politely. The ash-pale sky testifies that he's gone. The dubious thing is what kind of a father that just was. I can't remember his voice and nor can my sister. We fail miserably every time we're asked to describe our father's voice. What kind of German did he speak? Good? Clear? With an Austrian accent, because he polished it in Vienna? Was his grammar impeccable? Was his vocabulary large or measly? We don't know at all, even though we ought to—I was eleven and my sister thirteen.

Did he launch right in when he spoke or start hesitantly—we don't know. Did he speak in loops, as if slyly securing himself—we don't know. Did his speech proceed in jerks, was it smooth, was it fast, was it lame—no idea. Did he have that bad habit common to many foreigners of accelerating his speech when he no longer mastered the grammar? And his voice? High, squeaky, throaty or did it come from the barrel of his chest? The choir of patriphiliacs that once surrounded us tries to make us believe our father spoke wonderful German, so wonderful it was pure poetry to listen to. Above all, they had it, he sung so wonderfully it was barely bearable.

We've taken to holding our tongues when we hear that kind of thing. One of the rare cases in which my sister refrains from her famous smile. The choir of patriphiliacs has now thinned out noticeably, thank goodness; there are few ladies left alive who knew our father personally. Now it's up to us to establish who he was. When we were little, leaping about the garden with our pigtails flying, we were watched by strange women who came to the conclusion that we had turned out rather weedier than their magnificent Orpheus, barely worthy of being called his daughters. And now the question bounces back from our lips—is that weed even worthy of being considered our father?

Let's establish that our father was a typical Bulga-rian. A typical Bulgarian is hirsute, has perfect white teeth, eats garlic and grows as old as the hills. Our father's hair was thick and black, though he rarely ate garlic. The typical Bulgarian retains his hair into old age, only going white late. Our father did not pass the age test, however, so we have no precise information on that matter. Only that when a friend cast a last glance at him and stroked his head, hair came away in his hand by the bushel.

Where else was there hair? Left behind on the furniture? Was there fatherly furniture? Motherly furniture?

The furniture dozed on deep pile carpets in shy insubordination. Blue carpet in our parents' bedroom. Lacquered wooden furniture. Eggshell-coloured carpet in the living room. Our father had reserved the little sofa in the balcony room for himself. Whenever he sat on this sofa he felt safe and seemed to get by without the slightest mite of temperament. In essence, he required little cubature for himself. Only a space large enough to fill with his sadness. Sometimes, though, he paced irritatedly across the balcony room, baring his white teeth. He was obviously screwed up deep inside. It was no surprise then that a battery he left lying in the sun, on the table in the balcony room, exploded a few years after his death, spewing its horrible chemical stench over the red sofa.

He maintained only fleeting contact with the people who surrounded him. Focusing on someone once, committing them to memory, was enough—after that it was fine for the rest to be unfocused. He always wore a bonnet of melancholia. He considered his inner darkness incomparable. And the family supported him in that belief—oh, the family satellites held regular brooding contests on the inscrutable darkness of a fatherly, masculine Bulgarian soul, of which the example haunting us was a particularly monstrous specimen. This darkness glowed in the abstruseness and sensitivity of genius. Why on earth, though, did no one look at the man's dull expression and come to the conclusion that he was—no, not the wreck of an artist—a sordid wreck of a doctor?

He did not grow unapproachable and morose over the years like the fathers of most of our school friends. When he fetched his sagging waistcoat out of the wardrobe we knew what would come next. The world around him was extinguished for two months every spring, and we were condemned to extinguish along with it. Creeping past his locked chamber, shy taps at the door, hesitant enquiries as to whether he'd like anything to eat, and no response. If we opened the door a crack, something so musty came wafting out that we quickly closed it again. He lay on his sofa as if putrefied.

We hoped our mother, an athletic woman, a skier, a climber, the owner of an ice pick, would wrench open the door and slap her corpse of a husband resoundingly in the face, either awakening him or sending him off to the grave for good, or at least forcing him out of the terrible waistcoat with the moth hole over his stomach and burning it. Nothing of the sort occurred. We stopped pinning pointless hopes on our mother.

There was no motherly furniture. And what would a woman whose every fibre was aligned to her husband do with furniture of her own? True enough, she did choose which items of furniture from which highly respected manufacturers came into the house, from Schildknecht for instance, 1960s furniture with the nimbus of the upscale and the well made. But she only ever chose it for his sake, to cheer him up, never for herself.

Lacquered wood! A hundred reasons to bash your brains out on a lacquered wooden bookshelf! Lacquered wooden bookshelves, with the works of Uwe Johnson, Max Frisch, James Baldwin and Albert Camus standing in rows like obedient soldiers, summon up destructive instincts. Hand me an axe! Pass me a saw! Tear out the pages! My sister though, such an unswerving sleepwalker, strolls calmly past lacquered wooden bookshelves as if they were the most natural thing in the world, even if they contain closable elements, little doors with waffle weave patterns, little doors with little brass keys, behind which the brandy and its brandy glasses, the whisky and its heavy tumblers lead their discreet lives.

If only our parents had devoured the books of real drinkers—Lowry! Faulkner! Cheever!—they might have taken a detour around Schildknecht and its lacquered wood. But no, if you go looking for unhappiness you're bound to find it sooner rather than later.

Our father remained moderate when it came to alcohol. Being a nocturnal fighter, he didn't need it. As it was, he could hear from the furniture what people don't usually hear, he could smell the desperation. The nightly threats died down by day, but in his head he had cultivated a bed of hearing, planted with sensory apparatus capable of perceiving the finest and most distant vibrations of such threats.

When we speak of finely and finest-tuned hearing, don't we automatically think of angels?

I'm tempted to hold a lecture on angels for my dear fellow travellers. If it weren't so barbarically noisy in the body of this little Daihatsu I'd tell them about the angels closest to God's throne. Their hearing is infallible, it's said. Excessive listening goes on in august angelic circles, not only around the all-singing, all-lyre-beating Orpheus. God sometimes pipes up incredibly quietly, quieter than a newborn amoeba (we could never guess how quietly in a hundred thousand human years), and sometimes as loudly as if Father's Day had broken out up there (and then it gets loud, eardrum-splittingly loud for us little people of all colours and creeds).

Angels are the bearers of truth, I think up against the Daihatsu with stubborn force. They have to pick up even the tiniest grains of messages in the words floating, drifting, fluttering on the draught. Anyone who listens that intensively, right into the midst of silence, might not actually understand. Let's assume God said *officially*. It mustn't take too long for the angelic brain to run through all the possible varieties of *off* and *fish* and *all* and *lee*, along with all the piscine occurrences in the Bible, and come to the conclusion that the cod, the sardine, the tuna are mere red herrings swimming on the sidelines, so to speak, a cheerful shoal of fish accompanying the word through the aether.

A terribly silly example, I know (and I retract it immediately. We can ignore the issue of literal hearing of literal words but one issue we can't ignore is the lack of evidence that God speaks German, plain and simple. Or Latin or Greek or Hebrew. We can count out Bulgarian, however. By no means does God speak Bulgarian!).

Hey hey, Big Sister, don't look so bleary-eyed. I'm thinking about angels, and you lean your head to one side and fall asleep on me, just because it's evening and the road's emptying out.

Emissaries, Big Sister! Evening traffic, fluttering in the sky. A host of signifiers!

Emissaries are there to deconstruct the divine gobbledygook. To collect, sort, examine, group, connect. To listen—what else? The orders sealed within as if in amber are to be passed on to everything with ears to hear. Even if there should be signs of fluctuation in the Divine Will, if the Divine Will should despair of itself, as it were. There must be no mishearing. The tidings must be correctly received and correctly conveyed.

In our father, the outside connection was blocked. He only ever listened to himself for his imperially immediate purposes. Let's not ask too precisely from what region the things he heard came. From his intestines, I think. From his heart, thinks my sister. She's such a dirty old romantic.

As soon as the gynaecology office was empty, as soon as no one was there to make carefree noise around him, his hearing bed showed what it was capable of.

There were holes in his brain, and into them leapt a dark imagination. Paper-thin leaves of nothing began rustling in his head.

Only yesterday—Big Sister, wake up! The leaves!

Yesterday, we admired the paper-thin crown of leaves of a Thracian princess in the Sofia Museum. Forged out of gold, as thin as fingernails. We exchanged blinks of joy by turns around the display cabinet. In our memory, the gold stays gold but is drawn thinner into ever more delicate and fantastic leaves. And so it stays bright, bright and cheerful, and does no damage, what leapt into our brains of the unknown princess's miraculous headdress.

We are not our father's children. The proof? Our father would have stared at such leaves for a matter of seconds, and in the blink of an eye they'd have grown into a threatening phantasm. Only seemingly made by human hand, they would have grown rank into the devil's work. Secretly, the leaves would soon have rustled inside his head or, even worse, begun to wind around the outside in a dark wreath. Soundlessly, not to forget. A winding and wrapping of leaves as an immaterial machination, invented—by whom? and why?—to torture a five-foot-eight-tall Bulgarian.

As if anything delicate transmogrified into something cumbersome, lumpen, as soon as it found entry into the paternal head. He battled against it with swarms of words, only internally, never out loud. To no avail. And by no means could the words sent into battle serve the purpose, the extremely ridiculous purpose, of brushing off the crown of thorns admired upon him by an unknown enemy.

ADMIRED ONTO HIS HEAD! the Dresden judge Daniel Paul Schreber would have shouted, thundering the words and showing his enemies that he was still a man, no matter what God or Doctor Freud had to say.

Our father said nothing in such cases. Not a peep, not even in Bulgarian. Might there have been a girl inside our father?

Hurry-scurry, improvement work in progress inside his head. We could tell how speedily the work was progressing by the clouds of smoke rising above his cranial sutures, despite all the hair that covered them. Oh yes, oh no, it went to, it went fro, and it never came to an end.

His crown, as I have said, was covered by a wealth of black and noosed into the hereafter.

Let us propose boldly that we are not from this father. Nor from the mother alleged upon us. One hundred per cent not. Yet, there's a slackening of our intellectual capacity when we cast about for a possible father, a possible mother. Perhaps Zeus? An immaculate conception? No no, not by the woman—by the man! That's just plain infantile, we hear the scoffers scoff, pathetically infantile. True enough, a not-right father, a not-right mother are guarantees of permanent infantilism. But please note the energies that drove our still-tiny limbs to escape the labyrinth we were imprisoned in by mediocre parents who claimed to be the real thing.

Childhood has nothing of a treasure to be preserved, as people say. Pure inability in the heart, pure mulishness in the head, the ancient childhood preservers babble away. All we wanted to do was get childhood out of the way as quickly as possible. Learn to run as quickly as possible. Learn to read as quickly as possible. Run out of childhood, read our way out of the mendacious diminutive, never to return. Even ever having been children is embarrassing to us now. Every year that helps us rush closer to old age is precious, as it takes us further away from childlikeness, childishness, childhood; in short, from every idiocy held so high elsewhere.

My sister's striving for love began at the age of five. Her palms pressed against the bars of the garden gate, her tiny fingers clutching at them, she watched her beloved. There was building work going on in our street. No, she didn't fall in love with one of the small, rugged Italians who swung the heavy Bosch hammers back then, but with a German. If there were such a marvellous term as *blonde bombshell* for a man, this man would have earned such an accolade—plain old *blond man* sounds less than attractive. A muscular body, hair of sun flickering gold about his head, as the Greeks loved to adore their heroes, there stood the man in the ditch, clumps of earth flying from his spade.

By falling in love with this particular spade-swinger, my sister showed an early instinct for power and authority. He was no average builder, but the future head of the Epple construction company, the first-born son training on the job in Wurmlingerstrasse.

My sister paid no heed to the different ages drifting along our street in adulating clouds of chemicals. Only sexual pedants claim there's a difference between five and twenty-five. They have not the slightest idea of love's flying gallop through time. My sister (in brisk anticipation, not yet knowing Homer at the time) related the great Greek storyteller's words—she thinks me no daughter of mere mortals, but of God—to herself, and that meant anything was possible and anything permissible.

The only thing that bothered her was me. Was it jealousy? My sister, otherwise so patient, lost no time in biting me away from the gate.

MEAT!

Large, lonely cable drums by the wayside. Plenty of silence in the hinterland. Rumen is positively chirpy, beating out a tune only he knows against the steering wheel. The hair around his crown is standing up in a cheerful pattern now. We'll be in Veliko Tarnovo in about twenty minutes. Not a trace to be felt any more that anyone is annoyed with anyone else in this car.

But here comes a hindrance. Flashing blue lights everywhere—a road block. A refrigerated truck with a bustling crowd of policemen around it. We are waved past, without having made out what the problem is. It doesn't look like an accident, at any rate.

That large, ugly thing in the evening sky, drawn out like a smudge of dirt—it's not our father, is it? A red margin on the horizon, above it blue darkness building up, coming closer and closer, and directly above us this steamrollered stain. Why so much talk of our father here, and so exaggeratedly malicious to boot? We didn't talk about him for years, for years he only bothered us in secret, if at all—a faded hero from a time-blurred story. And next to nothing left of him. Not even a skull. The human material in which he once wandered the earth now consists merely of dilapidated crumbs.

It's true, isn't it, Big Sister—a little pile of granules made out of shock-frozen and shaken-apart crumbs of skull and bone, about the amount that would comfortably fit into a pickling jar? And, of course, I get no confirmation from my sister, or nothing I could take for confirmation. Her folded jacket against the window and her head lowered upon it tell me she's nodding off, has simply drawn her sleep skins over her eyes—because there's so much empty road ahead of us, nothing but motorway dotted with a few peaceful drivers for once, leading straight to the evening sky.

It's time for an explanation now though—what demon is driving the two of us, vocal abhorrers of the land of our father, to criss-cross around it like good little pious Christian girls? Money, money, money. Seventy thousand euro, thirty-five thousand each, to be precise. And a crazy idea behind it, not sprung from our own minds but from the incredible mind of an eighty-eight-year-old man. He was no great friend to our father when he was alive, merely a companion in times of need, one of the nineteen stopgaps in the general national loneliness of the Stuttgart émigrés.

For this flowery and thorny story, we'll have to take a detour back to the year 1945, slightly before and slightly after. Twenty Bulgarians, among them one Orthodox priest and one sole woman, had come to sunny Swabia, to Stuttgart. The men grabbed the first blonde bombshell they got hold of and settled down. Their social origins, political motives, their war experiences were miles apart, different too the degree of fascination or reluctance they had displayed towards the murderous German Nazis. After all, Bulgaria had been an ally of these Germans during two world wars, and by way of thanks the Germans had done their best not to cast the Bulgarians as an inferior Slavic people, instead seeing in them a higher hybrid nation offset with Aryan blood, far superior to the Russians. Not that it stopped them from measuring our father's skull while he was a medicine student in Tübingen.

In semi-defence of our otherwise indefensible father, I do have to mention that he was a supporter of Willy Brandt after the war, when the subsequent chancellor was still referred to derisively by the name of Frahm, a taunt at his illegitimate background. That made our father a left-winger in the eyes of the solidly conservative Bulgarians, albeit an enemy of Stalin. My sister and I, two pessimists of the obstinate kind, don't believe in our father's purity, don't believe in anything for lack of clear evidence, neither good nor bad, and leave the judgement to divine authority, which will one day let us too know who we are and what we are. Whereby my sister has grounds for hope for a mild judgement, and I have to be prepared for a tougher sentence; that much is clear even now.

But what about our father's Bulgarian buddy, now octogenarian, neither friend nor foe? He was considered a curious fellow, a man with political relations to all sides. A photo in our possession shows him with four lads lounging on the ground, leaning loosely against each other, one of them our father, and on the right, not quite part of the group, is Tabakoff. His face the kind of face you instantly forget. The good thing about it perhaps is the curls tumbling over the right side of his forehead, which were never to be seen again once his business began to flourish. We only know Tabakoff with shorn, badgerly hair.

He undoubtedly possessed a marvellous instinct for money, which gave him the idea of bunking up with the Sovietophile regime in Bulgaria and building up a brisk export–import business. What exactly was being exported and imported, we don't know. But it couldn't have been only sunflower seeds. Sunflower seeds and feta cheese wouldn't make you the kind of fortune that gradually moved into the millions and has since passed the one-billion mark.

Despite that, Alexander Ivailo Tabakoff can't be mistaken for a happy man. He may have been happy in his younger years, when he fell in love with his designated blonde bombshell—and a mighty fine specimen she was too! With sparkling charm, her thick hair curled into permanent waves, clicking, rattling golden links dangling with lucky charms around her wrists, lips that every Bulgarian man longed to kiss, although her meticulously ladylike manners rejected any such desires with a provocative pout.

As children, we were her greatest fans, always hanging around in her vicinity and flattering her. She smelt wonderful; every living thing came into its own alongside her. She possessed a generosity of the flesh that our mother lacked for us.

Alexander Ivailo Tabakoff married a woman with Hollywood qualities, a cross between Marilyn Monroe and the alleged murderess Vera Brühne, albeit with the flaw of a broad Swabian accent, marking her out for those in the know as a child of East Stuttgart. This origin, and the thick ankles from which she suffered all her life, prevented Lilo Wehrle from trying her luck in Hollywood. Instead, she married a very promising Bulgarian and gave birth to his son. We can barely remember that son. Only that he died of meningitis at the age of six. There were nasty rumours that he had died of exhaustion because his parents, ragingly in love with him and ragingly ambitious, had sucked the very life out of him. The subsequent birth was an unfortunate one, at any rate, and did not make up for the damage—a daughter.

Oh, how the righteous suffered! The child's only purpose on this earth seemed to consist in torturing her parents. Lazy, dishonest, sullen, superficially pretty, the moody child grew into a horrible teenager and later a vulgar woman, of whom little remained after four failed marriages than a messy pile of hate, taste for revenge, greed and another son, whom she presented to her parents as bait, only to whisk him away again and simply demand cash should her parents wish to see their grandson. What dreadful score was being settled there we do not know, nor do we wish to know.

The once divinely fleshy mother ended up in her grave at the age of sixty. The father saw no way out but to do without his daughter and grandson entirely, with-drawing to Florida a bitter man. How he lived there, whether lonely or in the company of jolly American ladies, remained a mystery. At any rate, he reappeared in Stuttgart around a year and a half ago, with a plan in mind, a plan of the kind one dreams up by night and for-gets the next morning. No one believed he would ever bring it to fruition.

Here we are, says Rumen, pointing at the remaining walls of a fortress, lit up by a rotating battery of red, blue, green and yellow spotlights and planted in the darkened sky like a ghost-train backdrop. The town we drive into seems to be collapsing into two halves, around the base a belt of dilapidated tower blocks and on top the older part with crumbling tiled roofs.

My sister has woken up, her delicate head rearing up with its partridge-coloured hair. Oh, she calls out, how pretty! Her overly mobile face twists and turns to the sides as if there were something amazing to discover. She praises Rumen, patting his arm and seeming rather excited all of a sudden, as if we were young again, smok-ing our first Gauloise as we drove into a French town. Her hair flying in the wind, she turns around to me, those hazel-brown eyes glinting with pleasure—Well? What does the backseat have to say?

Veliko Tarnovo, says the backseat in a pernickety tone, as if someone had to make it clear that we're not in Avignon. Although I'd intended to find Veliko Tarnovo horrible, it's not quite as horrible as I'd thought. We wind up the hill around curves and bends, and yes, there's something about it, at least by night when the seediness shrinks back into a merciful approximation.

Rumen parks the car in a walled area high on a hill, from where we can survey the view. Up on the left, on the opposite hill, are the remains of the ghostly fortress in its artificial colours. A red seam of the setting sun on the tips of the forest, in the distance an abandoned river winding its way along the valley. Behind it more hills, hill after hill, no doubt green in daylight but now woven into the darkness without contours. A raucous din of music interrupted by announcements wafts over from the fortress.

A narrow road on the right leads to our hotel. To our great joy, it has recently been renovated. And it seems to be clean as well. The person at the reception, half surly, half friendly, barely looks up from his papers. The entrance clad in shiny granite, plastic bouquets, a television shrieking from the top left-hand corner, instantly according us the pleasure of hearing the Bulgarian language from the mouths of bottle-blonde Bulgarian beauties.

Having slept so much, my sister is now a live wire. She taps me on the nose with one finger, taps the edge of the reception desk and jerks back as if she'd had an electric shock, taps the crest on the back of Rumen's jacket, so gently that he doesn't notice, taps a pink plastic flower and makes its blossom nod, turns on her heel, and in the next moment her swarming fingertips, her skipping eyebrows and her lips contorted in all directions are translating the men's conversation into a nervous mime show for the deaf.

All for me. My good, kind, hardworking big sister. No sooner do I laugh than she feels she has done something useful, and she puts an end to the performance.

Passports are deposited. Signatures are provided. Keys with wooden key rings as large as billiard balls are handed out.

Rumen, who has engaged the reception person in a highly important conversation and brought said conversation to a satisfactory conclusion, feels capable of all manner of gallant deeds. He loads himself up with our two heavy bags as if they were only stuffed with newspaper, picks up our suitcase and climbs the stairs with graceful, almost choreographed movements. My sister follows him, a smile floating on her face. I trot along behind them as usual and inspect the sharp edges of the bare steps. It would surely end in tears if ankles or heels were to get too close.

My sister and I occupy two different rooms. Our sisterly love is not strong enough to make us take a room together. Nor do our habits allow it. My sister sleeps at night as if under strictest orders. She has the necessary lightness of conscience. I'm cursed with staying awake, wandering around, not finding an end between lights out and lights on, watching advertising lights and headlamps criss-crossing the curtains, hearing even the most distant sounds, which are made specially for me because someone out there is furious at me but is not willing to expose themselves as my darkest enemy.

It's too early to contemplate sleep. We march out again, walking over dilapidated cobbles past overflowing trash cans, in the vain search for a restaurant that fries with less oil than usual. Cats roam the streets, instantly capturing my attention. Whenever a cat crosses my path I grow whiskers of my own, and a netherworld spun out of dark corners and heavy scents tries to make me slink on all fours.

Rumen is showing off his funny side. He has cranked up his optimism generator, which thrusts the jolliest prospects into his brain. In the heat of his hunger, he inspects the facades strung with lanterns like a picky brothel visitor, leaning down to the menus on display with a knowing air. My sister, blowing with every wind like a mood-sock, allows him to infect her, even taking his arm and laughing along with him, as if I'd never been born.

We end up in a place with ear-splitting music and an overly challenged waitress.

And now Rumen's favourite ritual begins, prompting my sister's mirth but driving me into a frenzy of sheer rage. He unfolds his reading glasses, a chic pair of spectacles that usually reside in a tight cocoon. With the dignity of a nine-teenth-century luminary, he devotes himself to studying the menu. His eyebrows are raised and lowered alternately, his expert pout makes an appearance, a disparaging or benevolent *mmm* (hummed in a low register) or *hhhmm* (on a rising note in expectation) accompanies dish after dish. In a running commentary, we are informed of the favourite dishes in the Apostoloff family, in which the mother bears the crown of unsurpassed cooking fairy—

although the widow Apostoloff is blind and gout-ridden, barely capable of standing, and the kitchen on the fourteenth floor in the Sofia suburb of Mladost is held together by dirt, as we have seen for ourselves. Now Rumen's hands are imitating activities such as the rolling of vine leaves, the crushing of imaginary spices between his fingers, his thumb forming a circle with his index finger to indicate exquisiteness. One of the famous Apostoloffian recipes is included on the menu and must, of course, be tasted.

But that's not all. To my great annoyance, the menu is particularly long, and Rumen won't be held back from translating everything on it. Listening to him in all this noise is pure torture. Though we both shake our heads at the very first section—surprise pizza, four-sector pizza—we still get a relentlessly precise recitation of the collective misery of Bulgarian pizza choices.

We order what we always order—for my sister grilled mincemeat kebabs with salad, one of which she gives to me, for me the salad with feta cheese, a safe option with no risk of surprises, and for Rumen four or five small dishes for us to try from. The waitress has to be veritably shouted at, even her young ears having trouble hearing above the din. Everything tastes repulsive, unsalted, unspiced, overly oiled. The cheese, tomatoes and cucumbers are edible. Not that our order is brought to us speedily. It takes a desperately long time, even though the place is barely half full.

The only spectacular thing is the waitress. As the newly hatched moneyed generation is convinced that women over the age of thirty are bad for business, they employ pretty, obscenely young summer waitresses, who sway around on high heels, plates aloft. They have a look of licentiousness about them although they're hard-working girls, with feverish red mouths, spatula-shaped fingernails in glittery varnish, their skirts ending two centimetres before their underwear becomes visible, provided they're standing upright. Another speciality of the waitresses, and of Bulgarian women in general—they are very fond of eau de toilette. My salad, otherwise a rather neutral matter, smells as if it had spent the night in a Parisian perfumery.

We don't stay any longer than we have to, and then we walk around the narrow streets, up one and down the next. It's only ten but the town is already ready for bed. Where a light still shines, it's televisions flickering through the windows. Our printed travel guide recommends strolling to and fro between bars and nightclubs to round off a pleasant day. At least the loudspeaker in the fortress has been turned off, thank goodness. A handful of English pensioners, the spindly descendants of indomitable colonial officers, are still actually on their feet. Without pith helmets and tropical suits, the English are more ordinary than one would like. They seem very keen on the old royal city—we meet them here, we meet them there, they have houses in the region with backyards straight out of *Homes and Gardens*. We would never have guessed that Veliko Tarnovo was once an important seat of the tsars, as Rumen assures us.

At the hotel, as we weigh the wooden balls in our hands ready to retire, Rumen is magically drawn to the television set in the corner. He orders silence with a wave of his arm, an unusually dramatic gesture. The news is on—a refrigerated truck by the side of the road, flashing blue lights, policemen scurrying about. Rumen slaps a hand to his forehead, stammering, first in Bulgarian, then in German—it—it—it can't be true! We step closer but we don't understand what's going on.

This time we welcome Rumen's translation skills. The refrigerated truck that he's still pointing at in amazement is the same one we overtook on the motorway. A Romanian truck, full of meat, *twenty-year-old meat! From Ireland!* Rumen can't believe it, we can hardly believe it either, but no, Rumen's not hearing things—twenty-year-old meat, halves of beef from Ireland in yellowish coats of fat, sealed in plastic. Swathes of dry ice waft out of the truck's hatch. Twenty-year-old meat! Even the news-reader can't help repeating it, as if to convince himself of the fact. The receptionist has popped up again, and he and Rumen provide a running commentary on the news, holding their heads, groaning, cursing, laughing hysterically. Rumen orders a beer, downing his glass in one gulp to master his agitation.

My sister's stomach turns, thinking of the tasteless kebabs she's just eaten four of, and I only one, thank goodness. I told you so, I call out in triumph, there's nothing you can eat in this country but salad.

Romania! is Rumen's angry riposte—the meat was meant for the Romanians! He's absolutely incensed now, and I ought not to goad him. Not interested in the rest of the news, we leave the men alone and withdraw upstairs.

My sister struts past me wordlessly in the corridor, giving a flirtatious wave of her left hand without looking back, so sure is she that not one of her movements eludes me.

It's raining by now. I fling the windows wide open. The raindrops fall in straight lines, with soldierly accuracy. That's fine by me. Raindrops stop insects from flying. Night rain clears the air and helps to fall asleep; night rain spreads silence, drowning out all unpleasant sounds. If only it weren't for the cold. Ever since they bought our permission to dig up the remains of our father and hand them over to a Bulgarian–Swedish firm, I've felt a mysterious chill in my bones. What my joints never did before, they're doing now—they're sending out phantom pain. Thousands of pinpricks, helping me to understand how the skeleton is connected. Only provisionally, the pinpricks tell me, and easy to take apart.

HOW MUCH?

Rumen receives us with his usual morning squeamishness. His back is aching, his neck is aching, perhaps a tooth as well, a stomach, a knee, a toe—who knows. He begins his neck stretches with his eyeballs rolled to the ceiling, sighs, clears his throat, swallowing the saliva he's projected upwards. Madonna, Our Lady of Sorrows, how she suffers and wends in her pain! I giggle and he gives me a stern look. Mysterious morning rituals from the Apostoloff family are performed; between them we reap accusative looks for failing to do something Rumen is accustomed to. Did his mother leap up, back when she could still walk, and massage his neck? Did he divorce his wife because she didn't?

A middle-aged waitress, who looks as if her clothes aren't quite holding her together, brings our breakfast, a cigarette clamped between her fingers, from which ash falls onto my sister's plate. A chin of iron, the lumberjack type. This thoroughly hard-bitten creature has planted herself in front of us and is looking down her nose as if she'd been ordered to knock us down if we even think about making a complaint.

My sister is indulgently lethargic in the mornings. People throwing down gauntlets can't shake her off balance. The cardboard-like bread, the grey coffee, the tomato aged over seventy in human years—she surveys the delights with composure and asks Rumen to request a sharper knife. Thank you very much, she calls after the woman, who has long since turned away.

Her methodical instinct seems suddenly awakened. The plate is raised off the table and the dusting of ash blown after the back of the waitress as she stomps away, a soundless and concentrated act. As soon as she receives a new knife, my sister gets down to work. She is the mistress of precise incisions, a surgical talent with not human flesh as its object but breakfast ingredients. The tomato is dismembered using all the tricks of the trade, and seeing as I would never manage to slice a tomato without producing an imbalance of thick and thin slices with unattractively fraying edges, my caring big sister passes me an immaculately cut slice of tomato before continuing on her own plate, layering bread, cheese and tomato tranches and fixing them with her fork so the knife can go back to action. Eight similarly sized pieces invite the eater's eye. She puts down her cutlery for a moment to bask in the perfection of her work.

Well, that's that done, says my sister and raises her coffee cup aloft, as if to make a toast.

I press the slice of tomato into a torn shred of bread. I'm perky and nimble—this is my best time of day.

An outing to the tsars' castle is on our schedule today. We walk down the hill, our attention called to the famous National Revival buildings. Ottoman rule, I crow merrily into ears that certainly don't want to hear it, was the best thing that ever happened to the Bulgarians! Rumen stares stubbornly ahead, instantly drawn into a more agreeable conversation by my sister.

The Bulgarian National Revival refers to the liberation from the Ottomans in the nineteenth century. The tawdry name proves we're dealing with a land with an operetta-like sense of grandeur. Puss-puss, I say to a dog, my need to make fun of the Bulgarians extending even to the country's pets. He listens attentively, unlike my companions whose turned backs tell me to keep my mouth shut. Puss-puss, I feed the dog with lukanka sausage from the breakfast table.

The Bulgarians raise their heads when they talk about the National Revival. Their torsos stand tall, every Bulgarian's favourite hero taking a seat within them, having stepped out of a magnificent line-up of heroes, stiffening and stretching their Bulgarian bodies, and the smiling, gentle-mannered man of a moment ago now has eyes that roll around in their sockets with a good dash of fury. Hristo Botev is one of those favourite heroes—Botev, the great liberator of the Danube. An operetta hero, the perfect model for a film or a stage comedy that has never been made. Botev, the poet with the voluminous beard. He spied the future of Bulgaria with his fiery eye, far, far beyond the date that we have reached, and his zest for action was great.

Kozloduy, 1876. One of those low-hanging October days that encourage decision-making. Botev and a group of patriots had boarded a steamship disguised as gardeners. Barely on deck, the patriots laid down their rakes, secateurs and flower baskets, tore off their costumes, only to astound the passengers with their even more magnificent under-costumes, with golden cordons across their chests and golden lions decorating their helmets.

They had guns with them too, and they used them to force the captain of the steamship *Radetzky* to send messages of liberation to the civilized world. The patriots disembarked before Rousse. Not a single hair on a single head was harmed. Yet the inhabitants along the Danube, whom Botev and his men had intended to roil to jubilation and insurrection so that they would procure arms and beat the Ottomans about the heads, stared in amazement at the golden-decorated squad and returned *tout de suite* to their fields to bring in the rest of the harvest.

There's a house with monkeys on the facade to be admired. It is delightful. What do you think, I ask Puss, who won't leave my side—did this house belong to a Turk before a New Revivalist snared it for himself?

Veliko Tarnovo is characterized by an unusual harmony of architecture and landscape, enthuses our Bulgaria guidebook. It oozes sweet touristic nothings with an iron will, coolly ignoring all the hard work put in by communism, here and everywhere else. The part that calls itself the old town clings to the tip of a hill, encircled by prefabricated concrete tower blocks.

We cross a bridge to reach our destination. The other two have generously decided to allow me back into their circle. The fact that Puss has joined the expedition party annoys Rumen at least, but he doesn't say anything. Behind the cabin where the tickets are on sale is a performance with child-sized plastic models, in German, English or French depending on the tourist groups. Rickety armour, a horse with almost no hair left. I like the way it neighs. The cassette tape is distorted, the stubborn nods of the horse's head remain silent, its whinnies only audible once the head stops moving. Shrill, scratchy voices tell the story of the knight Count Baldwin of Flanders, how he was taken prisoner, how he unfortunately fell in love with his captor's lady wife, how the two of them were caught in flagrante and Baldwin was beheaded. Rumen frowns, embarrassed by the performance. I find it amusing, and my sister laughs.

Visiting fortresses is not one of our favourite pastimes. Unfavourable memories lounge on every ruined stone we look at. Drives to the Swabian castles in the area were among the thankfully rare Sunday excursions we were forced to undertake with our parents. We put up stiff resistance every time, not wanting to leave our grandmother, whose house we all inhabited. It was no use— we were spirited away against our will.

We sat silently on the soft backseat of the Citroën. Our father was an excellent driver; his clothing that of a 1930s motorist—open-backed leather driving gloves and a cap. He never speeded, drove neither slowly nor jerkily, never swore. Yet I still felt sick every time, and it was my sister's job to report to the front when we had to stop. As always, I sat on the right so that I could open the door swiftly, vomit routinely and return to the car. Everyone was used to the procedure.

After that I turned boisterous, acting the clown with my sister, soundlessly. We played finger-wrestling, arm-pinching and Chinese burns. Not a word slipped out, at most a suppressed giggle, instantly interrupted if our mother turned around to us. We were forbidden from saying anything. Our parents would probably have enjoyed a little cheerful noise from the backseat; it might have perked them up a bit. But we had sworn not to say a word during the drive. We were the most practised silent sisters in all of Degerloch. In united muteness, we exacted our revenge against the false parents who thought a ridiculous fair-weather excursion would convince us they were acting like real parents.

We had never felt more powerful—our little arms crossed, our feet bobbing, our tiny chins buried stubbornly onto our chests and not a word spoken. We were as one in our tough defiance. My great love for my sister comes from these fights we fought together. How I'd like to be sitting on a wall next to her now, defying all Bulgaria with the same attitude as back then. But my big sister has long since grown up into a sleek and supple adult, who takes everything as it comes and—very unlike myself—forgives almost everything.

Teck Castle was just as boring as the three royal castle hills at Staufen, Stuifen and Rechberg. We yawned, stared demonstratively at the ground when we were ordered to look up at the ruins, and wandered behind our parents in murderous obedience, hand in hand.

Compared with the pitiful remains here, the Swabian castles are impressive constructions. Inscrutably enough, my sister is acting as if she were in the midst of an eighth world wonder; even the pale, peachy hairs on her arms seem to sense the presence of the mythical tsar. With her grace and her permanent beatific smile, she has moulded Rumen into a wax man with whom she can do whatever she will.

I'm horrified by such feminine shrewdness. The only thing that interests me is the execution cliff. The condemned men were thrown off it alive, their corpses a gift to the birds and the worms. It soon became a dump of tangled bones, as one can easily imagine. A pale field of curses, on which the bones rattled in expectation night after night: Is someone coming? To arrange us? To beflesh us anew, so we may grow veins, muscles, tendons, nerves?

I sit on a wall and let the other two pass by. Puss has abandoned me for an Englishwoman, who is feeding him white bread. A crow is strolling around, far away from its swarm. Apparently for no particular reason. A dignified reeling gait with no recognizable destination.

Tip tap, and it's father cutting in again, pressing his fingertips to his mouth as if to consider something. His black hair so neat and accurate, as if the dream had combed it for us.

Take your time to think about it, he's trying to say. Don't be so forward, my daughters. No one believes a word of it when you pretend to know it all.

All empty words of course, as usual.

We don't know much. So what? It's clear enough—even if we'd majored in Bulgarian Studies, Feta Cheese Production and Indo-German Suicide with a focus on the psychopathology of male gynaecologists—we'd still be out of the question to serve as magistrates on the matter of our father. Even in a shabby, old family court held in a portacabin. To say nothing of high-court judges. My sister and I step out either side by side or in confrontational mode, *en face*. If we wanted to climb to heady heights and pass judgements, we'd have to conform to the seating plan in the Supreme Court, a semicircle, open to the world like an amphitheatre and, at the same time, the navel of the world. They say the seventy-one judges in the Supreme Court can look each other diagonally in the eyes from the side but are never to turn their back on each other or take a full-frontal look up-close.

Mackerel clouds in the sky, gently riffled. A judge gathers strength when he looks up and delights in the sky. He had to have a quick look out at the green between one patient and the next, our father claimed when he was still hanging out in his doctor's coat. And what do you do in the winter? we promptly asked him, not getting an answer.

If my sister hadn't headed off with Rumen, I'd unfurl judges' questions before her and refute her responses.

No, Big Sister, that's where you're wrong. Don't say the seating plan is a secondary matter. Quite the opposite—it's essential for finding a fair measure. Now, for example, as I'm alone and watching the wandering crow through the lenses of my sunglasses, with no human face in semi-, quarter- or three-quarter profile calling me to think of the consequences, I could judge merely by the crow's legs. Follow the legs to the next bend in the march—the last leg put down will count. Right leg: call in the executioner! Left leg: not guilty!

It's impossible to communicate when you're sitting side by side in a row. Beckett proved that. With unbeatable humour. Once and for all. Remember, Big Sister, how you read the passage out to me and we doubled over in laughter? Where was that again? The committee meeting? In *Watt*? I think so. *So Mr Magershon turns to Mr O'Meldon, to find Mr O'Meldon looking, not at him, as he had hoped, but at Mr MacStern, in the hope of finding Mr MacStern looking at him*—and so on and so forth. The contortions of the heads, the looks cast at backs of heads, ears, neck hair, collars—dizzying! What the gentlemen are concerned with is of no interest. Why should it be—it's impossible for anything sensible to come out of it all.

Of course, a semicircular seating plan and viewing plan alone does not guarantee that justice is administered. It depends on the judges. If you want to hold such an office you have to have learnt to control your passions. You and I, Big Sister, as anyone can tell, do not control ours. A judge must not fall for the charms of temptation, nor for the lure of mental experimentation. We have succumbed to such temptations more than once, and succumb to them over and over again. A man free from the immoral services of Eros, free from an immoral drive for provocation, as little enchanted by charity and forgiveness as he is driven by a desire for revenge—*that man* may be a judge.

Surrounded by a bed of roses separating them from common sin, the judges of the Supreme Court hold court and pass their judgements. Their judgements are benefactions, shining in the darkness. If a death sentence is to be passed, there must be more than one vote weighing down the scale.

No and no and no again, we are not suited for *that* office; not you, Big Sister, with your propensity for lenience and forgiveness, nor I, born with a gavel in my hand, always prepared to call for the death sentence. Our hearts are too soft and too raw and have never been protected by that legendary bed of roses. The weeds run amok in the secret gardens of our souls; we must fight for every rose petal on which innocence and reason live together in perfect harmony. Having remained childish against our will—although we are constantly claiming the opposite—we honour our mother and father poorly and find no measure to judge them, to judge ourselves, to judge anyone at all.

What now?

I'm still all alone. A cigarette, take off my sunglasses, put on my sunglasses, hop off the wall, a few paces up and down, hop onto the wall.

What, apart from the memory of holding hands, connects us sisters nowadays? Books. While our parents delved deeper into their misery downstairs, we slipped into our beds upstairs and read. We still read now, reading and reading to escape the impositions cropping up at every turn. The difference is that my sister loves big fat books, while I'm a Speedy Gonzales of a reader. Gutzkow! My sister burrowed her way phlegmatically through the complete works of Karl Gutzkow; I still don't understand how her delicate wrists managed to hold up those Gutzkow heavyweights for hours on end. I, on the other hand, love a good chop and change. I like to follow up an Ellroy, mean and greasy and blood-soaked, with wanderings through snow with Adalbert Stifter. After a book entirely free from human beings, illustrating the fig in all its natural states, comes an Indian novel chock-full of characters.

And there's another difference. It was when we began reading that we got the dachshund. An argument flared up between us as to whether he belonged more to her or to me, a battle that was easy to win by exploiting the dear beast's greed. We weren't allowed to take the dog to bed with us, of course, or give him snacks secretly. But I found ways to sneak the dachshund into my bedroom. And there he lay by my side, snoring and sighing, while I switched the light back on and read. Though I haven't had a dog for years now, all I need to do is open a book in bed, and I instantly feel the warmth of a dachshund ear twitching against the back of my hand.

And otherwise? What do I have in my sister?

I have a sister in a magnificent mood at the touch of a button. A chameleon who knows every trick in the book, but I mustn't complain—in the case of Tabakoff I've profited from her skills. She's irreproachable when it comes to money, at least with me. She shares perfectly correctly.

O come, night, o silent laden night, and shake down your talers into my shift.

Tabakoff has gone crazy! What on earth does he do all day long? It can't be true, can it? The ears of Stuttgart's Bulgarian children grew warm from all the telephony when Tabakoff came out with his idea. People who only knew each other by name and hadn't seen each other since they were children got agitated all around the globe. Few of them had stayed in Stuttgart. Tabakoff's gone crazy in America, the Swabian Bulgarian widows told each other, at least those not yet buried next to their husbands. Who is this idiot, do you know him? asked the children and children's children. The storm in a teacup sloshed over to Frankfurt, Mannheim, Berlin, Copenhagen, the Allgäu, Mexico and Cincinnati.

Those who talked to Tabakoff face to face certainly did not get the impression they were dealing with a senile old man. Quite the opposite. Tabakoff came across as energetic, sober, straightforward. He didn't hold long confused speeches, aside from the easily explained fact that English words slipped into his German at regular intervals. He had sun-browned skin, sinewy agility and a thirst for action that he came up with in precise sketches. His now bald skull glowed with energy. His idea seemed to be keeping him alarmingly young.

Pompous, megalomaniac, grotesque. What was it the man wanted?

He wanted to bring home his one-time companions. All nineteen of them. It was for them that he'd abandoned the sunshine shores of Florida and returned to his old house in Stuttgart, the one he'd once shared with his poodle, his wife and his child, a hundred and thirty pairs of ladies' shoes and fifty different types of nail varnish.

Bringing them home—Tabakoff meant it literally. The Bulgarians lay scattered across the graveyards of Stuttgart, some relatively fresh corpses, some ancient and decayed, all apparently waiting for nothing other than Tabakoff to take charge of them. He, the last of the Stuttgart Bulgarian club, had come to gather up their last remains and translate them to Sofia. In a dignified train of limousines, naturally, with a first-class Orthodox burial awaiting them.

The idea was so ridiculous that everyone thought he was pulling their legs.

My sister, who had driven all the way from Frankfurt to Stuttgart to meet Tabakoff, must have sensed that this crazy idea would give rise to unforeseen things. She was probably as dismissive as all the rest to begin with. Then she raised issues of piety. Of all people, my sister, who has not visited our parents' grave on a single occasion! Who gives about as much for the hereafter as a rat does for the moon.

By claiming I was in France, she cleverly ensured that Tabakoff did not bother making direct contact with me. My sister knows I'm drawn to adventurous ideas, and I'd have given the crazy guy my permission out of curiosity alone. But she played hard-to-get, mentioning the sacred peace of the dead and telling him how reassuring it was for us to have our parents' grave nearby. Until Tabakoff finally made her an offer. A modest one to begin with— ten thousand euros for her permission. Now, I wasn't there—but my sister must have played so hard-to-get that she managed to haggle Tabakoff up to eighty thousand.

But then came the bartering blow. Tabakoff threw the suicide card onto the table. An expensive, special case. If the transfer took place, the garrulous Bulgarians would start talking in Sofia as well. He could predict plenty of trouble for himself and it would cost him a packet to convince the priests to house a suicide in consecrated soil. It was no use my big sister detailing the trauma her little sister would go through if the body were dug up, especially because it was a suicide.

We could pay for a first-class trauma specialist out of the money, with plenty to spare, was Tabakoff's cool response. They agreed on seventy thousand, on condition that my sister tell no one about the deal. She called me up that very evening.

It later emerged that Tabakoff had provided a financial sweetener for other descendants. But no one had got nearly as much out of him as my sister. What everyone had thought at first turned out to be wrong. Tabakoff had fallen prey neither to a fit of religious orthodoxy nor to a passion of patriotism. Or, at least, these were not his real motivations. The driving force behind his project was that everything had to take place in a clean, dry and odour-free manner—for him it was all a first-class business idea.

Patriotism and orthodoxy were more like embellishing cherries on the top.

He had run into an old acquaintance who had once worked on a secret project in an adjunct office of the Sofia Academy of Sciences—mummification of foodstuffs. Strawberries that looked like fresh, scarlet fruits but crumbled to dust the instant anyone picked them up. The Bulgarians provided the Russians with food of this kind, which they had liberated of all liquid by means of cryoengineering, without taking the taste away. Cryoengineered carrots, tomatoes, peaches and chicken breasts flew into space in portion packs and vanished into the bellies of Russian space travellers, who kept a vain watch for Lenin's soul and gradually went mad because they had no vodka and the heavenly revolutionaries stubbornly refused to manifest themselves.

Blagovest Kondov now worked for a Swedish funeral company with a sophisticated method of disposal of human bodies. Cryoengineering could not only be used on foodstuffs, the power of science could also dismantle a corpse into tiny parts, barely larger than grains of rice. All ecologically correct, of course, without firing up a single incinerator, which tend to make some people feel uncomfortable although they'd rather not know why.

The Swedes had a systematic, clean and modern method, almost enabling them to banish all elements of the eerie. When dealing with intact corpses, they were first frozen at minus eighteen degrees Celsius and then lowered into an immersion bath of liquid nitrogen, coffins and all. And then came the adventurous part, the actual innovation—what had previously staunchly maintained its shape was now placed on a vibrating plate and gently shaken, prompting it to crumble into millimetre-sized pieces. Any gold teeth, copper or iron still in there were removed. What was left behind was a few kilogrammes of last remains, which could be transferred to a space-saving burial site.

A state-of-the-art method that solved several problems in one fell swoop. As yet, the funeral laws in most countries prevented it from being actually used but that would soon change. Tabakoff was determined to start the ball rolling in Bulgaria, once the pioneering land of cryo-engineering, with the aid of the Swedes. As a pennon leading the way and the simultaneous culmination of the undertaking, his old Stuttgart companions would be the first to be treated to the new treatment.

The craziest thing was that Tabakoff actually managed to put his plan into practice every step of the way, with even the tiniest details becoming reality. And so Stuttgart's Bulgarian children set out on a very special mourning journey. It ended last Sunday in Sofia, although not for my sister and me, because we decided to spend a few extra days in the country.

And so here we are, Rumen, she and I.

Clean, dry and odour-free. The process could almost have been invented in Swabia. It was certainly efficient, but in our father's case it seemed like trying to kill a dead man, or at least mighty exaggerated. He had long since rotted away and his cryoengineered remains weighed light. At the age of forty-three, he was the first of the Bulgarian club to die. If we are to believe his fleeting hints in retrospect, he had the suspicion that the body was beseethed by mysterious vermin. They acted on higher commands, marching, crawling in columns, butchering each other in running battles. They were apparently whitish creatures, drawn out like threads. With increasing effort, our father tried to banish them from his body. How fruitless his efforts were! It's no use, silly Papa, I hear my sister calling, I hear myself calling, and I see us waving and wagging, you must, Papa, yes, you can, Papa, even live a comfortable life with a vermin infestation. Just don't take any notice. Life's so easy if you just live it.

Our arguments are no use now. The worms have gnawed away all the hirsute Bulgarian flesh on his bones, long before the Swedes got their hands on his remains. You can count on vermin, I say to the crow, raising an imaginary glass to the health of the subterranean cleaning crews.

HERE'S BURNING AT YOU, KID

Here's burning at you, kid, says our father again. His who-knows-what-it's-like face with its smoking eyes, which he wants me to lay a wet cloth on—old familiars from dreams. They're all too out of place here. It's broad daylight, painfully bright, and I'm still sitting on the wall with my sunglasses on.

An airy mosquito squadron dances in the light.

Did he ever read the Bible? Not that we knew of.

We saw him reading the newspaper, in his armchair. Fingering the pages of his ghostly medical books, on his red sofa. Very much against my will, I'm overcome by a jolly memory, concerning only me; my sister doesn't crop up in it and that's tantamount to betrayal.

Our father loved it when I read to him from the *Stuttgarter Zeitung*—before I learnt to read, that is. He was royally amused when I unfolded the newspaper with stately precision and looked through it for a suitable article, chortling when I began to read, spurring me on and rewarding me with a tender kiss at the end of my presentation. I enjoyed this privilege so much that I spent entire days occupied with little else than thinking up what I'd read to him that evening.

But my little newspaper show was only performed when he was feeling well. It came to an end when I started school. From then on he became more and more of a sinister character. A sinister character who darkened the hearts of his children. And all of a sudden my sister was essential again, holding my fearful hand as we watched him toss his keys.

Our father had a tick of tossing his keys up in the air. He stood in front of us, looked up and threw the keys up towards the sky.

Now I know—the man was acting like a temple servant defiantly quitting his job and throwing the keys back to his past master. Let Him up there see how He took care of His business. To all intents and purposes, our father was waiting for a miracle. Had the keys floated on air, only *one* time, everything would have been different. Our father would have entered into revelation mode—first his hair would have stood on end, he would have fallen on his face and got back to his feet with the aid of an angel; then the Kristo unworthy of salvation would have been elongated, a longing, listening, feeling would have thrust him heavenwards—our father would have entered the empyrean.

But no. Either he caught the keys and carried on in the same mood as before or the keys fell to the ground and his mood sank. We stared at him. His games were not meant for us. This wasn't a merry father clowning around, trying to show his daughters the proof of the heavenly pudding.

Oh yes, he vexes us, me more than my sister, me with a sack full of reasons in mind; with my sister, the vexation feasts on her streaky heart chambers.

He made no use of the salvation within his name. Found no balance between too much God in his name and too little God in his life. Over and over, he immersed himself in an ominous vacuum, fishing in it for blame that was not to be escaped. Nothing there could ever be concrete, ever find a name for itself to be rid of it. We could see the horde of dismal thoughts coming over him, his head lowering onto his chest. His hands lay folded over his stomach, not relaxed but in perplexed flaccidity. A ridiculous hat perched on his head, as a small jagged-edged photo proves. Next to him his wife, exaggeratedly perky, her legs stretched out in a casual pose.

Let us take a closer look at the case. He may have been acting on orders (ha ha, you don't even believe that yourself). He may have been put to an intricate test. A false command, a wrong order had been given—annihilate yourself, you swine! (a swine who thinks of such a thing)—and he didn't listen quite precisely, failed to hear the giggles accompanying the command. No one's claiming it was a command from God, a command from his adversary. Nonsense! All our father was dealing with was the whims of a child-god, practising his commands and giggling as he did so. That giggle was meant as a suggestion—there's nothing easier than wiping yourself out in laughter, just as a test mind you, and why not take your wife along with you, your children, your patients, your mother-in-law, father-in-law, Auntie Luise, Auntie Emma, Auntie Clara, the dog, take them all with you. You'd be a swine, swine, swine if you didn't laugh at that, all your own fault. You'd be a fool to take your own swinish flesh and hang it up on a hook.

The suicide-to-be that our father was at that moment had no idea at all of the absurdity of suicides, their ridiculous poses.

If my sister were here now she'd call me to reason— our father never used the word swine, and certainly not of himself; and if the child-god did whisper the Bulgarian equivalent of swine in his ear, well then, we're at our linguistic wits' end anyway. She's right as usual, my big sister.

In fact, our father had always taken his possible hanging into consideration. More philosophically than swinishly. Did he not make notes on his favourite Nietzsche passages, those that concerned the tragicomedies of human life, which, played over and over by new actors, were astoundingly resistant to boredom. *Although one might think that the entire audience of the earthly theatre had long since hanged themselves on all the trees out of tedium.* Ha ha, our father laughed out loud and wrote in the margin *Tedium! Tedium! How very funny!* And in his excessive annotation fever he added the word *Jawohl* with three exclamation marks at once.

I now suspect our father was one of those unworthy of salvation, one of St Augustine's *massa damnata*. He was expected to behave as a name-bearer potentially worthy of salvation, to one day come into question for refilling the heavenly choirs thinned out by the fall of the angels. Someone had even made provisions and given him a beautiful, melodious voice, which he could have begun training in the here and now for its final purpose. But no. He refused to sing along. He hotfooted it straight out of the furrow that his name had intended him to stick to. He insisted on his own disgraceful physicality, forfeiting it and the heavenly realms along with it. A chosen one gradually degraded to a doleful domestic tyrant, an apostle of sensitivity, a miniature man of sorrows who revelled in his own woes and glooms. His life was not attuned to Jesus (aside from minor errors), not: *Although I have been separated from You, yet I return again,* oh no no, his botched motto was: *Although I have been separated from Me, yet I return again.*

On the other hand, we don't want to ignore the fact that many a commentator claims the treasury of the satisfactions is immeasurable, large enough to suffice for the devil and easily large enough for the *massa damnata* gathered under his dark pinions. According to this interpretation, our father would be off the hook again after waiting for a tiny aeon of time.

Have I mentioned that we sometimes receive calls from him in the middle of the night? We concentrate with all our might on understanding what our father wants to tell us. But as we no longer have any imagination, as I have said, which might present the paternal voice to us in an instantly recognizable form, we regularly fail to decipher the nightly messages, uncertain if it wasn't just the man next door butting in on our dreams. Our father doesn't speak Bulgarian in our dreams, of course—that would fall on deaf ears. Seeing as his German is no less dubious to us, he now speaks Hamletish.

Corpsing, says our father with a laugh, we've gone and caught him corpsing again.

Although my sister likes to announce in general that our father does not play a part in her dreams, one night, recently, she was almost about to grab him. She was walking towards a building that she first took for the Kaaba and she instantly began worrying whether she was even allowed to approach it, being a woman. She was not wearing a veil, only her pale-green summer suit, which displays her legs up to her knees. The cube showed no signs of its legendary blackness, and there was not a Muslim in sight. It shone out moss-green, an intensely glowing green, dressed in plants, as if refreshed by subterranean waters and moistened by the morning dew. Where there might have been windows, black-painted arches were inserted into the walls. With a myriad of eyebrows but no eyes, the cube lured with shining brows and yet dashed hopes with them, for there were no openings below them, for neither an out nor an in.

You do remember, I interrupted my sister as she was telling me about it, how boldly the paternal eyebrows curved—even though we're his sworn enemies now, we must not withhold this fortunate characteristic of his.

My sister paid no heed to my interjection. According to her, the cube was squatting on a rotating platform and in its nether workings there were dubious deities, wall flutterers, as my sister said. They wanted to flutter out of the nether construction but all they had were wings of sackcloth, and behind those filthy wings, subterranean wings, our father seemed to be scurrying to and fro. My sister grew faint in her dream, no longer capable of looking behind the sackcloth wings. And so she lost our father again.

I pointed out that the word sack left scope for dubious interpretations in conjunction with our father but she merely laughed in her usual, throwaway way. And that was that. I'm still fascinated by the building's improbable green colour.

The crow performs a poor take-off and flies away.

Here they come again, the two of them. Submerged in cheerful conversation, Rumen's gait elastic; both in a marvellous mood. A patronizing look at the evil-tempered little sister; someone's obviously feeling strong enough to deal head-on with rebellious little people as if they were cute little hedgehogs.

There are moments when the world is simply beautiful and nothing else, says my sister, wagging her crown as if this realization were just too much for her pretty little head.

When you see the landscape spread out around you, when that panorama can take its full effect with nothing to disturb it, all the fuzzy trouble and strife fades away, she continues, stretching so unexpectedly upwards that I can't help thinking she'll fly off any minute.

With the two of them standing so close to me, I feel pressed in and can't rid myself of the fear of falling backwards off the wall, so my hands clamp tight around the stone edge.

Perhaps the Bulgarian soul hasn't quite discovered itself yet, says my sister.

I forget all fear in sheer amazement. My sober big sister and the word soul don't go together; soul is more suitable for my linguistic compartment. Even though it's a delicate word, one with ruffled wings so to speak, it tends to seduce us to exalted, vague usage. Please be careful when using this word.

Rumen also appears to be in an unnaturally buoyant mood. He emits a weighty sigh, which comes across as rather ridiculous from a man whose black chest hair is spilling out of his shirt.

Let's not talk about that, he says, eyeing the ground meaningfully as if we were standing on the trapdoor to a secret chamber full of the most magnificent treasures of the soul ever collected by humankind.

Bulgaria may be a degenerate culture at the moment, says my sister, but I think that will soon change. It will find strength from the past of which it knows nothing as yet.

A degenerate culture? Am I hearing things? What on earth has got into my sister? If it goes on like this I'll be all at sea. Like a doctor examining a maniac, I look her in the eye. Her pupils are small. The whites are immaculate, shimmering porcelain and not a single burst blood vessel to be seen. A provocatively healthy whiteness.

No alcohol, no cigarettes, a good night's sleep, a clear conscience.

They're still the same brown eyes with their subtle sprinkles of green, kept miraculously moist and therefore warm in tone but austere in expression if you look at them for a while. And my sister's delicate face with the little mole on her cheek is still the same face, always at risk of drifting slightly into uncertainty if the fine lines around her mouth and eyes didn't hold it firm.

Bulgaria is so beautiful in unexpected places; it's not a country you can think about, says my sister. It suddenly comes over you like a gaggle of geese settling on a field.

Now she's really on a roll, stretching her neck suspiciously again, as if she were searching the sky for her white flying companions.

She puts one finger to her nose to help herself think. Her brows draw together. Rumen's waiting, I'm waiting. We're waiting for the excessively intelligent thoughts about to be born.

It's too soon to put such delicate experiences into words, she says, and after a pause in which no actual geese are to be heard but at least crows, she looks me straight in the eye. There's no point thinking about a maltreated country like Bulgaria, it's pointless talking or writing about it. Singing would be the only appropriate thing to do. Strangers ought to come and sing odes to this land!

Now she gives me a cheerful wink—I don't mean us. You're unlikely to find two people who sing worse than we do.

I can think of at least one—Tabakoff.

My sister throws open her mouth and displays her even top teeth in a smile. In an exaggeratedly moansome voice, she sings the opening lines of 'Mi Buenos Aires querido'.

What with the two of them seeming to float on air, I start feeling more and more uncomfortable on my wall. I see myself squatting there in stocky adhesion, while breadcrumb-sharp stone surfaces cut into my palms.

As if she'd read my thoughts, my sister detaches my left hand from the wall and pulls me down. Now I feel well and truly like a child that has got some nonsensical idea into its head, from which it must be tugged away. A moment later my sister lets go again, and while my body finds its way back to its usual adult proportions, she turns on her heel and walks a fleet-footed zigzag down the hill towards the exit.

Rumen looks up, as if he were thinking of something great and important that will determine the future of Bulgaria and then follows my sister like a carer, cautiously, as if he mustn't divert a mind-walker from her path. I walk on behind at a distance.

Something must have happened over the past twenty minutes. It's been a long time since I've seen my sister this emotionally clouded, more than twenty-five years, and that was when she'd just met her atrocious Persian.

GOLD

Part two of today's excursion. We're driving to Arbanassi. Forests, hills, delightful clearings. I don't say a word on the journey. The landscape would like to pass by slowly and silently but the Daihatsu's not built that way.

Beautiful, oh yes, it really is beautiful. We get out of the car on a gravelled heap of weeds. A few steps onward, everything changes.

The convent greets us with a vine-encrusted court-yard. Everything around us is blossoming and thriving—in pots, in tin cups, in furrows as straight as arrows, on small terraced slopes and wooden supports; wherever the eye wanders, all is green and budding and aflame. Even the pillars of the cloisters are climbed by abundant magnifi-cence, stretching blossoms to the sun in a riot of unleashed colours. Blue flickered through with mosquito gold. Drag-onflies hover past like lines from a song. Simple wooden benches whispering—abide a while. A buzzing and a twit-tering in the air, almost indecent, a wagging of tails, a rustling of leaves, a darting, a flying, a humming all around and past us three people, busy as bees with our own matters.

We take a seat and a deep breath and a stretch of our legs. Behaving like triplets born most gently, in a miraculous birth, as yet incapable of distinction and spite. Wanting to savour this rare state of being, none of us say anything.

A hunched nun with a bucket and secateurs comes along the way and welcomes us. Rumen stands up and bows and the two of them walk and talk together, laughing, Rumen carrying the nun's bucket and shears for her. Shadow-flecked in the aisle, flowed about by light at the corner, they move off until they disappear.

Our sisterly hearts slip softly across this beautiful world, sailing into the blue of the sky and off with the last of the clouds.

I'd actually wanted to find out how my sister got into such a bustled-up state but right then Rumen comes back and waves. He slips into an entrance and we follow. All of a sudden, we're in an anteroom and have to accustom ourselves to the damp, clammy atmosphere and the darkness. We're surrounded by frescoes—red, blue and umbra—with figures rather naively painted at first glance, nimbi around the heads of saints whose names and legends we don't know. We are not initiated and suddenly fearful about knowing nothing at all.

It seems as though the figures were whispering to each other, in poorly masked anger, consulting with saintly lips pursed and murmuring into their divided beards about us, odd daughters of Kristo, walking in here, bold as brass. Before my eyes, the closely crowded saints blur together, nimbi and all, as if a light mist had softened their contours. But I can make out the earnestness of the brownish faces— you can always count on earnest faces in an Orthodox church.

Rumen strides ahead into the main room. Are we even allowed in? We put one coy foot in front of another and, all in all, behave very, very cautiously. Who will describe the uproar the moment our eyes race around the room?

There's a flash from the front. We're standing like toy dolls set out at arm's reach, not stiff but softened up. A tumult on the wall, the likes of which have never been seen nor heard.

It's not simply gold brooding to itself in heavy clumps, it's inspired gold, sparkling with every widening of the lungs, shimmering and extinguishing with every outward breath. Enraptured gold, awoken gold and then slumbering gold again, sinking in the darkness. As soon as we take a few steps, that which we were just resting our eyes on is veiled again and another section unsheathes itself, flaming up like the Day of Judgement.

Reflexes upon reflexes, created by candles and oil lamps, lend a momentous shimmer and a cloaking twilight. It lives and converses and sleeps and dreams by turns. A saint raising a finger only moments ago is now submerged in the flood of shadows. I feel as if jagged questions were being asked but calm answers given. In the next moment everything seems to be drawn to the magnetic core of silence, bat's ears pricked up.

The extremes are at closer quarters here than elsewhere and have forgotten to fight. Alongside an icon of the Virgin Mother placed on a table for kissing is a rusty tin bowl full of wilted flowers sinking towards the tablecloth.

Rumen has turned around, and now we see her too—an elderly nun sitting at another table, in front of her bundles of candles, long and thin as petrified threads, a pile of devotional pictures next to them. One after another, she looks us in the face through water-pale eyes before she responds to Rumen's address. It looks to me as if she's missing a few teeth.

She whispers, automatically drawing Rumen closer until he bends down to her. We don't understand a word of course, yet it's clear that Rumen's not listening only out of politeness but increasing curiosity.

We step back and take a closer look around. Our past has vanished; we're examining with industrious minds. Have we fallen for a spectacle? No, no—even when we move around the room more boldly and begin the sober business of inspection—it's a cabinet of miracles, not a place of artifice. Never, not in the best museum in the world, can icons, no matter how good they may be, have such a startling effect as here. Icons are companionable, clasped together they want to tell important tales from the testaments, flanked by local saints who help show and tell, unrolling parchments and promising protection.

Now I finally realize what others have known all along—icons are only in possession of their rights when they glean out of a consecrated space, but only briefly, then they ask to be restored to the darkness, disappearing as secretly as they came. Only hesitantly, in this emerging and disappearing again, can something kindle on their painted skin, in auspicious cases that un-created light that hits the observer as transmitted light, reflecting the trembling shine of the candles and lamps sparingly and festively by turns.

It's difficult to talk about it with my sister. Her soft, benevolent heart is entrenched in the steel cage of Protestant atheism. Pictures are art for her to all intents and purposes, to be judged high or low depending on their value. Pictures belong in a museum, otherwise they'll be stolen. What human fingers have made has no part in the magic of the inexplicable for her. Gold is gold, a valuable material that glints prettily in the light, but from which unearthly lights never sparkle and leap into human souls.

It's cold and damp in here, says my sister, freezing cold in fact. Do you think that harms the pictures? She looks up as if waiting for applause. She's a picture of concern and responsibility now, and in this strange atmosphere her eyes have an unimagined depth.

I play down the topic. The pictures have survived here for centuries after all.

She comes closer and whispers her worries in my ear—the black jeep below the gravel driveway, the one with tinted windows. The man in black leathers leaning on the bonnet, the one with the cauliflower ears. Hadn't I noticed him? Almost certainly one of those Mafia gorillas checking out the territory and waiting for an opportunity to dash off with the icons. The way he followed us with his eyes was just creepy.

Hmm, I say. It looks like it'll be a while before your dear Bulgaria's cultural regeneration after all.

Intense frowning, which indicates that my sister is extremely dissatisfied with me. Only her eyes are still the size of a child's. But her annoyed furrowed face suddenly has the look of a bunny-rabbit professor wondering what punishment to impose on her little bunny-rabbit pupils.

We could use a drop of incense to get us back in the mood. There's none burning at the moment though. While myriads of hovering, glittering particles spread around the room, the atmosphere mellows, and then the heart and mind go off together on a long journey, floating off on the sweet fumes. All incense aside, there's just no telling my sister that there are places that invite people to transform themselves. Here we are in such a space, more spacious than almost any before; we're invited to breathe with our lungs wide open, perhaps even to sigh a little.

Can't you tell how everything's different in here, down to the very atoms, than in secular spaces, different than in secular air, in which everything happens as if harried?

Five minutes before, on the bench, the same invitation was whispered, answers my sister. She refuses to be distracted from what the man in leathers is doing outside with his car.

Oh him, I say, he's just Witiko, cleaning a jeep for a change instead of his iron-grey horse. Witiko jokes have always worked on my sister, ever since we had a running battle over Stifter's book of that name decades ago, constantly pretending enthusiasm as we read it, even exchanging Witiko blessings by telephone, of the type—may you savour today what your house is able or as it happens to happen, thus let it happen or so it arose, and now accept God's gratitude—until we finally admitted amid peals of laughter that we found the leathery knight's adventures dull, magnificently dull and nothing else.

Witiko's not working at the moment. My sister is more and more on the retreat with her sullenly twisted face.

Please don't be so stubborn, I say. Take a look about. Move around the space. Imagine a choir singing. You don't have to look at the singers' open mouths, always an absurd sight. The choir's resounding from above, from a hidden place, just like music from the heavenly spheres, which never puts up a front when it sounds out either. And then please, enjoy the sensation when a breeze blows fresh about you, concealing nothing other than the coy embrace of an angel.

If we wanted, we could lead a more melodious life than before, never mind our dead father and mother, I murmur to myself—my sister is not fond of me trying to persuade her, especially not in the name of angels. By now she's turned round and gone outside to see about the man in leathers. I follow at a leisurely pace, finding her on our bench. We are silent like sworn enemies who have known each other for too long to have to talk. Rumen joins us, unearths a squashed pack from his pocket, offers me a cigarette and lights up for himself and for me.

If only you knew, he says, taking a deep breath and grinning. It's pretty incredible but you wouldn't believe it anyway. He leans back and acts as if a story this incredible

could only be told to the mosquitoes. We turn to him obligingly. Go on, tell us.

Our blouses crinkle gently, our eyes twinkle merrily
to soften up this old mystery-monger.

Rumen maintains it's a story for Bulgarians only, for
proto-Bulgarians.

Bulgarian Bulgarians?

Rumen smiles a mischievous smile and wags his
finger.

To be strictly accurate, we're not allowed to be told
the story at all because we weren't rocked in real Bulgarian cradles and don't know how to listen with pure ears.
We turn away, disappointed.

But Rumen won't let it go and is getting into his
stride. He talks about bad times in which Bulgarianism
was on its last legs. (We picture Bulgarianism as wilted
flowers.) Back then there was a monastery near here, but
it was burnt down by the Tartars. (We picture a trampling
horde of barbarians.)

In the midst of the general misfortune lived a monk,
who saw all of it coming. A tough, imperturbable hermit
who lived in a hut by the monastery and subsisted on
crumbs of bread and occasionally a piece of feta cheese.
(We picture a lunatic with a rank growth of beard, a
Father Ferapont with a scratchy voice, seeing devils at
every turn.) He broke the most important icon out of the
icon screen and buried it, only days before the monastery
went up in flames. (We see a Tartar fire raging across all
of Bulgaria.)

You see, I say to my sister, breaking icons out of walls is an old Bulgarian tradition that the Mafia is simply continuing today.

Rumen tells us more about the monk, who was killed along with all his brothers. On that very day two hundred years later, a farmer was walking across his field when he heard a voice.

Rumen leans forward and wafts something up from the ground with his fingers, cigarette and all, looking up at us from below.

Come on, you idiot, dig me up! he curses with the voice of what's buried in the ground.

The farmer gets a shock but finally gets his wits about him and starts digging. As he burrows away, he comes across a black box, covered over and over in— Rumen searches for the word *pitch*, and we find it. A cussing and a complaining comes out of the chest; the farmer carries it home in trembling hands. There he takes his pliers and pulls the nails out of the lid. Out comes an embroidered cloth and, once he unwraps it, the archangel Michael, who incidentally stops cursing once he is unwrapped and on the table. Being a pious Bulgarian, the farmer knows what he has to do and hands the treasure over to a priest. The monastery was rebuilt on the very spot where the chest was found. And now the archangel Michael hangs there, the most beautiful icon of all.

We gaze wide-eyed at the sky and feel stupid. Can it be that winds are rising and grabbing at our hair from all sides? We overlooked the angel.

I imagine the archangel as we finish our cigarettes. He comes flying down on mighty wings and reaches for his sword. Our father's shadow slips off the next bench. We file back into the church. Rumen buys several candles from the nun, which he lights in the iron holder in front of the icon wall so that the angel may appear to us.

How could we have overlooked him?

He is standing firm upon the body of a rich man. With golden platelegs, a golden chest plate, veritably spraying sparks of red, violet and pink and gleaming with ribbon-like tips, his red cloak dramatically waved, a blue cloth slung around his immaculate thighs, he stands with both golden feet upon the rich man's back. Although his wings are not quite as impressive as I'd imagined, his sword makes up for them. A magnificent sword, with which we, too, could behead anyone who got in our way. He's holding it in his right hand, drawn from high above to plunge it into the profligate sinner with all the more might. In his left hand he's holding the newly fled soul of the half-dead man by the hair—a tiny naked figure with a shock of long locks.

Two devils are doing their best to wrench the body from its splendid bed with a long iron hook, hoping to disappear to the depths of a blazing red hell with their booty. A goatish figure is showing off the collected jewels in a pouch. How useless that pouch is now. His family and servants, magnificently dressed like their exanimate master, realize with horror what is going on before their very eyes.

Looking more carefully, the suspicion arises more and more urgently that the rich man might be Tabakoff, although it's unlikely, seeing as Tabakoff was still wandering among us and chatting heartily over Sunday breakfast. Look, I say to my sister, and point out the similarity. She looks at me with an amused frown but doesn't contradict me.

The relatives are beginning to look familiar now too. They are wearing more sumptuous clothing and different hairstyles to Stuttgart's Bulgarian appendages as I remember them from the sixties, seventies and eighties. But time is thought differently here. Unlike what we're accustomed to, yesterday, tomorrow and today are permanently changing places here. It may well be that my sister and I have long since been captured here, although we feel far too full of compulsions and lifeblood to be mere depictions.

Tabakoff's wife for example, Lilo, is leading the dance of dismayed onlookers, not with her varnished fingernails and Marilyn Monroe curls, of course, but in a golden, green-embroidered cloak that covers her hair. And there, the small girl with the ferocious face, that might be the terrible daughter, and even the peculiar poodle is leaping out from behind a pillar on the right. There are at least two more of the rest of the Stuttgart Bulgarian bevy— but yes, Big Sister, look, there's Zankoff, Zankoff without a doubt, the brothel owner, and next to him his friend Gantcheff, who leased a car salesroom on Olgaeck. Only our father is missing, and our mother too. Perhaps because they never worshipped Tabakoff, reacting to his riches merely with a shrug rather than envying him his fortune. But perhaps they're missing because they have no place in a sacred shrine, for reasons unknown to us.

My, what a day, on which the Stuttgart Bulgarians appear to us, wives and children and all, and only father and mother fail to show up.

The black jeep has vanished; no one saw it drive away. No sign of the man in leathers. The car's as thoroughly and absolutely gone as if it had never been there. The grass is as teeming, champing, brightly green as if it had gobbled up everything that isn't grass in an instant and turned it into grass.

Let's turn around, says my sister, and drive after him. Rumen doesn't understand what she's talking about, not having noticed the car earlier.

We parked the Daihatsu in the middle of Arbanassi. And what we'd just experienced instantly began to take its leave for the realms of the unreal. After two failed attempts, we've found a restaurant where they welcome us on a garden terrace. As we've missed the lunchtime shift in the kitchen, we're warned our order might take a while. My sister decides to visit the shop next door and Rumen has disappeared inside the restaurant, presumably to entrap the waitress in conversation.

The terrace rests on the back part of the building but seems to be suspended above a valley. Cold shadows have filled the valley, making me shiver. I take my sister's jacket from the chair, hung accurately over the back like our mother taught us. I sit there with my neck drawn in and my fingers cold, letting a tiny spider crawl along my sleeve.

If I look out beyond the spider into the distance, the view is really rather charming and well-ordered—moderately high, wooded hills with mute, stony crowns, green fields, roads snaking between them like on mediaeval panel paintings. Looking down, the view is a seething mess. Collapsing wooden sheds, rusty water tanks, plastic sheeting, abandoned car wrecks sunk into bushes, tubs spiky with withered stalks, dented cans, a workbench with a saw, splintered trellises, toys strewn around and then forgotten, a hutch perhaps housing rabbits. Behind that the garden plot of a rich neighbour. There everything has been cleared away, the garden newly planted, the mighty old stone house renovated with wooden balconies. And blue, so blue you'd want to fall right in, is the kidney-shaped swimming pool, work still being done on its surround.

I suddenly miss blue-and-white striped awnings. Our little balcony in Degerloch, also suspended out into the back garden, was protected by them. When you sat there a confusing diversity was revealed—it was by no means easy to understand how people could live so differently in a space of a few hundred square metres. To the left of us was a vegetable gardener and amateur mechanic with all kinds of appliances in and alongside his garage, another seething mess, albeit not a Bulgarian mess but a well-considered, Swabianly stubborn mess. The arrow-straight vegetable beds were lined with wood shavings, topped with manure in winter. All the extending branches of the pear tree were propped up on stilts; in summer it hung heavy on its crutches, in winter it stood its ground, iron and stony. It haunted my dreams in the form of an old man of many arms, who swung to and fro in a threatening motion, shaking the snow off himself, raising his crutches and suddenly breaking into a run.

Directly opposite, weeping willows rained down on a garden pavilion and a cleverly arranged rock garden with austere plants sprouting out of gaps, not a common sight in Degerloch, twisted its way up to the house. Next to it grew a huge fir tree, which rustled in the wind as if it were talking to its sisters in the Black Forest. A gravel path ran around the perfect square of lawn, on which basket-work chairs and tables stood in summer, guests rattling their coffee cups. This was the realm of Sniffy, a black tomcat with the nonchalant bearing of a lion, with whom our dachshund, Snacky, had a menial relationship, having immediately thrown himself down on his back the first time Sniffy came to inspect him.

Even the garden houses on the three plots of land could barely have been more different. Our left-hand neighbour had a functional shed for tools; ours was a delicate structure of thin black branches surrounded by a bench, covered in moss and damp and empty but for the cobwebs in the corners. Nearby waited black spiders, their bodies perhaps only pea-sized but in our childish imaginations as large as the palms of our hands, which meant we avoided the garden house. The other neighbours had a fancy thing on stilts, topped with a flat roof slightly raised towards the front, its interior walls lined with weather-resistant raffia. The sole decoration was a mosaic showing a Greek flute-blower, dancing snazzy steps but slowed down by the black outlines beloved in the fifties and also by the coyness of the colours—ochre, pale blue and green, offset with a weakish rust-red.

Beyond the rock garden was a garden no longer bordering on ours, which was enough to make you think the war was still on—corrugated iron and a high wire fence protecting the shed and the bare run for chickens and rabbits, which Sniffy and Snacky would all too dearly have loved to hunt down together.

For as long as our father was well, my sister and I vied in telling him stories about the adventures of Sniffy and Snacky, a very odd couple. It was par for the course that they crept through their owners' two gardens; the cat dignified and measured, the dog eager with ears a-fly. Every few days came the same strange spectacle. Sniffy took a seat high on a post and stared downwards. Snacky approached him cautiously, his belly to the ground like a seal. He stopped prone at the foot of the post, daring a brief devoted glance upwards and immediately lowering his eyes, only the twitching of his ears hinting that his senses were sharp. The cat on the post was Stalin, our father explained with great pleasure, folding his arms and putting on his impenetrable Stalin face. We had to tickle him until he put out his claws and hissed a Russian curse, at which the two of us leapt away with squeals of laughter.

Another small jagged-edged photo shows our father sitting on the edge of our balcony, thirsting for action, young, slim, with flashing eyes and a victorious smile. Not a trace of gloom about him. As if nothing and no one could harm him. Without a doubt, he looks like a seducer willing to pursue a long career in the field. He seems to be dangling his feet, with no fear of falling off backwards, for instance. In front of him is a bulbous basketwork pram, with me leaning out beneath its hood, curious about the person taking the photo but already with the dour look of someone who doesn't love life. There are no awnings as yet.

No one in the neighbourhood had a pool. It was probably Tabakoff who built the very first private swimming pool in Stuttgart in the garden of his house in Sillenbuch. It wasn't a modest tradesman's house like ours, it was a solid sandstone house from the turn of the century with a highly respectable entrance hall.

We were invited to the housewarming party and instructed to bring our bathing suits. In the car on the way through the woods, past the television tower, our parents grumbled about the bombastic kitsch that awaited us chez Tabakoff. Back then they were united in their aversions. He acted amused when she imitated Lilo (née Wehrle, she used to say, which soon became Neverle because we children misunderstood her); née Wehrle, Neverle, who raised the ends of her sentences unnaturally high and drew them out exceptionally long, especially her married name, to give it an impressive dash of flair, was our mother's favourite target, and our mother was an expert at shooting darts at all her friends.

Lilo had a naturally high-pitched voice but made an effort to speak an octave lower and above all slowly, which made her listeners restless. She loved long sentences, initiating a downward curve after one or two clauses—which sounded slightly snotty, as if she'd suddenly caught a cold—only to end unexpectedly high on the full stop. Speaking in a shrill voice was frowned upon, at least by the wives. They saw it as a speciality of Bulgarian women. The Swabian wives never tired of telling each other horror stories about Bulgarian women.

They were despised for their high shrieking and pointed emotional outbreaks, particularly by our mother, who was very proud of her naturally low voice, gnawed away and depraved as it was by smoking.

There was a jolly atmosphere in the house, with plenty of guests already present. Tabakoff junior was presumably still alive at the time but I don't remember him being present. We were quite young back then—my sister could swim but I could only paddle about clutching a rubber animal. In we strolled with an inflatable swan and our dachshund. Lilo greeted the guests in a voluminous dress and bolero jacket, a delight in pink, cream, yellow and turquoise, with plenty of gold around her neck and wrists; her perfectly varnished nails stroked through our hair and she gave us each a kiss (the only person outside our family from whom I tolerated such behaviour; my sister tended to accept such assaults with indulgence).

The garden looked as if it was in America. Hollywood-style swing seats stood around the square of blue, ornate decorative tables were on standby, a tea trolley with drinks was wheeled out by a dainty fairy in an apron and bonnet. As soon as she turned around we all saw a huge white bow, its ribbons falling coyly over her behind. What impressed me though was the poodle. Snow-white, with eyes like black buttons sewn into his fur and a delightful little crown. His curls looked freshly bathed and blow-dried. Cherie wore a glittery diamanté collar and acted in such a ladylike manner that it was impossible to believe his gender. As our dachshund Snacky got on well with all breeds of dogs, we were allowed to bring him along. Cherie barked him out every time, trembling up to his crown and performing cute, decorative jumps on his curly-haired legs. Snacky stared at him in confusion and wagged his tail. Two minutes later the old acquaintance was back in balance. Snacky descended upon Cherie's bowl and drank up all his water, and then they went off to make mischief in the garden. I longed to be the third dog in their gang but the two of them wanted nothing to do with me. Despite her many guests, Lilo noticed my sadness and lifted me up—oh gold-rattling, sweet-scented queen of my heart, how I miss you!—onto her lap.

Zankoff was already sitting by the pool. In a bathrobe, plastic sandals and shorts. His unhappy family had taken up their positions round him. Dark-blue blazers with golden buttons—inside them the twins, not yet boarders at the prestigious Salem School but being prepared for the experience. The wife in a fiery-red suit. She had put her hands around her husband's neck, as if she wanted to give him a massage or strangle him right then and there, as proof that he was all hers. Which was by no means the case by that point. Zankoff lived separately from his family in an apartment with his favourite whore, and every one knew it. He rarely saw his family, he hated his wife and people tended to agree with him, although most looked down their noses at him in a mixture of envy and disgust.

Zankoff delighted in showing off his hairy chest, smoked cigars and tended to snort and slap his thighs when he laughed; he ate garlic with no inhibitions, in amounts that the others would never have allowed themselves, concerned as they were with their reputation as Bulgarians. His wife was generally regarded as malignant through and through, while people believed that Zankoff did have his good-natured side, although there was no concrete evidence to back it up. The fact was that he owned a brothel that he supervised from a bar. Other than that he was a fence, carried his money around in fat bundles and had a passion for counting large bills of money in public. The instant Tabakoff came close to him, Zankoff grew nervous. He was overcome by irritation and spoke overly loudly, no doubt because Tabakoff had more money and a more beautiful wife. Our father, though, he referred to as Doc and behaved as if our father were the apple of his eye and he himself were his personal patron saint. He also sent his whores to our father's gynaecology practice.

One thing about Zankoff, however, was extremely odd, and it was only revealed after his death, which caught him on the hop at the age of forty-five when he smashed his Karmann Ghia into a pillar. (He was the second Bulgarian to take his turn at dying.) In the living room of his apartment, which neither his family nor his friends had ever entered, was an entire built-in library of nineteenth-century literature—Goethe, Schiller, Kant, Hegel, all the big names lined up in complete editions. No one was aware of him being interested in books; after all, he could barely read and just about write his own name. The books were made of wood. But that wasn't all. If you took Schelling's *Ideas Concerning a Philosophy of Nature* off the shelf, a rust-brown dummy with a green label, which looked on closer inspection as if it had been rubbed with shoe polish, it revealed a hole through which you could spy into Zankoff's bedroom.

There's a red-fringed cloth on the table, on top of it a bread basket. Rumen and my sister are back again. How caring and concerned my sister is! She immediately rubbed my shoulders to warm me up. And did not say a word to ask for her jacket back, although she'll soon be cold herself, no doubt.

To warm us all up I make a few blonde bombshell comparisons. Rumen is now as familiar with the Stuttgart Bulgarian tribe as if he'd known them from an early age. My sister arranges a threesome of salt cellar, pepper pot and oil pourer for our Paris, introducing the characters as if in a children's play—Ladies and gentlemen, boys and girls, may I present to you Zankoff's wife, with the woman they call our mother, and here, a round of applause for the beloved and respected Lady Neverle!

Strange pain, to reincarnate three dead blonde bombshells in their strange sins. Even stranger that there's suddenly so much talk of our mother, whom we haven't mentioned for years.

When she talks about our beloved, my sister enters the realms of ecstasy just like me. She literally makes Rumen's mouth water, feeding him with this woman's magic, for she's not dead at all, she's just emerging from the pool down there and shaking her locks. Astoundingly, everything artificial about her (and she was more artificial than the other two) immediately turned back to nature. Née Wehrle seemed to have been born with red-varnished fingernails and toenails. All three women had perms but only for our Neverle was this the only possible, the only suitable hairstyle, to which she wisely remained loyal her whole life long. What looked like yellow-painted concrete on Zankoff's wife radiated an indestructible lustre on our favourite. She was the strong-headed, strong-curled blonde bombshell of our childhood, not plump although her ankles were unarguably thick (we accepted this blemish with grace, loved it in fact, as if two delightful bulges had deposited themselves around the thinning bones for their protection), they never seemed vulgar although her joints were decorated with vulgar charm bracelets.

Without a doubt, our mother had the most elegant legs of the three, long and slim, but what good did they do her? She had by far the better jewellery, but what was it good for? She had more brains too, but why have brains when they make you neither wiser nor kinder? We'll leave Zankoff's wife's legs out of the equation—they were thin as rakes and instantly forgotten by all around her. No one ever noticed her having brains. When she joined in a conversation it came out confused and abrupt and mean, in later years slightly slower, clouded by alcohol. All the gold she hung from her ears and around her neck, the glinting baubles, prompted merely pity: How could such a small person weigh herself down with such senseless ballast?

Curiously enough, Rumen puts in a good word for our mother. He's a real gentleman and he won't tolerate anything bad being said about any mother. His eyebrows shoot upwards in all the respect which our mother suddenly engenders in him. How admirable, how clever is this woman that Rumen is talking about; he knows her from a handful of photos but we don't appear to know her at all.

The other two were mothers as well, we sisters chorus, but Rumen's strict answer is: but not yours!

To prove he's made his choice, he takes a toothpick and sticks it into one of the two holes in the pepper pot. We laugh, perhaps a little too loudly, keen to show we're not churlish about people making dirty jokes in our presence.

Two falcons circle above. Our necks slump tired over our plates. A good day has been had!

Outside the town hall, not far from our car, is a parked jeep with tinted windows. Is it the same one as before? My sister thinks it is. She surveys the square with narrowed detective eyes. Hundreds and thousands of possible hiding places. I'm not sure it is the car we were suspicious of—it looks smaller and more harmless to me. And nor is the man in leathers anywhere to be seen. And what (my sister doesn't explain it because there is no explanation), what would a fully leathered man who happens to be leaning against a car while we visit a convent want from me, from her or from Rumen?

BLACK CASINGS

Tonight there's no rain and I can't get to sleep again. Perhaps I'm in too much of a good mood to sleep. Reading doesn't help this time, certainly not by this dim and dingy bedside lamp. I've got *Koba the Dread* with me, a gruesome but excellent book about Stalin, and I took the sentence *The laughter should have stopped around then* as a hint to put it aside. It won't be of any help to me tonight. I normally pick up a Martin Amis book in the evening and don't close it until I've finished it the next morning. Then I read it at a slower pace again later. But tonight there are too many fathers and sons whirling through my mind—Tabakoff and his dead son, Stalin and his surrendered son, shot dead against the barbed wire of a German camp, Zankoff with his curly-headed twin sons and our father with a phantom son, a third child unknown to us.

Frivolous laughter is lying in wait. What if there'd been an exchange of moustaches from one corner to the other, with Old Mother Hitler ruling over Russia and Old Father Stalin over all of Germany—fie! I gurgle with laughter and toss myself with elan onto my other side, as if struck by an electric shock.

Now let's get down to things one after another.

Back to Tabakoff. Tabakoff with his crazy plan that's brought us to Bulgaria. This Tabakoff, whom we all underestimated because his wife's gorgeous flesh pressed so much into the foreground that he remained as if hidden behind it. And yet he'd always been pulling the strings in the background. Pulling the family strings back then in Sillenbuch too, I'm sure of that now. Tabakoff showed us all what surviving means, casually demonstrating what a measly Bulgarian can manage all on his ownsome, although there are plenty of historical examples to be had.

If Tabakoff was the kind of person interested in history or literature (which he isn't), he would have come up with two role models for his plan—the funeral processions for his relatives scattered across Europe that Philip II had arranged to El Escorial, and the transport of Hermann Göring's first wife Carin from Sweden to Carinhall.

Black cortèges all across Europe, beating hooves, creaking wheels, clouds of dust on the horizon, the scent of sweat from the decked-out black horses, peasants doffing their caps by the wayside, criers on the towers, swinging clappers ringing in, notables in black velvet doublets and golden chains at the town gates; then three hundred years later the drone of engines, torch-lit parades, flagged convoys, escorts of uniformed men with raised right arms, wreaths suspended, determined arms outstretched by mayors, sonorous voices on the radio, proclaiming unshakeable loyalty one of the virtues of the North.

All dead, much deader than they thought, deader than declared and invoked.

Tabakoff, so long overlooked, such a hard-headed man, thought up his personal itinerary for the dead, acting on his own account as usual. It gave him great pleasure to work everything out down to the tiniest detail. He chose the travel route, chose the hotels to house the baggage train, negotiated with the owners of limousine fleets, negotiated with the authorities in Stuttgart—and once again I'm overcome by giggles: the very idea of Tabakoff battling his way to the heart of the Stuttgart senate chancery, where he comes across a prime minister armed with pointy milk teeth and gradually transforms the haughty figure into a trusting little puppy, makes me flounce myself onto my other side.

Steady as she goes, you silly moo.

And now keep going with Tabakoff in an orderly manner because that's by far not all his heroic deeds. He negotiated with the metropolitan in Sofia, an earnest man who was swiftly persuaded, however, by means of a weighty donation; he spoke to several Orthodox priests; chose the graveyard, the wreaths, the restaurant for the funeral reception and of course the grave monument, which had to be made to order on the basis of his scribbled sketches, whereby the incompetence of the bricklayers and stonemasons offered him the greatest resistance. Ha!

Our man had had an easy time of it with the bureaucrats, all the way across the five countries involved, but not with the Bulgarian tradesmen. The work progressed slowly between one temper tantrum and the next, with Tabakoff forcing them to tear the thing down, several times over, letting only the concrete foundations remain as they'd originally been poured.

The monument's main attraction was this—when the Stuttgart Bulgarians flew out of their caskets all together on the day of resurrection, the first sight they would see was the snowy peak of the Vitosha massif. Tabakoff imagined the whole thing absolutely topped with snow, although it only rarely snows on the Vitosha now and possibly will not snow at all in future.

And another thing—as everything was always about America for Tabakoff, his religious ideas had been infected by a consoling childish faith, in which all was as pale pink and blue as on his poolside garden swings, not dark and strict like in the Orthodox surroundings where he'd grown up. Over dinner at the Principe di Savoia, his rusty voice informed us of how he pictured the resurrection—in one flying whoosh. Delicate clouds in the sky. God would wait in a pink tunic. The little doors would leap open, as would the lids of the caskets, and whatever crumbs remained in there would fly out, transfiguring into light new bodies. He himself would be among them—by that time he'd be long dead of course—but not only that: he would fly on ahead of the team. They were his students and he their captain.

Stalin was scared shitless of flying. He only flew a single time, escorted by seven fighter planes, cramped up in his seat and as white as a sheet.

Onto the other side, this time without giggling.

So let's establish once and for all—Tabakoff had no idea about any dry bones whose journeys had come to fame in the past. What he'd come up with was a muddy newfangled muddle, a modern whatchamacallit made up of both funeral processions. Despite all that, our man had every right to feel like a pioneer in all his innocence. He was only vaguely aware of the melancholy Spaniard who had once held sway over a huge realm. Göring he knew better. The fat Reich Marshall in his leather doublet and boots—oh yes, he was all too present in his memory, in his various costumes topped off by his tufted hunting hat. But Tabakoff knew nothing at all of his Swedish wife. And so he had no need to worry that both men had achieved something similar to him, albeit on a far more pompous scale.

Black. That deadly, chic, universal colour tone.

Of course, black was Tabakoff's first choice as well. In America he'd come to value the comfort of stretch limousines (tomorrow Rumen will have to explain how they get by with only four wheels without sagging in the middle). Eleven worm-length, black limousines with dainty anthracite curtains in an intricate Escher pattern, which I'd had eight days to ponder. The limousines, a German and a Bulgarian flag fluttering on each of their front flanks, drove out of Stuttgart with some forty people inside them, the drivers not included. At the vanguard of the procession were two even longer and beefier cars, special designs with decorated lids to crown their otherwise smooth roofs.

Our eyes popped when we first caught sight of the things! In fact there was a historical role model that had been honoured after all. As we later found out, Tabakoff adored the Argentine singer Carlos Gardel. He absolutely idolized Gardel and had once engrossed himself in a glossy magazine showing photos of Gardel's funeral in Buenos Aires. The Avenida de Mayo thronged with people. And right in the middle, drawn by a team of eight feather-bushed black stallions, a coach that looked like a huge, drawn-out sugar bowl with a massive lid on top. Black, of course it was black. But that wasn't all. The vehicle was entwined with ornaments, its glass sides as if spun over and over with black sugar, and inside it lay the badly damaged Argentine Sleeping Beauty who was driven past the mourners to La Chacarita, his temporary resting place where he was to sleep for a thousand years.

Tabakoff made an exception for Gardel. He did not imagine his beloved singer's resurrection as much in flying mode as in a singing miracle. With outstretched arms, 'Mi Buenos Aires querido' on his lips, Gardel would climb out of the opened coffin. Jesus, how Tabakoff tortured us with that song! He sang it and hummed it at every opportunity, not once as out of tune as we feared every time he started again.

But perhaps it was something entirely different that had awakened the pompous funeral idea within him, an experience from his younger days, with the death of his beloved Gardel arching romantically over it. At the age of twenty-five, Tabakoff had witnessed the much-loved king of Bulgaria being taken to his grave in Sofia. Boris III had died of heart failure on 28 August 1943, still young, only forty-nine years of age. He had returned from a dramatic state visit to Berlin two weeks earlier. The Bulgarians immediately suspected that Hitler had had him poisoned. Even today they persist in believing it, although no evidence has ever emerged and it was hardly in Hitler's interest to kill a wavering but all in all compliant ally.

As so often, the Bulgarians have constructed a huge theory around a single detail, in this case a complicated murder theory—the king had gone to Berlin in civilian clothing rather than in uniform, wanting to demonstrate at first hand his political tactic of keeping his soldiers out of the war as far as possible. Hitler, they say, had received him in a black mood and dismissed him in just as black a mood. That may well be the case but it's not enough for a murder. And the Bulgarians are all too eager to forget how highly Hitler regarded Boris.

Boris was also popular with the Bulgarian people. Through the alliance with the Germans, Bulgaria had swallowed up large swathes of territory without having to fight for them. Which is why Boris was celebrated as the Unifier. Apart from that, his style of government was regarded as less despotic than his predecessors. And on the occasion of his funeral there were more people out and about in Sofia than ever before. Among them Tabakoff.

The great day of mourning is extolled in verse. The people wept, even the sky donned a veil and shed tears, bitter drops falling on the coffin of the beloved king, who could no longer protect his country from spiralling into misfortune.

Tabakoff recited one of these poems to us by heart, his eyes glinting with emotion and his outstretched arm clutching at the air, while the fingers of his hand opened up as if they'd just lost hold of a tail of the tsar's coat, long since translated to the realm of myth.

Tabakoff obviously considered a complete ornamentation of the two flagship limousines exaggerated, so he made do with a special design for the roofs, those lids at the sight of which—hardly had we recovered from the surprise—the tongues were set a-wagging. Not mine incidentally; I'd found the entire undertaking likeable from the very beginning.

Likeable. Now would be the moment to pat my pillow into shape, find the ideal position and set off in search of slumber—*likeable*, a lovely word like that would be ideal to take along with me, or perhaps rather a vague tra-la-la, a melody word?—No, likeable is just fine, why not likeable? It glides across all that's desolate, likeable Bulgaria, likeable Rumen, likeable sister, likeable Dimitroff, Zhivkov, Zankoff and who knows who else—

No, it's not working, my bones are—no matter which way I toss and turn, somewhere there's a bone in an unfortunate position; I simply can't get to sleep with my bones all wrongly ordered like this. There's nothing for it—light on, book open. I'd rather laugh with Koba than feel my own bones.

Abandoned dogs howl in the distance, and each of their cries sounds as if the most perilous hour in the universe had come, the time of impotence and vulnerability.

And only a few unhappy souls are awake or a few entranced souls like me. Desperate lights of lonely lamps in the pitch-black Bulgarian night, which had once coalesced with Stalin's long nights, in which Stalin's copycat henchmen and torturers had knocked at the doors.

Expect the Judgement any time of day or night, our Swabian grandmother had impressed upon us, or it'll take you by surprise and you won't be prepared for it. But the judgement our pious grandmother was awaiting was a harmless one, a joyfully absolving one, or at least not the judgement of Stalin's kangaroo courts. The very placidity with which she stroked our heads as she gave these speeches of hers proved that we had nothing bad to fear.

On the first arrest the body's chemistry produces a sudden heat—*you are burning, boiling,* says Amis, writing in Solzhenitsyn's wake.

I'm cold, and this book is really not a sleep aid, so the book gets closed and the light goes out.

Black.

Our cortège in broad daylight spawned by the night. When night came it disappeared into the garage of a large luxury hotel or the belly of a ferry; by day it drove out again. We couldn't see into the two limousines in front. Their windows were blackened. For good reason. Inside they were less ornamental, less ebonied and copper-mounted than one might have expected—more like in a temporary hall operated by a delegation of the UN tribunal at Srebrenica. The remains of the deceased were transported on simple wooden pallets, packed in black plastic to ward off the air, some sacks flaccid, some full. They all had a pocket sealed on top of them with a transparent square for inserting the necessary paperwork. Most of the relatives who had decided to make the journey were spared this sight.

So there were thirteen cars in total. We started out from Degerloch, because most of the Bulgarians had lived in Degerloch and Sillenbuch and it wasn't far from there to the motorway. Even negotiating the place where the convoy was allowed to set out had been no easy undertaking. They agreed on the broad expanse outside the forest cemetery, which was practical enough, as until recently most of the deceased had been slumbering there in their silent beds, edged with oaks and linden trees and mosses and ferns and hedges.

It's time to make sleep contact with them, to sleep alongside them under dissolved oaks and linden trees and mosses and ferns in the great We. Just look how eyelessly this We is sleeping, and the universe too, sleeping in its black cave of retreat. We're all sleeping, kept safe in there with sad smiles, like bony old maids saving themselves for the divine lover, who perhaps even comes but decides after a brief glance not to wake us, seeing as we're so devoid of charms.

THE WALLFLOWER

I resurface because wild boars of all creatures were chasing through my inner undergrowth, from which I fled in a slow retreat, my gaze boring into their small, black, evil, perfectly round piggy eyes—

It can't have been more than ten minutes. The section of window between the curtains is still dark, a slim carving of moon barely suitable for illumination. Give me sleep at last, erratic Morpheus, do you hear me, sleeeep, it can't be all that difficult, night is outspread, the stupid and the wise alike asleep, the witty and the dumb, tap me on the fingernails, Morpheus, and count me out in consolation, only please don't let another sounder of boar traipse through my dream, please not those beasts, of which I'm madly, truly, absurdly afraid.

What do I have ears for, as finely tuned as a wild animal's? No one's hunting me. There are only isolated barks outside now, the answer from one kennel to the next with a gap, a doggy pause for thought, and after that a feeble grousing, the dreary dutiful barking of aged dogs. The tired doggy throats have had enough for the night, they're sick of choreographed chorusing to show who has his territory where.

Alive wild boars—I know them from films, I'm not scared of them then, and I've seen them dead with my own eyes. A costume designer once told me a story of made-up wild boars. It was harmless. Only a tiny bit of cruelty to animals, hardly worth mentioning. An olfactory story. According to the script for *La Reine Margot*, the hog had a turbulent performance to put on. At first all went well, a black-spotted boar fulfilled all expectations. Weeks later though, on the outdoor shoot, the pig was sick and they had to use a different one. As there were none to be found with similar patches, they used make-up to put spots on the new boar. With the side effect that the dogs, which were supposed to launch themselves barking at the boar, went gallivanting around it in confusion. The wild boar didn't smell like a wild boar any more, it smelt like a human in make-up, and that didn't get the dogs barking and slavering. The poor beast may well have smelt like a troop of perfumed Bulgarian women, so I'm surprised the dogs didn't skedaddle straight out of there.

I saw dead wild boars and a pack of excited setters and pointers on a hunt as a child. We owed the excursion to one of our father's rich patients. We were invited to spend the weekend with the von Wefelkrodts—the entire Degerloch clan: father, mother, the eight-year-old and six-year-old daughters and the dachshund.

The high, keening choir of the pack of dogs. There it is again, effortlessly recalled in my mind, that exulting choir of lust echoing out of every corner of the forest. Our dachshund was absolutely beside himself. But he wasn't allowed to join the hunt, our father had to keep him on the lead.

Disconcertingly, our father hiked across the field in hunting dress too, a strange hat with a tuft of hair perched atop his head. He had even been given a rifle, which he didn't know how to hold. Could he shoot at all? Probably not. He had never been a soldier, and he certainly hadn't learnt to hunt in Bulgaria. At any rate, he did not look like a born huntsman, our father, as he disappeared into the woods, the open rifle cradled in his left arm, dragged along by the dachshund pulling at its leash on the right.

At some point the men came, hunters and forest workers, steaming in leather and loden, sweating in boots, streams of sweat running from their foreheads and down the backs of their necks, came back out of the forest, and the worn-out, happy dogs got their teeth into their share of the bag. The kills were laid out along the edge of the woods, pretty piles of leaves and branches making a pro-visional death adornment for the slain animals. There lay sixteen wild boars, sixteen bristly mounts with their gob-bling bellies, a good few red deer too, a hart with its head twisted on its grassy bed as if he were terribly surprised, all the way up to the tips of his slanting antlers, at what had happened to him, and a handful of hares, swift run-ners presumably hit in the midst of a leap.

My sister and I were ear witnesses to the hounding, eye witnesses to the previous perforation of a bevy of beasts. We couldn't tear our eyes away from the kill; I can still hear the gurgling sounds escaping from the distended stomachs. Did that gobbling noise come of its own accord or because the animals had just been broken open and gutted? I can't remember. Of course the hunting horns were blown as well, short and clear at the start, in between separate signals, sounding the mort at the end. All the gloomy rituals of the hunt, rescued from generation to generation into the sixties of the past century, came to enactment.

The evening's entertainments were equally strange. Greenish wallpaper, which had presumably survived several generations too, horizontally striped with flowers, their long stems criss-crossed, the voluptuous blossoms changing colour from stripe to stripe, standing out in salmon-pink or vanishing in pale-rose—if my memory serves me right they sheathed the large salon where one gathered after dinner, good-humoured, red-cheeked and tipsy, a society consisting mainly of aristocrats and only a few commoners. The entertainment was charades. The adults devoted themselves to the game with childlike exuberance. They were as keen as mustard, much to us children's amazement. Even more disconcerting was that the great huntsmen and their wives called each other names as silly as Fritzi, Beppi, Dolly and Dotty.

We squatted timidly against the wallpaper on high-backed, red-flowered chairs and suddenly turned into miniature copies of our mother. Next to me, at about ankle level, was a hole in the wall, the wallpaper torn out all around it. I stared by turns at the middle of the room, at my sister, at our mother and at the hole, in the hope that a mouse might appear in it.

An insane hope—that the animal only I'm expecting runs straight across the room and everyone stops thinking what they're thinking at that moment. The whole conglomeration nailed to their seats. Then uproar, commotion from the men, commotion from the women, understanding calm from the children. What Father, what Mother? Allow me to introduce myself: Miss Mouse. She pays her respects to me and whisks me away to a place where there are neither parents nor dead animals. The child and the mouse are agile enough to go roaming the world hand in hand.

Sad common sense pushes Mother in a smoke-grey Chanel suit back to my side, sitting there motionless in her gold-buttoned rampart.

Up to this weekend, our mother had never had any close social contact with the aristocracy. What she thought of the aristocracy was presumably—if we allow ourselves to think our way into the maternal mind by way of exception—of petty bourgeois romantic nature, a stew so to speak of nobility and nobs with a few poisoned chunks of meat floating in it. Aristocrats were born on a mountain eyrie with golden nametags around their necks, but they had to earn this gift of advantage in retrospect, compelled by an unrelenting upbringing, by climbing up again from the bottom (at the bottom in terms of human drives, for in the Swabians' eyes human nature was a very, very low thing) to their high beginnings. They had to be tough, hard-working, earnest and strict and they had to submit to rules at the dinner table ten times more complicated than we were used to at home, so as to be aristocrats, gracious, winning, wise and kind aristocrats who had earned their aristocratic titles. Were they even allowed to laugh?

No wonder the entire European aristocracy disappeared into this yawning chasm of human impossibility.

How they slapped their thighs, how the young, old and ancient laughed until tears ran down their cheeks— this boisterous band of rascals in the green salon upset the entire applecart of virtues dreamt up for them. Our mother responded with stiffness. Had she had a head of black hair and worn a mantilla of black lace, she could have played a part in Fellini's *Casanova* as one of the Spanish ladies who don't bat an eyelid, frozen stiff by the Italian Casanova's obscene theatre of salamandrine tongue undulation. Mother and daughters all, we sat there like pillars of Pietism.

Unlike our father. He fooled around like a schoolboy, suddenly liberated in a way we'd never seen before. When he was given the task of acting out a wallflower, he played it with such captivating charm that he garnered a round of applause from all directions, with the exception of us three. His hands mimed the bricks of a wall, then a plant pot with a tulip inside it, perhaps, then he pulled up a chair and sat down on it instead of the wall, pushed his knees together, made awkward curtseying movements with his legs, pressed his fist to his mouth, sighed, cast bashful glances to all sides and gave a brief giggle, bubbling over with pleasure as if he'd been playing charades his whole life long and intended to do so again the very next day.

There was a certain young woman, a rather doughy, very fair blonde with glimmering hair and the kind of skin that comes out in red patches at the slightest touch—the host's wife.

As was whispered to us later, much later when all those involved were long dead, our father was said to have had an affair with this woman. Why, there was even tell— and now we are entering the territory of feral Balkan speculation once and for all, for this whispering reached our ears along a circuitous route, via our Bulgarian aunt, our father's sister who lived behind the Iron Curtain at the time and never once saw a single one of these people. So this aunt claimed to have heard of the scandal (or rather the scandalous incident, as there are millions of its ilk) via a former school friend who lived in Switzerland and was allegedly acquainted with Zankoff's respectable older brother, and this respectable brother, in turn, claimed to have heard from his feckless younger brother, the pimp, that—well, a child, a son, existed. And as befits every *chronique scandaleuse*, our father is supposed to have sired him with the glimmer-haired hostess and she in turn is supposed to have cunningly managed to foist the child upon her husband, without him (according to Zankoff, an idiot) ever smelling a rat.

Supposed, claimed, alleged, heard. So we allegedly had a secret brother. Do we?

Of course, we were shocked when we found out. Being the only member of the family with a heightened sense for the true embarrassments of life, I asked after a brief moment of zealous consideration—So? Did Zankoff say anything about whether our father played the obstetrician?

Red-faced flinching all around the table and no answer.

Our agitation was soon dispelled. We remembered the Bulgarian tendency to believe in rumours—fail-safe betting systems, miracle diets, conspiracy theories, UFOs, astrological abracadabra—and to disseminate the stuff with raised index fingers and eyebrows aloft. We contented ourselves with opening up the Stuttgart telephone directory, establishing how many von Wefelkrodts there were, and then slamming the book closed again.

Either way, even if this brother were more than a phantom, we had no right to look for him and set a strange family in disarray with a drama of pure conjecture.

One thing that does place the story somewhere in the vicinity of credibility is our mother's stiff behaviour on that evening of charades. The fact that her ideas of the aristocracy came into confrontation with reality is hardly reason enough for her silent, motionless posture, her strict refusal to take part in anything at all. Usually, our mother grew aggressive in uncomfortable situations, seeking to get over her insecurity through witty, jaunty remarks, drinking too much and lighting one cigarette from another. Did she smoke at all that evening? Not even that, it seems to me—a sure indication that there was another worm gnawing at her other than charades.

Now I see our mother's elderly face quite clearly in my mind's eye, for the first time in years—her nervous, wanton face with a slight squint behind thick lenses, framed by an enormous white mane of hair. I see her slim, carefully manicured fingers with their many rings, fingers with cigarette smoke rising from them, and everything behind the smoke stays secret, not to be deciphered by me or by my sister.

We are part of a secret family machinery, which perpetually produces misfortune—the dead father scares the children, the surviving mother scares the children more than the dead father, my sister in turn scares her children—only I don't scare anyone, seeing as I'm less of a secret. As my punishment, I hear the secret cockroaches in this very secret Bulgarian hotel and feel the Bulgarian disease beseething my skin and seeking an open pore to creep into.

Secrecy and conspiracy, the ailment of all Bulgarians! A gift from the rumble-headed fathers, a gift from the mothers chit-chattering in high voices to their children, for centuries on end. We always got fresh samples of this disease delivered by our relatives in Sofia. Their plot-seeking brains grew most agitated when it came to our father's death.

Zealous cracking of sunflower seeds, the piles of shells growing swiftly on their plates.

Grandparents, great-aunts, aunts, uncles and cousins were (and still are, those who are alive) convinced our father was murdered by the Bulgarian secret service. The theory is simply too good to be untrue. It is lodged unshakeably in their minds. One would have to tear off their heads to take it away from them.

It was of little use for us to describe the tortuously drawn-out years of his destruction, the two attempts to kill himself in the bathtub before his hanging. The only effect was that all the espionage withdrew for a moment, whereupon our relatives shrugged their shoulders as if it had never been of any concern to them how the man had happened to die, and then silently switched to another of their favourite theories, which they refrained from mentioning in front of us out of politeness, or at least never spoke of directly.

Through bizarre insinuations, which we learnt to piece together over the years, we figured it out. *His German wife murdered him*, was the short version of theory number two. The how and why played no role at all. The theory drew its strength solely from our mother's unpopularity. She was unpopular with the Bulgarian family because she was two months older than our father. That meant he had married an old woman, a disgrace for a Bulgarian man.

A childish murder theory. And because it's so childish, we nourished it too for a short time while we were growing up, regardless of all the facts. At least I know I nourished it; I think my sister did too. Oh yes, in our childish minds our mother had somehow, at some point, by some means, killed our father. However, the fantasy never managed to establish itself properly; barely born, it withered on the vine, simply shrinking away because experience left it too little space. Experience had taught us that our mother was too ineffective, too indecisive, too uningenious and, above all, too impatient to put a murder plot into action. She was absolutely out of the question, regardless of the answer to the vexing puzzle of whether she had ever loved her husband and if so, whether she still loved him by the time he died.

The patient paternal fingers, the impatient maternal fingers. My sister glides through life with incredibly calm fingers and toes, while I'm perpetually riddled with twitches. No rest for the wicked—by night I'm tossed and turned about, basking in murderous ideas, in naively lisping childish innocence of course. No sermon nor gentle childhood lessons resound. Allow me to introduce myself: Miss Mouse. May I help you to get rid of your family altogether? It's a secret of course, but I'm sorely tempted to drag my sister out of her legendary calm, at least once. She'd frown at the most if I told her I'd spent hours of the previous night killing her with the aid of a mouse. A mouse? I hear her asking incredulously. How would that work?

For the Bulgarians, nurturing secrets of the imagination is both a pleasure and a duty. It therefore only took a few hours or days for theory number one to reoccupy its rightful place and for the sunflower seeds to be maltreated in the accustomed manner. In the meantime the theory had grown stronger, more radical, more artful, more plot-like than ever. To give credit to our brave Rumen, however, I ought to mention that he never believed this nonsense, even though he was force-fed with plenty of it, seeing as he grew up next door to our grandparents.

It was certainly exciting to watch the secret service creeping into the little house on Wurmlingerstrasse, in the form of two inconspicuous men (inconspicuous to such a degree that one thought of fairy-tale cloaks of invisibility), who opened the garden gate and closed it obligingly behind them, who put the dachshund out of action with the aid of chloroform (not being aware of the dog's character, our relatives envisaged a furiously barking, snarling, sharp-toothed defender of the home and hearth; we refrained from revealing that he greeted strangers with a friendly wag of the tail and would have led the most sinister of characters straight into the house in return for a string of sausages), only to climb the steps to the front door—unnoticed by us children, at that moment practising with a ribbed blue hula hoop next to the porch (me) and hitting a ball against the wall with an old tennis racquet with sagging strings (my sister). So the two men opened the front door with a few skilful secret service tricks and closed it silently behind them, slipped across the hall behind our grandmother's back as she was scraping *spätzle* noodles from a chopping board into a saucepan with the kitchen door open, past the shoe cupboard and the coat rack, dashed around the corner and up the stairs—

Stop, stop, stop—no secret service man would have dashed willy-nilly past the shoe cupboard and certainly not a Bulgarian secret service man. If need be they'd have knocked off our beloved *spätzle*-making grandmother, just so they could dedicate themselves to the cupboard.

Impossible! The very thought of it makes me punch my pillow and switch to the other side. Are you gentlemen from the council? she'd have asked in her trusting way, then served up two plates of roast meat and *spätzle* with gravy for them, after which even the wildest man in the world could never have killed the dear woman, for she cooked so very well and was so very gentle.

The shoe cupboard! Oh yes, the relatives may well frown, for they hadn't thought of the cupboard at all. Simply because none of them ever set eyes on it—apart from our Bulgarian grandmother, who was the only one to get permission to travel in the 1960s and had once visited us in Wurmlingerstrasse. And this four-foot-seven tall, wizened, Nivea-scented princess, who was either busy with her own business or ogling her beloved son with her wide owlish eyes, had absolutely no talent for descriptions.

It didn't look at all like a shoe cupboard. It looked like a secret cupboard for diplomats from the Austro-Hungarian empire. A Swabian amateur inventor had come up with it as a patent cupboard. You could turn a crank on the outside and eight horizontal-format doors opened, and if you then turned a smaller wheel with a locking mechanism and lowered the lever into the slot with the number 3, for example, you would set a mechanism in motion that stretched out pair of shoes numero 3, polished to a shine and kitted out with wooden shoe stretchers by our Swabian grandmother, through the opened hatch as if on a protruding tongue. The cupboard was our father's pride and joy. He'd bought it from the Middle-Class Relief Fund, where people got rid of their old furniture after the war because it suddenly looked elephantine alongside their brand new low tables and chairs with protruding steel spider's legs. It was a magnificent piece of engineering but much too large for our hallway.

Go ahead, I tell our relatives, currently lying in their Sofia bunks and probably snoring, their night-warm heads pressed into their sweat-drenched pillows, while my sister, sleeping in the next room, knowing and disapproving of my penchant for drastic acts, raises a warning finger so that I don't start swearing. If you like, go ahead, you tough-jawed old Bulgarian seed-biters, so your secret service men are on the stairs—

Stairs, such a harmless curving Degerloch staircase, a fuggy family staircase treated to a vacuum once a week, carpeted in red (not exactly recently), and—I can't look without reaching out a hand—they've come loose at the bend as usual, the two brass rods that always slip out of the mounting, the staircase where the fourth and the ninth steps creak if you don't jump over them—

But yes, oh yes, your secret service men are very neat and tidy, so they put the brass rods back where they belong and they're cunning enough to jump over the two creaking steps, and our grandmother hears nothing, nothing, nothing, absolutely nothing. She doesn't hear them arriving on the upper floor, assailing our brooding father in the balcony room, gagging him, dragging him into the bathroom, running the bath, holding his head underwater, slitting his arteries, waiting until he's unconscious, then quietly, quietly, tip-tapping back the way they came past everything and everyone and very nearly getting caught by our mother coming in from the garage loaded down with shopping.

My dear relatives, I'm sure your theory is ingenious enough to explain why this attempt, and the second one too, went wrong. Though I must admit the secret service had an easier time of it the third time around. Hanging him from a heating pipe in his empty surgery was child's play.

A proto-Bulgarian doesn't kill himself—that's your favourite argument. And you've come up with all this balderdash because you can't get it into your heads that you raised a worn-down creature in the swamp of your very own family, a wimpish, selfish mollusc of a soul, who started trembling at the slightest day-to-day stress. Do you know the story about the washbasin? The washbasin that began crumbling away from the wall in the surgery? Our mother spotted the damage and got into such a panic that she immediately sent her husband on a skiing trip to Davos so that she could get it repaired secretly. Why? *Because the sight of a washbasin coming away from the wall would have been too much for him.*

His filthy blood all over the bathroom. How amazing that it gave his daughters a cleanliness tic. You can eat off the floor, the tiles and the bathtubs in our bathrooms. My word of honour—there's not a drop of Bulgarian blood in there, nor any other kind of filth. Not in our bathrooms—that's guaranteed by Ata, Vim, Domestos, rubber gloves and protective goggles we don specially to clean our bathrooms.

Our father has been exploiting eternity for thirty-nine years. If we were supposed to take revenge on his behalf he'd have let us know by now.

Perhaps—but this perhaps and what it draws to mind is an extremely tentative, a not yet logically thought-out confusion still in a primordial form of thought—perhaps the fact that my sister and I employed Polish cleaning ladies, with whom we were very satisfied (although we did clean after them by cleansing our bathrooms twice over with the aid of Ata, Vim, Domestos and rubber gloves, not to forget the goggles, secretly every time so as not to offend them); furthermore, the fact that these two Polish women employed separately in the cities of Frankfurt and Berlin, who had no contact with each other whatsoever, indeed had probably never even heard of each other, committed suicide within only five months of each other—first the Frankfurt cleaning lady in Frankfurt and then the Berlin cleaning lady in Krakow—whereby the age the two women had reached flanked that of our father at the time of his death, if you will, for the lady who died in Frankfurt was a year younger than our father at forty-two, while the lady who died in Krakow was a year older at forty-four—perhaps these mysterious double cases are trying to shape into a wave of the paternal hand, which—

Well, what?

Which is nonsense. A conglomerating and then re-nebulizing swarm of idiotic thoughts. And now it's time to sleep, quick-sharp, faster than it takes the end of the rope to vanish behind the father who's already vanished into the wall.

There's no joy in staring out of the window. Your eyes go dumb, the landscape is dull, the road is straight. Those two in the front are in an appallingly good mood, twittering and giggling and chattering away. I'd like to know why but not even that gets me agitated. Everything's simply grazing me from a distance now.

No worries to carry around any more, a dull state of having exhausted my potential for annoyance, no thirst for activity, no hill to climb, no valley to descend, just dog-tired. My head dangles limply against the headrest. A discarded chandelier with only one bulb left, perpetually burning, the dear, loyal light bulb of family hatred. Which at the moment, however, for lack of energy is only glowing, threatening to go out soon due to increasing sleep-limpness.

How I miss Tabakoff's limousine, in which we drove across five countries, that miraculous sleep-generating vehicle. You could whisk me all the way around the world in it, like Raymond Roussel did it in his day, and I'd sleep, daydream, listen to the noise and not look out, not even if I were being driven through a lively market quarter, even if it were old Marrakech in the days of Hollywood miracles; I'd turn away and enjoy the sounds of the market criers as I slept on.

Mind you, the slumbering Roussel (a rather jolly genius as long as his money lasted) had his extravagant reconstruction of a birthing cave, replete with a bed and damask eiderdowns, all to himself. Staff dashing together at every destination took care of the cleanliness of his linen, the table set immaculately for every meal, fruit as gorgeous as jewels and chicken drumsticks glistening with jelly. I had to share the limousine with my sister and a bag of gummy bears, most of the time with the Zankoff twins and sometimes with Tabakoff too. At least Tabakoff wasn't stingy. He did things in style—that is, he had the limousine's cooler filled up with champagne bottles and other posh drinks from station to station. The Zankoff twins poured large amounts of champagne down their gullets. I didn't though. I don't drink champagne, I don't drink any alcohol with the exception of advocaat, and this eccentric preference remained unknown to Tabakoff, so I made do with a glass of still water or a Coca-Cola from time to time.

In principle, Roussel was right—being driven around the world with the curtains closed and never getting out to look at anything is well worth emulating. It's not on the cards though, there's too little gold in the coffers of the Degerloch inheritance and too little courage for such a wonderfully snotty gesture of disdain for the world.

This ugly Daihatsu with its stupid rattling of plastic. A Händel opera would be welcome right now. Händel leads us to other realms, away and above the usual trials and tribulations; Händel sets the fingers of even the tone deaf secretly conducting along; Händel is a first-class travel companion. *Giulio Cesare in Egitto*, how it waves and weaves, bobbing a hundred heads in time, that brisk zigzag of violins, fiddling up and down again, snappy, cheerful grasshopper music, just what my tired old brain could use right now.

But look, the family light bulb is still glowing. A wan craving for Father wavers through the car. There's no room in a low-mid-range car for a sprawling proscenium but outside on the stage of cloud, huge, lofty, thunderous like in the good old days of Olympia (I'm still not looking) our three-centimetre father is being put on display. Standing there with dangling arms, a bit of doctorly stuff around his neck, the pompous idiot. Despite his tiny dimensions, this father seems to possess something we don't have. He has in his possession a hugely significant Hölderlin notation in his terrible handwriting, which he's now extracting from his breast pocket. *Will the audacious spirit, escaping its restraints, emboldened to vie with God, wrecked by its huge pain in and through itself, find light, measure and truth elsewhere, and how?*

And how, and how, gasps Father, coughing, doubling over, regaining his composure and laughing his lungless laugh so loudly it can be heard in all the heavenly regions. But Olympia is far from here, albeit closer than from

Tübingen, and Zeus is a god who sleeps and can't even be enticed to bellow a reply through brash translations.

We pass tall electricity poles; that much I notice. Birds on the wires, not caring about the electricity sweeping through beneath their claws.

One of the Zankoff twins is now a manager in the energy sector. I have disquieting ideas of what a manager in the energy sector might be and I preferred not to ask any detailed questions. We had barely arrived at the Degerloch forest cemetery than we were accosted by the Zankoff twins. They seemed to have been waiting for us, or at least one of them, Marco, the manager in the energy sector. We sisters climbed aboard one of the cars and sat down facing the engine, leaving it to coincidence who would join us, and the door was immediately darkened by the mass of Zankoff, that is by Marco, who squished himself into the car ahead of his brother.

Two and two makes four, said Marco, flopping onto the seat opposite me, a revolving seat that could be electronically adjusted into all manner of positions—which he tried out expertly with the scuttle-fingered curiosity of a child—on which he half lay, half sat once he had set up the backrest, armrests, height and footrest according to his requirements and fastened his seatbelt. A spread-eagled creature (male? female? sexless?), prevented from flowing across the seat by the seatbelt and by his suit material, an entity with rolls of neck bulging out of its collar and segueing into a pale clump of flesh upon which a small nose protruded only slightly, while the gaze of the deeply embedded eyes made its way out of the fat with astounding intensity.

There was space enough, thank goodness. But fate had sent me a chattering sack of flesh as a travelling companion, who was to follow me around for days on end.

Whoever would have thought it, he said in his lukewarm, ingratiating Swabian dialect, meaning the unlikely fortune of us meeting again so late in life. He instantly expressed his enthusiasm that we'd now be inseparable for a full eight days.

Whenever I see a twenty-three-stone man I immediately think of the difficulties involved in getting rid of his corpse. Why do the steersman of the world and his hard-hitting corps of angels let such sprawling bodies come about?

He had a mischievous way of treating me as his prisoner by putting one padded hand on my knee. We were trapped in the hosepipe of a limousine and, as expected, my sister appeared to be enjoying the situation.

Everything studies about twins generally claim was proven wrong by these two men. One fat, the other thin, but still identical twins. On closer inspection one did discover similarities—both had hair in a dark blond shade, rising to bushes on the backs of their heads, both had large mouths, a tiny wart in the hollow of the left wing of their noses and short, stubby fingers. The entire scaffolding of fat that Marco had constructed with aplomb and which he was lovingly continuing to expand seemed as though fallen off Wolfi's body, perhaps melted off his bones through a slow process of annoyance, presuming he'd been fat before, which we didn't know. Where one was concealed behind a fleshy fortress of reality, the other had something principally belted about him, something that tended towards the sharp, the thin, the pointed. His nervous face seemed troubled by nasty thoughts, while a haughty arrogance forbade him from wasting glances on us. They'd both been thin as children.

Wolfi's speech remained meagre. We could barely get out of him what he did when he wasn't driving from Stuttgart to Zurich and from there to Bulgaria in a stretch limousine. He certainly didn't give us the impression that he'd been missing us since the heady days of childhood. He left the chatting to his brother, as well as the laying on of slappy paws, the lukewarm fug of emotion intended to lull us into the certainty that we'd always been stuck in the same bowl of soup together.

Your mother was a fabulous little lady, terribly capable, said Marco, his fingers scrabbling at the cooler. And how long has she been dead?

He made a noise along with it, a ghastly sound between whistling and clucking, which set a great deal of saliva in motion. I instantly thought of *The Silence of the Lambs* and saw our mother shrink into a brown moth larva and disappear into the monstrous, dripping mouth.

My sister informed him that she'd died in 2001. Wolfi shot a swift glance at her in response and looked away immediately. Marco had found the champagne, bright delight overrunning his face. He liberated the plug from its wire confinement, making a weak plop, poured out four glasses, and simply refused to believe that I didn't drink champagne.

What? That can't be true!

He almost thrust the glass into my hand while I slid around on the backseat, darkly dodging like in my child-hood, then he spouted several remarks that he considered expedient to instruct me that I was missing out on the best thing the world had to offer, until he finally realized it was pointless and deposited the glass intended for me on his side of the cool box, as a reserve.

A touch of the electronic rocker control sent the win-dowpane down to half level. I had a dire need to let some air in, even, if need be, the cold motorway air between Degerloch and Echterdingen.

The air conditioning only works if we leave the win-dows closed, said the manager in the energy sector, and pressed the button on his right to return the window to its full height. I felt the air stand still, which made me first suppress my breathing and then make up for it in a hectic dash. I find the air in every enclosed space repugnant, always fearful I might suffocate. My sister shot me a quick glance and furtively opened the window a crack on her side.

Marco hadn't noticed her manoeuvre; Wolfi had.

Marco raised his glass and vigorously regretted that he hadn't been able to bring his little mouse along. At that moment I didn't know quite what he meant. Did this obese person really live with a tiny, delicate rodent?

But, of course not. Marco reached into his jacket and fetched out his wallet, an over-stuffed, multiply folding thing from which a lath pegged full of credit cards tumbled. He removed a photo from it—a short woman with her head tilted and a hairline low on her forehead smiled at us bashfully, as if asking for forgiveness for her existence and for stealing seconds of our valuable time. Juana, or Tita, as Marco said, a Colombian woman he'd met on a business trip to the US.

Very nice, very pretty, who'd have thought you'd end up with a Colombian. My sister and I chorused praise for Tita. Anyone who knew us well would have heard the subtle vibrations of irony with which we betongued the fact that such a fat man was permitted to have a wife.

He was happy, Marco claimed, and how. He'd got himself just the right wife—you don't find a woman like that every day, one who didn't keep bothering him all the time. The curmudgeonly face of Herta, the Zankoff mother, shoved its way through from times drifted away; her contorted, hasty way of speaking rose from the choir of women's voices silenced for ever, a manner with which she got attention everywhere, intervened everywhere and left no one in peace, least of all her sons.

His mousie was worth her weight in gold, he told us. She cooked like an ace, ironed like an ace, cleaned like an ace and she was capable in other areas too, he said, adding with a grin, always A1 at everything, if you know what I mean.

We had our doubts, but we kept them to ourselves.

You two would have been out of the question for me, said Marco with a wink and a giggle and swung his index finger to and fro. There was something prickly about you both, especially you (his finger pointing at me).

Then he pulled two photos of pudgy toddlers out of his wallet—Carlos and Nadja. First Carlos and then Nadja, each pressed up against a black-and-white spotty dog. What a delightful creature! Curious button eyes, two mischievous folds on its forehead revealing it was still young, its left ear upright with tiny hairs standing up in all directions and the other folded over. A first-class poser, a jester of a dog straight out of a William Wegman show.

We greatly regretted that it had ended up in such an ugly family.

The dog's so terribly pretty, I said spitefully. What's his name?

Minty, said Marco and put the photos away again. Wolfi made no comment on any of this, looking nervously about but mainly past us. At last my sister found the nerve to ask if he was married too. Wolfi graced her with a second swift glance while Marco answered on his behalf—Him? No, no! What would he want with a wife?

I can't remember when we finally got Wolfi to talk to us. It seems by now as if it took us days. There was no making out what kind of relationship he had with his brother, whether he hated him, disdained him, valued him, loved him, trusted him. Perhaps all those emotions were muddled up inside him, or he had none at all. It was obvious that he left the talking, organizing and in fact all conceivable activities to his brother and wasn't even bothered by Marco explaining his life on his behalf.

After much to-ing and fro-ing it emerged that Wolfi had been a sports and geography teacher in Heilbronn but had given up the profession (we didn't dare to ask why) and now accompanied elderly persons on cruise ships.

Always at sea, my dear brother, said Marco and informed us that his brother had a way with older ladies; he took care of them, mollycoddled them around the clock, but only if they had plenty put away for a rainy day. He earned a decent living out of it.

Wolfi grinned, which gave the pathetic impression that he was doing so under the disciplining rod of a facial streptococcus infection. Our distraught looks proved we didn't know what the world was coming to. What wealthy woman voluntarily takes on a travel companion who barely says a word? Wolfi made no further comment on his brother's insinuations and soon returned to his usual tense inscrutability, quite as if Marco were talking about someone with whom he was only vaguely acquainted.

I was stormed by a gang of images and thoughts of such senselessness that I had to stare out of the window for a while. In rapid succession, women and men flashed in and out of my mind's eye, including old man Zankoff, his hairy chest, and the smashed Karmann Ghia in obtrusive clarity; vulgar psychology dirtied my mind, childish fun and games interrupted, turning Old Man Zankoff into Zanki-Zocki-Zoffi, wee Wolfi had to work for his gold-bejewelled father as a child whore; I saw the twin masturbating on maps and smashing his mother's head with dumb-bells—mother, father, mother—was it his mother after all who had spoiled any pleasurable contact with the world of women for Wolfi?

As if he'd pulled the biggest fish out of the stream of my thoughts, Marco said, Mummy would have loved to have come along, but sadly it wasn't possible.

I spun around as if stung by a wasp.

She was bravely battling cancer with barely a hair left on her little head, we were told, which brought me out in a burst of laughter, hee hee, ha ha, only one hair on her little head! I saw the yellow plaster cast of her hair shattered on the ground; felt sweat breaking out around my nose and fell silent.

My interlocutor remained imperturbable to a frightening degree, as was his wont. My outbreak had caused not the slightest irritation. Your mum couldn't stand our mum, was his placid response, and ours couldn't stand yours either. What a crying shame, otherwise we'd have seen more of each other as children.

Our mother wasn't always fair to Herta, said my sister with an accusatory glance in my direction. It rubbed me up the wrong way even as a child. I was downright embarrassed by her behaviour, she added.

Believing she hadn't yet fulfilled her duty with this remark, she enquired at great length into the well-being of Old Mother Zankoff, even asking Marco to send her best wishes to her, for her recovery by telephone. She also asked in an emotively beatific tone whether there was a chance of her being rescued.

Federal cross of merit, said Wolfi.

That was all. What kind of bee did he have in his bonnet?

We fell silent. My sister plucked nonexistent fluff off her skirt. Marco emptied the glass originally meant for me and looked out of the window. Then he put headphones over his ears, turned his seat to face the engine and listened to something classical presumably, whereby his right hand conducted along with casual wrist movements—more hanging and waving than rising and falling.

It was suddenly silent, the excitement growing porous and collapsing in a heap. The only sound the even, warm-dark noise of the car, soothing, as is all right and proper for a funeral journey, and even when we overtook a truck the sound from outside only penetrated our cabin in muffled form.

My sister and I ruminated all the way to Zurich on what Wolfi might have meant. Secretly and against our will, he began to occupy our minds. Our thoughts flitted into contradictory corners. Did this man have a simple or a complicated nature? A mind objective or imaginative? Intelligent or stupid? The idea of him flirting with women to squeeze money out of them, let alone working as a gigolo, was inconceivable.

Women want to be entertained, or if a man does happen to be relentlessly taciturn then they at least want to suspect he's an unfathomable philosophical genius. Federal cross of merit? What was that all about? Had he intended to make a joke and actually meant Hitler's Mother's Cross? Or had he intended to offend my sister? But Wolfi was no joker. He wouldn't pass as either an entertainer or a philo-sophical catcher of illusions. There was something appalled inscribed on his face, a willingness for tumult that never broke out, instead trembling away to nothing in the narrow, furrowed zigzag of his web of wrinkles. Yet on the other hand, he certainly had confidence. At least when it came to his clothing. He was wearing a soft, olive-green shirt, along with a brown suit that also looked soft and had a slightly yellowish or reddish aura, depending on the light. The shoulder section was immaculately tailored.

Another strange thing was the aversion he seemed to have to my sister. It was no surprise that he didn't like me. Most men tend to avoid me so I'm used to that. It's a dif-ferent matter for my sister. She has a rather elastic manner about her. Passive but not lame. Even when they're not instantly besotted with her, men feel drawn to her. The reservation she exerts, her gracious figure, her pale, fine-featured face that has nothing challenging about it—all this never usually misses its mark. And then my sister's clever too. If she wants people to like her she knows how to use her means to precise effect. She dips into a huge reservoir of praise for the male of the species; it includes all manner of tender-hearted and finely targeted things, which she offloads very skilfully—with a bat of the eyelashes, framing green, sparkling and glowing flecks, a bat of lashes that almost make a large-eyed bug out of my narrow-eyed sister, while her voice (Big Sister, what pact with the devil bought you that voice?) is low-ered to an intimate whisper—and just listen, quietly,

quietly—breathed, aspirated, lisping discord like the snake in the Garden of Eden—her praise hits its mark.

But you only notice how much routine she has in the second after, while the recipient of her praise is still struggling with his debilitation and having to regain control of his fragile state of mind. All of a sudden, my sly sister switches back to narrow-eyed *modus* and stares into space as unfamiliarly as if she had no idea who she was dealing with.

Envy?

Yes.

And is that why I'm so moody?

Perhaps.

It was all in vain with Wolfi, at any rate. He never let the situation escalate far enough for a compliment to be due. How could she? Ought she to have praised him for rubbing his forehead with his fingertips like a man with a headache? Wolfi may have been as dumb as a bag of hammers but, I noticed the very first evening in the hotel in Zurich when Tabakoff held his speech over dinner, he was rising in my estimation.

We were a convoy of honour for his comrades of yore on their last great journey, said Tabakoff. He was glad that the Stuttgart Bulgarians' children had set out in such great numbers along with him. His wife was also among the comrades; he didn't want to keep that from us. His dear, beautiful wife (at this point he began to sob)— many of us no doubt remembered her, he himself recalled her vividly, and this loss was still hard to deal with. He could hardly speak her name, his shoulders twitched and his voice failed him in all his woe.

We sat there as if frozen to the spot. It was impossible for us to connect Tabakoff the businessman with an outbreak of this kind. The only reaction came from Wolfi. He got up from his seat, walked over to Tabakoff, took him tenderly in his skinny arms, poured a sip of wine into his mouth and gingerly stroked his bald head; and once Tabakoff had calmed down the silent Wolfi returned to his seat as if nothing had happened.

Aha, Shumen.

I haven't been paying attention. We're driving right through Shumen. The roads straight, concrete electricity poles, wind blowing, papers fluttering around, occasional tired pedestrians trudging with heavy bags, wastebaskets hanging half-torn from their posts. A place that no one visits, though not because it resists discovery particularly stubbornly. Idiots like us come here or dyed-in-the-wool Eastern Europe romantics, who greet every sheet of corroded tin with lambent, knowing emotion.

The usual decaying blocks with balconies rusted to a slant, long stalactites of fungus and rust, with pipes protruding from the walls in crooked hooks. Trickly-eyed moisture stains around the windows; every block without exception stricken by architectural leprosy, come into the world with state tumours, state rhagades, here with a triumphal peculiarity, however: these apartments were *glued* on top of each other. As the units were piled up, thick bulges of adhesive squished out between them. They remained the way they were. Beauty? What for? The official communist machinery considered all people equal—as blind vermin.

On we go along the parade road, a broad shopping street with cafes. Its only advantage consists in a row of crippled plane trees planted between the two lanes. We decide, or rather the other two at the front decide and I nod, to drive up to the plateau first to survey the scenery.

The monstrosity comes into view from a long way off. A huge concrete block on top of a flattened hill, a block with something about it of a skull knocked open and split, with something oozing out at the top. A road leads around the hill. Sparse coniferous forest, segueing into knee-high undergrowth. When we twist our heads and look up out of the windows, the thing menaces us from above.

Rumen cuts the engine off. We're alone in a car park the size of an Olympic field with a cabin at the edge, outside it a moped, a display stand of yellowed postcards and two dozing dogs. The wind blows cold and free, it's unclear from which direction. Inside the cabin Rumen buys the entry tickets, three tickets for *1300 Years of Bulgaria*.

We're standing in front of the monument to *1300 Years of Bulgaria*.

— —
— — — —

— —
— —
—   —   —   —   —   —   —   —
— —
— — —

Words fail me.

The usual evasion reflexes don't work. One ought to be able to fly away.

Filth. Filth of coercion. Filth of power. Filth of a people. The words that occur are of no use at all. Raw, brutal, monstrous—yes, they're right, but they apply to most monuments of the past hundred years, in the East and West. Thuggish, vicious, out of proportion—all correct, but this thing is harder and uglier. Desolate, repulsive, hulking—all true, and yet it can't describe the awfulness. Rough filth, miscreant filth, insidious filth, repugnant, extortionate filth—yes and yes again, but this monster cannot be stormed with words.

A broom for sorrows. Our Swabian grandmother used to sweep the pavement with a broom she called the *Sorgobesen*, the broom for sorrows. What's needed here is a heavenly broom for sorrows, with a handle a kilometre long and bristles of steel, to sweep the plateau clean so that the Bulgarians have a free view again, so that they get a vacation from their history of dictates, so that they never have to see these artefacts again, trying to persuade them their forebears were born as chunks of rock, and these chunks had slaughtered everything that crossed their horses' paths. The permanent wrath of these figures!

Why didn't they instal a loudspeaker system in their rugged tower too, to shriek at the land with yelling and screaming, with clashes of swords and trampling of hooves? Or build a fountain of blood?

It's ominously silent between the concrete walls, as silent as an abandoned, neglected site. Even birds avoid flying through the huge artificial cleft.

What's built here is not merely ugly—it's evil. Outside of the norm and evil. We are forced into this evil birthing crack, into this cracked open, knocked open, jagged open skull, in which the Bulgarian heroes of the past—no, are not lying sleeping in the beds of rock and growing lazily out of the stone, but storming out, exploding the concrete and crushing the flea-sized humans who, looking upwards, lame in the neck, groggy as if not in their right mind, are wandering beneath their toes. On cyclopean horses, with crests about their foreheads, poured concrete, large and crude like the storeys of a prefabricated tower block.

Let no one say Arno Breker was a sculptor of giants, oh no, Breker was practising at playing dwarves, and well-proportioned ones at that, compared to this battle-tsar and his throng of chosen ones.

A broom for sorrows, please, a huge one for a huge clean sweep. The prerequisite for the Bulgarians to be in good spirits again one day, for their ravaged land to find a balance and the paternal spooks to stay where they belong—up in the air. It would be better to have no reason for existence in history than such a fatally rigged and adjusted one.

Rumen is excited, I can tell just by looking. A hundred explanations on the tip of his tongue. His cheeks twitch.

He runs his hands through his hair, smokes, shakes his wrist with the watch buckled around it, strides here and there. He's sure to have anticipated my resistance but he was not prepared for my sister to turn away from him, and much more radically than I ever could. The one he adores, this woman hermetic through and through, is now deploying her main weapon. She has absented herself. Whoever's walking ahead of us in the dark-green cord jacket with the brown collar, it's not her. Not a word crosses her lips, not a gesture betrays what this creature is thinking. A nobody is walking through the monstrosity, and only the bag hung over her shoulder, suede brown, exudes any sense of life. A bogus body is wandering, wanting nothing, taking nothing, not even tipping its head back to look up, but sitting down on a stone and gazing, if you can call it gazing, down at the city. There is no link to me, and even less to Rumen. My sister, or whoever it is, seems no longer to know us.

Rumen's desperate attempts to make contact engender my pity. Should we have looked more closely at the mosaics? The gold? They used elements of the icon tradition and adapted them, interpreted patterns from liturgical robes as well.

To make him less alarmed and give him some annoyance to cling to, I contradict him in my usual way, albeit rather limp in tone, yes, they're particularly dreadful, the Bulgarians ought to be banned from making mosaics for all time. They're simply no good at it.

We have no idea, Rumen's voice accuses us, now also trembling like the whole man. Mind you, mind you, it was remarkable, more than remarkable, he can't find the right words for it at the moment, because it—even we ought to acknowledge it, even though we don't care about communism—it was remarkable that the communist party wanted to recall with this monument, and that in 1981—1981! the anniversary year!—wanted to mark Bulgarian history, and not only the history of communist Bulgaria as was usually the case, but the history of Christian Bulgaria, even Christian missionary history, Cyril and Methodius, those highly important monks who'd brought Christianity to Bulgaria, and Tsar Boris, Boris I, who was the first Bulgarian khan to be baptized. All of them and many more, of course the freedom fighters against the Ottomans too, they were all represented here, and that meant a great deal to the Bulgarians and was certainly something special. And also, he adds in a voice that is no longer obeying him in the slightest, and sounds nothing like Rumen at all, not like the Rumen we know, more like a teeny, tiny child Rumen, there's no arguing about aesthetic taste.

Rumen looks at me, blinking away the tears in his eyes. I say nothing for the time being but look at him more freely than usual, to show him I haven't forgotten his existence.

My sister, in contrast, seems to have woken up again. Whatever may have brought her back to the land of the living, it couldn't have been Rumen's explanations. She pays no further attention to him, concentrating instead on a piece of down, a small feather not quite blue, not quite grey, not quite white, which she has plucked out of the air and is now examining in all detail by laying it in the hollow of her left hand and stroking it gently with the index finger of her right hand, as if she had to smooth it out and bring it to peace, but then coming up with another plan, taking its delicate quill between her thumb and forefinger and engrossing herself in the sight of the wind pushing against the feather on one side and billowing it out on the other.

Poor Rumen. All over and kaput. The moral renewal of Bulgaria. Its fairy-tale powers. The man who represents these fairy-tale powers has instantly become a ridiculous Bulgarian, nothing more than a ridiculous Bulgarian.

We drove away again mutely, to a cafe we'd decided to go to on our arrival. We crept down the curves of the hill mutely and stared into the dead undergrowth, each of us differently silent and differently abandoned.

Now we're sitting closer together under the banner of misery, our joint misery at full bloom. Misery crystals blossom on our foreheads in place of sweat. Rumen is smoking silently; I am checking my hands silently as if they belonged to a stranger; and my sister is only provisionally with us, staring into space. None of us turns a head to the others.

There are glossy cardboard menus, as large as picture books for small children, the photos tinged red. What's on offer is listed in English as well, page after page of pizza and chicken nuggets, that kind of stuff on and on, but thank goodness, salvation at last, they have the salad with feta cheese that I always order. As a speciality, this cheese seems to have been pressed through a pasta maker; the photo shows a tangle of white worms on top of the chunks of cucumber and tomato. We order, and who would have thought it, my sister opens her mouth—pizza margherita.

And as proof that she's aware of the obligation to make conversation, she does it again—pizza margherita.

Not far from us is a telephone box with the door ripped off, a cable dangling from the cabin with no receiver at the end of it. Two old women with black head-scarves and bags big enough for market are sitting motionless on a bench, their calves crossed.

As we're talking so little, perhaps we're practising a kind of asceticism in secret. But I can't tell that it's leading to the spaciousness of the soul the masters of asceticism describe—a dissolved balm as if floating in a thousand tiny drops of oil, each drop shimmering with divine praise and mercy, filling the spacious soul and generating a delicate drift. No.

I can find nothing delicate or floating within me—I feel full to the brim with concrete. The horns of pride must first be broken, say the masters of asceticism; that is the prerequisite for an effective clearance of the soul.

My horns of pride may just have been broken, but nothing godly has taken their place, only the concrete misery that has spread from my stomach to my entire body and is actually too large for a human frame and would only fit comfortably inside an elephant. Such misery rarely befalls me by day. It normally attacks me in the middle of the night. I wake up from it, am encircled by it, subjected to a regular curse of misery, doggedly insisting, it'd be better if you'd never been born.

We're perching on plastic chairs around a plastic table, above us a Fanta parasol. Anyone seeing us like this must think: not a pretty sight, these people are lost, they're inconsolable, each sitting there alone, and all three of them are apparent corpses living on three different dead-end corridors.

The painted surfaces of the icons were cured with hare-skin glue, I say. A shy attempt to penetrate the isolation. Does anyone know if hare-skin glue is still made nowadays?

No reply from Rumen. It's possible he doesn't understand what hare-skin glue is. My sister doesn't even look up. I suffer an attack of faintheartedness that prompts me to chatter, a strange act of doing something in the guise of greed for knowledge. The year of salvation, when Boris I converted to Christianity (how eager the fussy swot's voice, how eager the head turning from one to the other with its hair all a-bob)—they call it the year of salvation in Bulgaria, I've heard (oh dear, another word is pushing its way to the front and wants to get out—vine tomato, they call it the year of the vine tomato, I've heard)— because it was the beginning of everything, or wasn't it? So when was that exactly? Wasn't Bulgaria actually a late bloomer in terms of Christianity? (Yes, you vine tomato, you deserve a clip round the ear for this nonsense.)

1981 minus three hundred.

That was Rumen. He flicks the ash off his cigarette.

My sister raises her head and sniffs the mood. She can even utter full sentences again, albeit only to me and not to Rumen. We know of Boris, she tells me, that he had his eldest son blinded, the son originally designated as his successor to the throne. Atrocious, isn't it? To have your own son blinded?

Atrocious, be that as it may, says Rumen (separately, to me). But his son wanted to ruin everything. Wanted to return to heathenism. Heathenism, right back to the beginning. Boris couldn't allow that. Son to destroy father's work. Younger son was better son; it does happen. Younger son, better son. Happens in the Bible too. Me too—younger son. Better for the succession. That way Bulgaria stayed Christian.

He speaks in a strange staccato, not yet our old, affable Rumen again, but a man who conceals his hurt behind a raw voice.

I suddenly experience an episode of happiness, a raising of my emotional hat. As the waitress brings our food, I'm overcome again by a need to share something, making me fiddle nervously with my cutlery. Do you two know what they say about Bulgarian heaven? (The tines of my fork pointing jerkily upwards.) It went through my mind on the way here. Imagine Bulgarian heaven as a funnel starting from the contours of the country and widening upwards into the airspace (the knife sketches a crazy criss-cross on the table). Think yourselves high up, very high, where your eyes can't reach, far enough away from the country's misery, where Bulgaria no longer smells of Bulgaria, where nothing recalls the wet, foxy fug, mixed with the reek of toilet cleaner and cheap aftershaves— high up in the clean air (I want to take my mind higher and higher, keeping my eyes closed and breathing deeply)—there's a crackling and a crunching, can you hear it?—all the time—crackling and crunching, because the angels' big wings are so close together—all of the sky stuffed full of angels, choirs rising up, choirs sitting down, choirs lying down in exhaustion, and their big wings are ceaselessly colliding, getting tangled, the entire Bulgarian heaven is full of gold-flaming wings crackling and crunching, you can even hear the sound above the songs of praise, which of course echo out just as incessantly, because there are always several choirs singing.

I put down my cutlery and take a sip of water.

There's a Mexican winged miracle too, you might have heard of it. It doesn't look much different in the Sierra Madre when the monarch butterfly spends the winter there. The high valleys are full of millions and millions of butterflies, a mass of black-veined orange wings. White dots between them, millions of flickering white dots, in constant gentle motion. The branches, the tree trunks, the mossy ground, everything bushelled and closely packed, the butterflies even perching on fern fronds, occasionally fluttering up sluggishly around midday, when the sunshine awakens their spirits. But why are there so many angels in Bulgarian heaven? Well, what do you think?

I take an artificial break, during which Rumen stares at me with his eyebrows drawn together.

Because the Bulgarians strived so intensely for the spread of Christianity that one fleet of angels after another was posted to Bulgarian airspace to support the battle from above, quasi with a combat of choirs!

Just eat your angel salad and be quiet for a while, please, says my sister.

Rumen has been looking at me as if I were two sandwiches short of a picnic. My sister doesn't let herself get distracted from cutting up her pizza, and now explains my state of mind to Rumen.

She has these moments at least once a week. There's no need to take it seriously, just wait until it's over.

I obey her command, stabbing at my salad and not saying a word, temporarily. My sister's description is certainly correct, but she doesn't know the true reasons for my behaviour. The only way for me to escape a sense of oppression is to deny everything around me. The easiest method is to abscond mentally, straight upwards in a heavenly direction. The first story I happen to chance upon comes just in time and I snap at the first word not contaminated by ugliness and dirt. It saves me, for I cling to it and chatter for all my life's worth.

Whenever I was alone in a room with my father, as a child, and he sat before me in his brooding, collapsed pose, an intense busyness came over me, I started chattering and warbling away like mad and hopping on one leg, as if everything depended on winning a Shirley Temple-style jollity competition. Papa! Papa! Look what a frog does! Look how a blackbird flies! Well, today it's no longer frogs and blackbirds, today it's the Christian constructors with whose aid I escape into a consistently organized heaven, a Swabian engineer's heaven, clean, orderly, every angel in his proper place, with a cleverly installed chaos component, however, so it doesn't get boring—this heaven is overcrowded, it's spilling over with singing, praising, flitting angels.

We may be more relaxed over coffee but all is not yet right again. We decide to go our separate ways for two hours and explore the city on our own.

No doubt it would be best to go to the Tombul Mosque, probably the only building in Shumen worth visiting. But I fear one of the others might have the same idea, so I simply roam around the depressing side streets—broken pavements and no chance of getting through, because no one stops the car owners from parking all the way up to the walls of the houses. Scurfy concrete, trash, rust, junk, a cat's cadaver, a filthy, sloppy little pile of fur, very much alone and no light burning beside the dead. Better prospects further along? There's someone with a scrubbing brush and bucket, at least. I turn back anyway and am on the main road in no time, where there's still space on a bench.

The poor are keeping watch here, distanced and withdrawn, men in rigid artificial leather jackets with heavy, red hands, women, most of them dressed in black, with large bags before their stomachs, both sexes magicked onto the benches as mute witnesses to the general state of misfortune. A man produces mucus but is polite enough to secrete it in his handkerchief. We're not in a comedy here, there's no need for laughter. All the people look like people who see themselves as washed-up. Their hopes have shrunk, the effervescent spring of youth dried up back when socialism still looked fresh and the Komsomol blouses billowed on parade.

Traders calling from far off; nothing to do with us. The people take no further notice of me, letting me marvel at them undisturbed.

Petite girls stroll past, some of them pretty, all of them appallingly dressed. They have picked out the sluttiest rags from the general trash. If there are men by their sides they are wrestler types with oily hair and ponytails, tattooed up to their chins, as broad as they are tall. There seems to be only one code available for each of the sexes. The women signalize: we're whores, and the men: we're brutal. We haven't come across one elegantly dressed woman or one man in a well-cut suit on the entire trip.

Sitting opposite is an elderly couple, he tall and she short. They've probably been together an eternity and have nothing left to say to each other. Just like our grandparents, except that our grandfather was better looking with his steel-grey and later white hair, and in their case the contrast in height was even more conspicuous. Our grandfather was very tall, you see, and our grandmother was tiny next to him.

We first met our grandmother in the early 1960s. The meeting took place at the garden gate of our house in Degerloch. It couldn't have gone more wrong. She was old and was allowed to travel, but not with her husband. It was the first time that a member of the Bulgarian family had managed to cross the Iron Curtain, so we were all nervous, especially our father.

I was a seven-year-old with a burning passion for the unknown visitor. I expected a grandmother similarly wonderful to our Swabian one, of course a tad more exotic, more fairy-like, perhaps younger? Even the name of our Bulgarian grandmother sounded enticing: *Nadja*—what a bright, magical name for a nimbly whispering creature swathed in rustling silks. For months I'd wanted to take on her name and get rid of my own, saving up for the bureaucratic procedure.

Appalling! A child-sized old woman wrapped in an absurd woollen cloak, helped out of the car by our father, teetered towards me. Her shrieks echoed in my ears as she pressed me to her and kissed me. The worst thing was the smell—rose oil, camphor, decay and pygmy wort.

A true dislike is formed in an instant. It burns into the skin like a brand mark, bursting into flame again at every new encounter. Even her huge black eyes that gazed at me imploringly could do nothing to change that. As soon as our grandmother came near me, I slipped off or ran away. Although her smell changed over the next few days—she developed a tic of applying Nivea cream every half hour and took the blue tin along everywhere she went; the house was soon Nivea-scented through and through, as if a pound of the stuff were lying about in every room.

My sister could abide our new grandmother as little as I could, yet she didn't run away from her embraces but put up with them with a contorted face. All that was left of my wish to be called Nadja was the money I'd saved. I bought myself a frog.

The deceased Bulgarians we took along in our retinue don't quite fit in with today's Bulgarians.

They certainly don't fit in with the ones sitting about on these benches. Very isolated, too, are the many characters that cropped up in the travellers' stories. Like a swarm of mosquitoes, they buzzed around our heads on the long journey; they accompanied us from Zurich to Milan, from Milan to Ancona, from Ancona across the sea to Igoumenitsa, and from Igoumenitsa across land all the way to Sofia.

Let's count up. Each of the forty travellers in the flesh had an average of perhaps fifteen ghostly individuals circulating around their heads, people they remembered themselves or knew from hearsay, which makes roughly six hundred dead but rather buoyantly circulating travel companions, including around a hundred stubborn fliers, while the rest only took a few turns and were sooner lost than they had come.

As fleetingly as this swarm flitted from near to far and back again, just as stereotypical was the decor from which the remembered emerged, to take a stand for a while with the aid of the words they draped around themselves. There were really only three or four varieties.

The fishing village. Nets and boats and ivy-covered courtyards are all part of the tableau. The sea is blue. A sleepy, watery peace of sun, sea, fish, wine and shadows spreads across the relatives. They don't lie half-naked on the beach like modern holidaymakers. At most their shoes and socks are removed and their sleeves rolled up. The women splash barefoot in the water, holding their ballooning skirts tight below their knees. They can't swim. And nor can the men.

In the countryside. It's boiling hot here. The people work hard and wipe the sweat from their foreheads with white handkerchiefs, stuffing them under their hats or their bonnets. Maize, sunflowers, chickens, goats, sheep, donkeys. Children scurry around. The tomatoes are close to exploding. The black olives glint, skewered on the blades of knives. The feta cheese doesn't crumble. It is smooth, moist, fine-pored, fresh, it shines in lamb-like innocence, neither too salty nor too watery. Its consistence is unearthly. No feta cheese of today can ever compare. Sure, Kolyo Vuteff sold the best feta cheese to be had in West Germany on his stall in the Stuttgart covered market, but there was a great difference to the mythical original.

Let's not forget the city apartment variety. It's set in summer in darkened apartments with voluptuous curtains, where the men, keepers of a bourgeois existence, perch behind meaningful desks. They wear richly embroidered velvet coats, true to the Ottoman tradition, a felt cone with a tassel on their heads. Velvet portières above the doors. Oriental rugs on the floors. Sometimes, secretly, one of these keepers of the family steals into the apartment of a cocotte and causes a scandal.

As a sadistic bonus, there follows the famous horror story of Alexander Stamboliski, the unfortunate prime minister who was murdered by a sinister clique of military men, freemasons and Macedonians in 1923. Head cut off and sent to Sofia in a biscuit tin. Hands that had signed the shameful Treaty of Niš hacked off and buried. Naturally enough, one of the chimeric relatives was present just as the lid was removed from the tin, the legendarily dangerous and legendarily bearded great-uncle of Ivan Nedevski, our gentle, chubby car dealer from Olgaeck, whose cheeks shimmered as tender and pink as the sides of a peach.

In their imaginations, the Bulgarians are wild. For centuries, they claim, they fought more wildly than all the Balkan peoples put together. Their imaginary organism pays no heed to numbers and probability. On closer reading, it transpires that they were actually dogged gardeners and traders (which makes them likeable, but that in itself is rather unlikeable to them). They keep the turbulences of recent history out of reach of their fantasies.

What's missing? The German Wehrmacht and the SS. What's missing? The Russian army. What's missing? The destruction of the country, the towns and the villages by the Soviet system.

The past seventy years seem little suited for fantastic embellishments. Bulgaria as it is barely occurs in the Bulgarians' minds. Only their bodies are trapped inside it.

I sit as limply on the bench as if the idea of roughed-up, dented Bulgaria had lamed me for good. What on earth am I doing here? There's still an unpleasant wind blowing, neither cold nor warm. How difficult everything seems. Only the Bulgarians' misfortune seems irrefutable, even if they rave about their good fortune like drunks in the rare moments in which they wake up.

Our grandparents' good fortune is one of those dizzying cases.

They were regarded as a happy couple. Philemon and Baucis on a park bench in the Doctor's Garden, feeding the pigeons, putt-putt, cheep-cheep, look at us, you unhappy couples of the world, look at Lubomir and Nadja whiling by the sparrows' dusty baths, above their heads the dim low-watt light bulbs of frugal old folks. The Bulgarian family clutched to this legend with great tenacity, constantly reinforcing it with the phrase about the *perfect happy couple*.

Rumen had our grandfather as his godfather, so he knew our grandparents from his very birth and spent countless afternoons with them until his family moved to a different part of town. It's thanks to him that we gradually came to know a different version of the story. He came out with it in chunks, after overcoming a good few inhibitions.

The thing is that they were strange, even in the eyes of a pious Bulgarian who, for reasons of sensitive patriotic feelings, is not keen to reveal certain things to foreign women, especially such mean ones as me.

Strange, very strange in fact. Our grandparents lived in Sofia back then, in one of the high-rise estates built in the 1960s on Lenin Boulevard, up on the seventh floor. Down on the six-lane road the traffic flowed, while up at the top of the building, boiling hot in summer, in a tiny two-room apartment, sat our grandparents. Rabbits hopped about on their balcony; pigeons cooed in the cotes made by our grandfather. A doll-sized, tiled bathroom was the apartment's gem, for out of the shower came warm water—a luxury.

Everyone—the neighbours, Apostoloff as a boy, all their friends, our grandmother's sisters and their husbands, the daughter and her husband and their children—came to our grandparents' apartment regularly to take a shower.

If her son-in-law was showering, if her two grandsons were showering, if little Apostoloff was showering, our grandmother couldn't keep still in the living room for long. She grew restless, started murmuring and then opened the door to the bathroom to admire the men and boys in all their nudity. Her son-in-law regularly bawled her out. She instantly retreated, closing the door as quietly as if there weren't even a draught about, but the very next week she'd go stalking again.

In other words, she wasn't in her right mind. Mumbled to herself, rolled her eyes so you could only see the whites, constantly crossed herself, muddled the names of even her closest relatives although she was by no means senile, always tapping restlessly about the place, plucking at people's clothes, not leaving anyone in peace. But still they used to say, *Grandfather and Grandmother were a happy couple.*

He: was prudish. He was permanently issuing warnings and instructions to the young generation. He was a graphomaniac, wrote like a madman.

She: hated it when he wrote.

He: did gymnastics with small weights every morning to keep in shape.

She: lectured at him while he was lying on the floor with his weights.

He: hated it when she disturbed his gymnastics.

She: loved icons and ardently adhered to the Orthodox Church.

He: abhorred every religion as a superstitious, backward-looking mode of thinking. Icons were repugnant to him.

She: scuttled like a bird and tired easily.

He: walked with long strides and had great stamina for walking.

She: hated it when he went away, which was unusual enough. But when he did, her theatrical talent came into its own. Unheard-of diseases blossomed, her heart started racing, she couldn't breathe, she was sent to hospital by the emergency physician, where she was released after three days of inconclusive doctoring about.

He: enjoyed a good rant. In letters to the newspapers. In letters to the philately community. In letters to the Esperanto community. In letters to the rabbit-breeding community. In his diary.

She: hated it when he wrote.

He generally ranted about sports, considering them too devoted to the pursuit of hedonistic pleasure. He also ranted about popular singers, as they encouraged base sentiments. In fact he ranted about mass consumption of all kinds. Consumerism was a plague, a case of corruption that came from the West and was infecting communism. His concern seemed rather adventurous in that he had never been a communist but rather a radical follower of the Tolstoyan movement. The simple, fair, rural life— that was what he strove for. A life without violence and above all without religion, at least organized religion. Where did natural requirements end, where did molly-coddling luxury begin? He was constantly occupied with such questions.

So much for the construct of a couple as we heard tell, whom we hardly knew at first hand. I met our grandfather at the age of nine, the first time I was taken to Bulgaria. A picture-book grandfather presented himself in the residential unit by the name of 'Victory of the Future'. He was dignified, slim, with very good posture, a man of reserved, benevolent character, or so it seemed. Unshakeable.

For days now I've been carrying around a folder that Rumen gave to us. It contains a number of papers written by our grandfather along with Rumen's translations of them, as well as a bundle of photos left to us by the family.

This awful wind! I have to hold the papers tight so they don't get blown away. Still time for a coffee. Just opposite is a cafe with a sheltering veranda. Almost all the tables are vacant, and for once there's no music playing.

The paper that our grandfather used is a sign of poverty. It is woody and has already begun to decay. As even poor-quality goods were in short supply, the entire surface of the paper, front and back, has been made use of in close-knit lines.

The lumberjack type. Burt Lancaster with bushy eyebrows.

In his youth, our grandfather is said to have been a hot-tempered, rowdy tyrant, an anarchist who abducted his girl to marry her against both families' will. The photos in the folder give the impression of a strong man, attractive in a wild way.

Our grandmother too certainly had her attractions. One charming photo shows a pale, silent-movie face with huge eyes and a mouth barely larger than the navel of an orange. There is something affected about this young woman; you can tell she'll never walk through life with firm, straight steps, she'll always be scurrying and scuttling.

The stories from our grandparents' young days don't quite fit with the pigeon-holed confinement in which they spent many decades of their later lives. They both lived very long lives, our grandmother dying first at the age of ninety-five and then our grandfather at ninety-eight.

She came from a wealthy family of merchants in Plovdiv and was the youngest of four sisters. He was under his mother's thumb, a resolute, power-hungry woman who lived to be a hundred and nine, wrote school textbooks and was involved in the introduction of the elementary school system in Bulgaria at the turn of the twentieth century. His father had studied several semesters of philosophy in Leipzig and Vienna, as testified by a small library that I've inherited. Rust-brown and blue-green-speckled hardbacks, page after page covered in our great-grandfather's notes, written with the sharpest possible pencil in precise Latin handwriting.

His son eloped with his bride with not a penny in his pocket. He began the adventurous life of a good-for-nothing who had refused all education but gradually rallied himself and worked his way to the top. First working on the roads, then as a clerk, and finally as the director of a cooperative bank, even becoming deputy mayor of his hometown of Pazardzhik, until it all came to a sorry end when the communists came to power. He ended up in jail and was then sent to a quarry, where he was allotted the modest position of a bookkeeper after years of hard labour. After that came thirty years' retirement, his pension so small that his children and son-in-laws had to help keep our grandparents above water.

How the transformation is supposed to have taken place from a ruffian to a prudish, bigoted bookkeeper who dreamt of a life in the country, Tolstoy-style, no one can tell us. Even the closest relatives have no stories to explain it, and so our grandfather's life remains obscure to us in large part. It seems to me to reflect something of Bulgaria's oppressive history, that radical mental shrinkage to the close confines of a paranoid treasurer's life.

Our grandfather ended up the keeper of an ingenious little treasury of his own construction. He held this very last post for over twenty-five years. He was very concerned about the lift in the building where they lived. To collect the money required to maintain it, he made a little box, which he mounted just above the doorknob. The lift door could only be opened if you put a coin in the box. Our grandfather kept an account of this treasury too. There were long lists of the sums he collected and the necessary expenditure every few years for maintenance work. Since our grandfather died, with no one collecting money for repairs, the thing has fallen into such decay that it's no longer useable.

Our grandmother's metamorphosis is no less puzzling. From a spoilt young thing with as good as no education and certainly no practical training, she became a scampering slave fearful of her husband's temper tantrums, but more fearful still of his mother, whose house she was soon forced to live in.

Her mother-in-law called all the shots and hated the young bride, whom she considered incapable, a burdensome idiot whose only purpose was for being ordered around. The relatives insist that our great-grandmother used to behead chickens with a sword, well into old age. That seems less than plausible to me. Beheading chickens with a sword? Is that even possible? No matter how exaggerated the stories may be, there is no doubt about the merciless personality of the lady of the small house, with its veranda, kitchen, five rooms and a yard with a shed, stable and vegetable beds.

JACKIE

The waitress is delightful. A slim wondergirl with almond eyes and long, very long but genuine eyelashes. She's shy and a tiny bit clumsy for it. A few drips of coffee have spilt over the edge of the cup and onto the saucer. She's terribly upset. I try to pacify her in English, raising a smile that transforms me.

I break out in a burst of enthusiasm. Oh, how supernaturally beautiful the Bulgarians are, supernaturally good, a conversation in their language might be veritably seraphic.

A brief honeymoon. The coffee tastes awful. The dripping cup mustn't stain the folder.

A special folder, rather slim, originally white and now grey, printed with the word *Kolektanto* and other writing forming a round signet encircling a stylized globe with a flaming torch within it: *Amica Rondo—Klubo de la Esperantistoj—Filatelistoj*. It was our grandfather's pet idea to link the philatelists with the Esperantists and gather them under the roof of Tolstoy's teachings. For this purpose, he produced a regular bulletin, most of which he wrote himself and had printed at his own expense, a bulletin that he sent out six times a year although he could hardly spare the postage costs. At the end of each working day he waited wistfully for reactions, which arrived, to his chagrin, only rarely.

There are still piles of ring binders in a broom cupboard in Sofia. They contain his correspondence in Esperanto; not only letters he received from various countries but also the neatly typed carbon copies of his own epistles, all closely written using the typewriter's maximum width. One can't help noticing that his letters are several pages long, while the answers he received were short.

The original sheets with the handwriting flailing like a tiny caterpillar prompt a slight panic as I look at them. Our grandfather used up even the tiniest space of paper. And all for nothing. Perhaps the message of these papers is: all writing is in vain.

I am despondent. I'm living in the certainty of my inferiority. I ask myself: Lubomir, why do you make a fool of yourself with your letters and petitions? Don't you see that even your closest friends no longer write to you? Borko Liakhov, Georgi Penev, Kolyo Gentshev, and even the man in whom you placed your highest hopes, Doctor Kantarev, even for him your 'philosophies' have become too much. He has fobbed you off with two or three lines in 'answer' to your long letters. Stoyan Batakliev doesn't even answer your questions, simply avoiding the issue and writing about his wife's rheumatism. Vlado Futcharov hinted that he found it unpleasant to correspond about social ethics or political matters. But look here, Chaim A. Israel, to whom I had written

about his article about the sexual education of children, writes
that my opinions are absolutely identical to his own. I feel flat-
tered. It means I'm not quite lost, at least not for today.

Prison labour. A prisoner sending letters out into the
world day after day, only to be read fleetingly in hurried
snatches until no one reads them any more, only the cen-
sor leaning over the letters with his eyelids drooping,
until they fall closed over this dull task and even he stops
reading them at some point.

The few fragments that Rumen has translated for us
from the countless diaries, epistles, petitions, complaints,
addenda, brief articles in specialist magazines bear wit-
ness to a man goaded into a corner, wearing himself down
for the sake of ridiculously petty issues, driven sheer out
of his mind by the inconceivable carelessness of his fellow
men, encountering a lack of comprehension at every turn,
suspecting betrayal at every turn and growing embittered
by it all.

He got into a dispute with the Sofia central associa-
tion of rabbit-breeders because chinchilla crossbreeds
were wrongly labelled as *chinchillas* at an exhibition, while
the *Vienna Blue* and the *Silver Angora* waited in vain for
acknowledgement. *The model cage on show at the entrance*
was of deficient quality. The tin feeding bowls were uncom-
fortable. The insemination box was far too small. And by the
way it was placed inside the bars, the female would have had
no way to get into its nest.

And then his monster of a diary. He wrote and wrote
and wrote. A thousand pages? Two thousand pages? Five

thousand? He stopped in 1965. *Difference between an apparent acquittal and a real one* is the last entry in the middle of the page.

After that the page remained blank.

Our grandfather was sixty-four when he received the news of his oldest son's violent death in Germany. He let his beard grow, which must have seemed very unusual for him, a man who valued a close shave and reached for the razor twice a day. After forty days, the usual strict mourning period, the beard was shaved off again. An atheist through and through, he even had a requiem mass said for his son.

During all the years he had left to live, he always spent the anniversary of his son's death in the same way. He got up early, trembling with grief, ate nothing, said nothing and left the house, returning after a long march and going to bed in silence, not having eaten a single bite.

In 1968 the diary begins again with the words *What seems impossible is possible for an American woman*. He was referring to Jacqueline Kennedy and the scandal that her marriage caused. A woman our grandfather loved to hate. She might have been his type, although he'd never have admitted it—short, petite, large eyes, vaguely similar to our grandmother in that respect. Her handbags, her tight-fitting suits, her hairstyle, the sunglasses, the shoes, her way of life—nothing escaped our grandfather, and he disapproved of everything. Whenever Jacqueline O. stumbled into his diary in a bikini and high heels, the writer grew heated and sounded the tattoo of virtue. It was as clear as day that the woman possessed not a single virtue but vices by the ton to make up for it.

She wasted money. The villa on the island of Skorpios only cost nine hundred and sixty million Swiss franks and was still too cheap for the new Mrs Onassis. If she didn't spend a million a day she had a nervous breakdown. She owned six hundred and fifty-seven pairs of shoes too many, and not a single pair among them in which she could walk properly. Her jewellery boxes were spilling over, and the money was not going to the poor. She flew to London only to visit the most fashionable luxury purveyors. She lived on lobster and caviar. She was cold and lonely, despite all the people constantly buzzing around her. Even though the violinists she'd ordered fiddled themselves out of their minds night after night, she lay alone in her bed, drew her knees up to her skinny body and wept. She didn't love her children and gave them neither her care nor a responsible upbringing. She was rotten to the core. Oh, wrote our grandfather, there was so much more to say about this deplorable case but he would hold his peace, for this woman would one day be her own undoing.

Looking at all the work Rumen has put into the translation makes me feel guilty. He did it voluntarily, presenting us with the translations as a gift. Our grandfather would have praised him for them, for Rumen did the job accurately and flawlessly. But I feel doubly reproached. Because I've barely acknowledged Rumen's efforts, have treated him with such disregard even though he's been driving us around and taking such care of us.

Because—dammit, my conscience unwraps the contours of a man, tall and bony with bushy eyebrows, standing over there by the concrete pylon or seemingly so, a few strokes holding him together.

His calm gaze a single reproach.

He'd disown me if he could. Disown—they like *that* word over on the other side, it gets a round of applause; from the side he's on, applause echoes weakly over and mingles with the asphalt sounds generated by the stream of passing cars; applause of the kind that escapes limp, boneless hands, for the people over there are putting the swaying man back in his rightful place. What the applause means is—we can't let any of us live on in your mind as undignified as that, as burnt down in his pride, not someone who provided your flesh and bones.

Disowning. Do the dead perhaps disown each other too? Or does aversion among them, if there is even such a thing, mean only restless fluttering apart?

No letters have survived from father to son, nor from son to father. Were there none written, or have they been lost? Perhaps they wanted to write to each other but their hands cramped up every time they wrote so much as the date.

Coming from behind, close to my ear, someone is trying to convince me he's now a released son and can do whatever he likes. Up there, the sons regularly gather in an army to bang heads with the fatherly army, he tells me.

And you? I ask. Aren't you a father too?

Daughters count differently, says the father, and apart from that you haven't died, so all I am up here is a son.

What codswallop! Dead people are thrust into old age irrevocably in a single stroke. No matter whether they died as babies, sons, widowers or grandfathers, they're much older than a living person can ever be. Their family ties? Irrelevant. I'm young, a spring chicken compared to every one of you up there.

Time to go. My waitress smiles so bashfully on taking the money that I take the smile with me.

My fellow travellers are waiting by the car, relaxed in a rather thespian way, as if an important instance had persuaded them it's better to keep the peace. That's fine by me; it means I can make myself comfortable on the backseat and pursue my thoughts. While I get in the car, the two of them are leaning eagerly over the bonnet, on which they have unfolded a map, their fingers speeding ahead to the Black Sea.

Rumen smokes and drives in his usual lax style, rapidly but interrupted by his abrupt brake manoeuvres. It's been decided at the front not to go directly to the sea, but to take a detour to the archaeological reservation in Madara.

Why not? Archaeological reservation, Indian reservation, reservation for residents in Bulgarian folk costume, Zhivkov reservation—I like all reservations equally.

We soon leave the city behind us on an uphill road, and then have to park the car beneath a rocky outcrop.

An empty, thin sky above Madara; the rider becoming hesitantly recognizable from a distance. A relief knocked out of stone, certainly monumental but delicate and modest compared with the colossus we viewed before. Like looking at a puzzle picture with objects hidden in it, there's a second's irritation before the appropriate parts stand out clearly and unimportant elements fade into the background. The horse is raising a gracious foreleg. The dog is jumping with its ears a-fly. Wind and weather have gnawed at the figures, especially the crouching lion. Here, the companion beast of *Saint Jerome in his Study* is slain, not tamed. Perhaps they didn't know the advantages of a tamed lion in these parts, a lion for example that can guard holy studies and is of no danger to pets. In Dürer's engraving the lion sleeps peacefully alongside a dog. Lion-killing— the privilege of the heathen rulers. Cruel in reality, here it looks porous, washed-out, sand-coloured, not reddened by blood.

What unique insights a tame lion has to give. Saints and philosophers count on the lion in that respect. Why is Hans Blumenberg such an exciting philosopher? He was a lion philosopher. By night he had a placable lion lying next to his desk, who did let himself in for the odd test of strength. Blumenberg grew with his lion. In the constant vicinity to a lion, even I would think myself more capable. His furry scent, still steaming from previous kills, the powerful breath escaping his muzzle, would inspire me with completely different ideas about our father, for example. Wild ideas and yet gentle too. A lion doesn't keep tally, it doesn't add things up at all. Father?

The lion would yawn, its head drooping to one side with tedium. Noose? The lion would bang briefly on the floor with the tassel of its tail, and that would be that on the subject for good.

The relief dates from the early Middle Ages. We stumble around a little more and look out across the land, then get into the car and drive towards the sea.

I've been to the Black Sea once before. It was a long time ago. On my first trip to Bulgaria, I went without my family. Lilo had invited me along and we were a party of three—she, her daughter and I. My sister, meanwhile, spent the school holidays at a children's home in the Swiss mountains.

Until we got to Sofia it was marvellous. Lilo drove a powder-blue convertible Mercedes. We usually drove with the top down, Lilo swathed in a rose scarf, with white, open-backed gloves and sophisticated sunglasses perched on her nose. Lilo was the dream of every truck driver and every worker who managed to set eyes on her on the dusty *Autoput* highway between Zagreb and Belgrade. The border guards assumed overly correct expressions as the car approached but she softened them up in a flash, right to the marrow of their stubborn border-guard bones. More for the joy of maintaining contact with her than out of professional obligation, they inspected the powder-blue fairy-tale car, opened the bonnet, opened the boot, had her show them the pigskin suitcases and couldn't get enough of this extremely attractive woman snapping the locks open. Silky underclothes, lacy undergarments, a Samsonite beauty case filled with nail-varnish bottles and jewellery, all sorts of things that sparkled and flashed like on opening the lid of a treasure chest; and all in the very best of order. How proud she was of her pretty things!

She had the patience of an angel, she found these things fun, she didn't see them as annoying but as a delightful adventure with uptight men in uniforms, in front of whom she removed her sunglasses with enchanting grace, shaking her curls and showing her white teeth with coos and smiles and yes, of course, you're very welcome, her passport and her driving licence too.

Very much in contrast to our parents, who drove up to every border with the most dubious of passports, as *homeless foreigners*—once displaced persons—our father red with rage, our mother hectic, she too absurdly branded a homeless foreigner because the two of them had married in 1945 before the new citizenship laws came into effect, back when a German woman who married a foreigner automatically lost her citizenship.

Brooding, in a cloud of misfortune and suppressed anger, they hunched at the front of the Citroën and acted like suspicious characters, our father in a dark mood for hours afterwards because of the humiliation he'd had to bear without resistance, our mother unable to stop her railing and cursing at the entire fascistic world. Travelling with our parents was painful, while crossing borders with Lilo was a genuine pleasure.

I spent most of the journey sitting or rather lying at the back. Voluntarily—the backseat has always been my favourite place. It was around the age of nine that I began to develop a sense of the agonies of jealousy. It was better to steer clear of jealous types, cleverer not to provoke them. Lilo's daughter, three years younger than me, was extremely jealous. The tiniest sign of affection that Lilo paid me made her lose her temper. So it did not seem advisable to move all too close to her mother, staking claim to a place that belonged to her daughter alone. Aside from that, I found the view of the road uninteresting and felt more comfortable on the backseat. There was a cosy pillow at the ready. If the wind blew too hard I stole under a blanket, my child's sunglasses protecting me from bright light. My hair was tied up in a scarf so the wind didn't flutter it up.

Lying in the backseat, with no inhibiting car roof between my eye and the sky, I could enjoy the drama up there in double motion. The Yugoslavian sky on show was a deep, dark blue and yet strangely glowing, presumably down to the tinge of my sunglasses.

Downy, pale herds of clouds moved across it, clouds with long drawn-out trains, clouds linked together by twisted umbilical cords, then compressed clouds again with huge blown-up heads, between them criss-crossing vapour trails. The opponent in their game was the sun, aiming hot rays at the clouds, burning all the clouds away, the sun blazingly standing its ground in the sky until a new group of clouds formed and grew magnificent.

The exhibition bouts in the heavens generated a sublime thrill in me. Everything has been arranged for my amusement—Lilo, Lilo's fluttering scarf, the Mercedes, the cream leather upholstery, birds flying above us, the pictures moving across the sky. A free, fluid, accommodating world. No parents, no sister, hooray! Everything moved for me, went like clockwork, roared for me, tweeted for me, made perfect pistons work in perfect time, sent me dreams, pressed me gently against the backseat where I felt safer than ever before. I must have been a terribly important creature if so much effort was put into banishing my misfortune once and for all.

I was happy.

That was all over in Sofia. They abandoned me.

Lilo might just as well have left me alone in the jungle. There I sat in my grandparents' rancid, overfilled apartment in a new misfortune that was at the same time an ancient misfortune. Sat on one of the high-backed black chairs from better days, upholstered in olive-green velvet, on which a large-leaved vine intertwined.

The chairs did not stay empty for long. Many, many relatives had come to welcome me, a confusing number of them, there was barely space for them all. The only one who seemed like a sensible human being was my grandfather, because he sat calmly at the head of the table, eyeing me benevolently and not saying a word.

I knew my grandmother already and avoided her as usual. To get me attuned I was given a saucer of *slatko*, a sweet dish, some kind of mummified fruit trapped in extremely viscous syrup as if in amber, brownish in colour, and the worst was the taste. The stuff was so sweet it hurt.

I pushed the plate away but there was no escape for me, I was trapped, doused, preserved and glued with the saliva of strange conversation and the caresses of my excited relatives.

I remember my grandmother's sisters particularly well. The eldest of them was very old already and could only walk with a stick. At first a calm woman biding her time, she then made her mark in abrupt outbreaks by clearing her throat as heftily as if a huge clump of mucus were waiting in her chest for its own time to speak.

Auntie Zveta led the troop of sisters, a cocotte with a cigarette holder. The instant I saw her mouth I thought of one of my Swabian grandmother's phrases, *the Whore of Babylon*. That mouth! It could only belong to the Whore of Babylon. By nature thin-lipped, it was painted well beyond its contours to create a half-devilish, half-Punch-like red pout, smudged at the edges, the colour stretching almost halfway across her cheeks, an overly agile, constantly moving mouth wide open with laughter; a mouth with bad teeth inside it, which I was terribly scared of because I was afraid I'd have to receive a kiss from it—though I didn't, thank goodness.

I must have been a deeply humourless child.

Auntie Zveta was odd, but I didn't recognize the desperate wit and pride she summoned up under the chastened conditions in which everyone dressed as if they'd been commanded off to a procession of ants, when she made her own fire-coloured, large-flowered dresses out of old curtains, defying the general dreariness all around her, shouting out her rebellion from her luminous mouth, ridiculing the communists' levelling uniformity with her provocative pout.

Auntie Zveta was an interesting person all round. She smoked to emphasize her profligate lifestyle, angering my grandfather. I didn't understand what she said because she spoke only Bulgarian, while a few relatives knew bits and bobs of German and some quite good French, which I didn't understand then either, but it was possible to make initial approaches in this Franco-German mishmash.

She was skinny and crooked-legged, not a naturally beautiful woman. But there were her greenish eyes and her rather fair, if not actually blonde hair, to which she lent a strawberry-blonde note with dye. Overflowing, over-lively hair of danger. Her eye and hair colour were sufficient to make her an object of desire for the Bulgarians, as fixated as they were with blondes. I later found out that Auntie Zveta had had a huge chest in her apartment, in which she kept hundreds of love letters from different men along with faded dance cards, pressed flowers, necrologies and piles of greeting cards with red and white bobbles that are sent to celebrate the beginning of spring.

An old, rust-red powder box with a fluffy tassel perched on the top as a lid, which smelt of old flour when you lifted it (the whole thing looked like a miniaturized pouf from the days of Toulouse-Lautrec), a tortoiseshell fan and a coral necklace, an embroidered washbag— these are what was left of Auntie Zveta, which I once laid hands on many years after she died. They said one man was so crazed with love for her that he killed himself.

I don't know why the childish Manichaean in me made such a strict distinction. Lilo, who played on a similar claviature of femininity, was allowed to do everything that was frowned upon in our home. Auntie Zveta seemed like a caricature of our beloved Neverle and that was why I found her so upsetting. And also, she was old. Different rules applied to old women. They were the rules of our Swabian grandmother and her eleven brothers and sisters, who could have been immortalized on an eighteenth-century panel without having to change anything significant about their clothing.

They looked like venerable Lutherans, all dressed in black, all buttoned up. Their heads rested on starched white collars, and they never revealed the slightest bit of skin aside from their hands and faces. The women were extremely clean and neat and never wore make-up, smelt slightly of soap with a drop of eau de cologne at the very most. They all wore their hair in a bun, without exception. To this day, that seems to me the only correct way for an old woman to look. It's imprinted upon me like the feeding master on one of Konrad Lorenz's hand-reared greylag geese.

Then there was Auntie Mila. A very different woman. Tall, broad, rustic and good-natured, as you could tell at first glance. She wore an apron and no make-up and was usually to be found in the kitchen, sweating and cooking, carrying plates to and from the table. The other sisters tended to abuse her willingness to serve as a drudge.

I can't remember how long I had to hold out in Sofia. Three days? Five days? Longer? The Sofia time stretched out to infinity. They took me on outings to the Vitosha massif, dragged me along to the ladies' department of a labyrinthine Turkish bath that led into a huge, steaming cave where there were drips and gurgles and naked women sitting everywhere, rubbing sausages of dirt from their skins under the supervision of corpulent supervisors, who refused to reply when you asked anything of them. The swinging of the raffia brushes, the slapping of the cloths, the voices of the women—it all sounded out from the mist in extreme focus.

It was the night I was most afraid of. At night, my grandparents slept head to head in a corner of the living room, in two bunks at right angles, the two walls above them covered in icons. A bed was made up for me on the sofa on the other side of the living room. At night the unfamiliarity grew to monstrous dimensions—they had locked me up with perfect strangers. The smidgen of sympathy that may have formed during the day was debunked by night. I was condemned to lie and listen to my own sounds and fight off strange smells. A snoring came from across the room. I lay motionless and silent with the backs of two fingers pressed to my nose to ward off the smell. My breathing, passing over my fingers, made a whistling sound. Every snore made thoughts rear up. Three oxygen consumers in one room. What was breathing inside me so urgingly and loudly?

At that time, my grandparents had not yet reached their full old-age form.

It had not yet happened.

There was a clear before and after effect. Afterwards, our grandfather relinquished his temper. He sealed himself in as an odd individual, while our grandmother lost all her shyness and finally held sway over everything. She paid him back for everything he may have done to her in their younger years. As his deafness progressed, she spoke deliberately quietly so that he found it more and more difficult to understand her.

By those terrible nights, my grandmother had already won the old argument between the iconodules and the iconoclasts. Although our grandfather detested icons, they hung above his head, his belly, his legs. He had to sleep below a Saint Elijah, from whom chunks of paint had peeled off when the icon had been thrown in a fire. A teacher in Pazardzhik had burnt whole piles of icons for demonstration purposes. Auntie Mila managed to rescue Saint Elijah ascending to heaven in his golden chariot, his discarded coat sailing down to earth, or at least saved part of it, and since then our grandfather had to rest his head beneath the semi-carbonized saint night after night.

The icon still exists. It's now hanging in our cousin Atanasia's cramped hallway. Originally no doubt a beautiful specimen, it is now as black as coal around the edges—the saint's face, his nimbus, the rear cheeks of his horse, the chariot and the clouded sky dotted with black-brown heat stains. Only Elijah's blue coat is magnificently preserved, flying down to earth with its pink, gold-threaded fur collar to land at the feet of a group of astounded witnesses.

And another icon in my cousin's hallway seemed familiar. It may have hung approximately above our sleeping grandfather's knees, back when he was still alive. A crucifix on a brown background. The suffering Jesus looks less suffering than usual, his feet resting on a comfortable little board, the holes in his hands and feet only hinted at, from which the blood seeps in thin threads. To the right and left of his hands, in the corners of the crossbar, are a sun and a moon, looking at the saviour's head with kindly round eyes more suitable for pancakes than for sublime luminaries. At his feet is a mediaeval town, painted in jolly colours, and beneath that rears a wave-shaped rock in which an array of skulls are slumbering with wide-open jaws.

Jaws open, jaws closed.

My sister spent a ghostly night sleeping on that same sofa many years later. She was seventeen at the time, on her first trip to Bulgaria. Our grandparents had gone to rack and ruin by then. They circulated in sufferance, a small bundle of bones around a large bundle of bones, in their rooms. *It* had happened by then.

Our grandfather's jaws were open by night. He snored. Which one night drove our grandmother to switch on the light and sit herself down on his chest. As he awoke fighting for air, she was wagging her finger in front of his eyes and hissing away at him. The epitome of horror. My sister told Rumen the story along the way. He laughed, having experienced similar scenes as a juvenile sofa-sleeper himself. What was that mysterious hissing sound? Our rake-thin grandmother, her hair unloosed, squatting on our grandfather's chest like a nightmare, *just wanted to make sure he was still alive.*

By day, once the nightly spooks had been driven out, I built up a little trust in our grandfather. He didn't ask anything of me and didn't drag me off anywhere. Though I did find his preoccupation with his rabbits and pigeons rather disappointing. At that time, of course, I knew nothing about Tolstoy and his ideas about the simple life. Had I been able to understand them, my grandfather's efforts to recreate such conditions on his balcony would have seemed all the more absurd. A balcony the width of a towel, which ran around the corner of the two rooms, from which we looked down at the six-lane main road, opposite at a hideous tower block and diagonally at a raggedy park with low bushes. It was so noisy on the balcony that it was impossible to hold a conversation. And certainly not with our hard-of-hearing grandfather, who actually spoke the best German of all our relatives, when he ever did speak.

On the balcony on Lenin Boulevard I longed for our garden in Degerloch. It seemed enormous, a terrain of freedom and adventure, an exercise zone for cat, dog and child alike. Visiting dogs were equally welcome. The dogs that came to visit with friends of our parents in particular were characters with bizarre traits, which we never forgot all too soon. But pigeons and rabbits? I failed to understand why an old man would make do with such dull creatures, although it did make an attractive sight when the pigeons paid tribute to our grandfather by settling on his shoulders, head and hands, and then he raised his arms as if exhorting peace and harmony, extending well over the concrete walls of his hideous balcony—as if he were inviting the heavens to a feast, or no, the other way around, as if the heavens were inviting him, about to grip him beneath his arms and whisk him away, pigeons and all.

Lilo and her daughter came to collect me several days later. We drove to the sea.

It's not far to Varna. Prostitutes line the dusty truck route before the city comes into sight. It's boiling hot. Sauna weather. The women are pitiful creatures. I've never seen such ugly, miserable prostitutes, their torsos laced into brightly coloured plastic, boots on their feet. Women of almost every age are selling themselves, standing by the rubbish-strewn embankments and grinning desperately at the drivers. The insane hope of being allowed to creep into the bushes with a man or clamber up to the driver's cab and drive to the nearest car park for a tiny sum of money. The torments of hell as Dante portrayed them seem suddenly harmless, mere poetic agonies, fires that don't really burn, boils that fester for poetic enjoyment. Here in the glare of the sun, everything is in sharp focus, the major adversities and the minor, sweat, sperm, urine, the abscesses, the blood, screams, blows, itching, flies, broken bottles, abandoned plastic, stinging nettles, ears of grain digging into the skin. The fate of these Bulgarian country-road whores is just as cruel as the fate of the lepers in centuries past. But no follower of Christ to be seen for miles, no one to anoint their aching feet or redeem even one of them.

The whores that Zankoff sent to our father's practice led a luxurious life in comparison. Although he made good money out of them, our father seems to have been incapable of overcoming his deeply rooted disdain for ladies of the night. As a former nurse of his confided in me long after his death, he once lost his temper at her because she had helped one of these particular patients into her coat, one who was badly ill. I could instantly tell the story was true. Whereas most stories doing the rounds about our father place him in the realms of the mysterious, the misunderstood genius, in this case it's an unembellished tale of a reaction and nothing more. There's no reason to doubt the reporter; she's a good-natured character and was devoted to him for eleven years.

Varna is more attractive than Shumen; that much is clear even on the way into town. The main boulevard at least is lined with palm trees. Around their unkempt fronds, swaying sluggishly to the northeast, is a hint of sea. But for a city on the coast, a very old city even, it's a bitter disappointment. There's not even the faintest echo of the famous French or Italian seaside towns. Where the gaze gapes into a spot that promises a little character, concrete towers block the view, brooding in their moronic omnipotence, and the yearning gaze glides back to the plucked palms for want of anything better.

We'd reckoned with finding a room easily enough—it's not the holiday season yet. But no, they turn us away everywhere. Of course there are vacancies in the monstrous block, the largest hotel in town.

The entrance hall would look empty even if twenty busloads of guests flooded in all at once. With its rhombus-patterned wall-to-wall carpet (greenish, greyish, aubergine, each big fat rhombus wearing two small rhombuses as petulant crowns on its head), it's reminiscent of the parade grounds to a monumental verruca hell. The lone member of staff behind the mile-long reception desk is difficult to reach. Will anyone hear us if we raise our voices for a shy question? Everything comes across as stale, run-down. And above all there's a smell. A penetrating smell of cleaning fluid, bucket-loads of cleaning slurry that I imagine being tipped over the carpet every morning, then the clusters of fungus are suspended in a soapy, slimy quagmire and use their busy little fungal arms, constantly opening and closing fungal mouths to convert the originally hostile chemicals into a friendly nutritious sludge.

A hotel for people who like taking risks. And it's not even cheap, as we find out from Rumen, who has trotted all the way back across the hall to us with his head hanging.

After many vain attempts, we end up in a small but no less ugly inn. It must have been years since the windows were last cleaned; a grey film on the glass transmits a poisonous reflection of the sunlight. Azotic air dominates the chamber. When the window is open the sound of the construction machinery opposite boxes its way in. My migraine, always lying in wait for accommodation like this, flickers in appreciative anticipation. Adapting a Buddhist motto—let the torments pass through your body without taking care of them yourself—I lie down on the bed and decide to spend the next two hours right here, come what may, not moving a muscle.

It may not be quite Buddhist to lie in an awful hotel and think of exquisite hotels where one has spent joyous nights, but it helps. Tabakoff, for example, can't be praised highly enough for the care he took choosing the hotels for our journey. Always the best ones in town, never the brashest. For that reason alone, the man's getting more and more likeable in retrospect. Indeed, he took truly excellent care of us.

In Zurich we looked out from beneath the blue-and-white-striped awnings of our balconies onto the great lake. The lakeside air unleashed a dreamlike exhilaration. It felt as if the lake were releasing a soft, iridescent fabric, gentle swathes suspended above it in the early morning. Rosy-fingered Eos touched the swathes, dabbing at the rippled surface where the lake lay free and gliding across it. In my room on the lakeside promenade, in the water-freshened air, the world was immaculate for a few hours.

I even thought forgiving thoughts about our father. In all the fatherly fluttering around us, there's a father above and a father below, there's the father aside, there's the chatty and the mute father, but above all the high and the low father. In Zurich, a cheerful father wafted over across the lake, mindless of all classifications, and inspected the room. He made tiny affirmative noises. The shadow of his index finger rested a while on a painting of stippled bird's eggs. I could almost hear him singing.

Even though we never want to hear a word about our father's beautiful voice and we wage war against any memories connected to it, perhaps it is time to put in a good word for him after all.

Even our father needs a direction that goes upwards now and then. A father mustn't always be leaning towards the end. He, too, sometimes led a useful and cheerful life, was bright and light. So up with him then, let him rise joyfully aloft.

What was that song you used to sing? I don't know, says our father, some song or other.

Beloved, rich, joyful, I say, why wasn't it always like that?

Responsibility, says our father, it's one big pain.

When something pleased him extraordinarily, he was overcome by a jollity that swept him along, and he started singing and humming. Unlike the much drier Swabians, unlike the dry nest of Wurmlingen where he'd made his bed, he possessed the dancing gift of lightness. He also had a sense of luxury and was always willing to spend large sums of money on it without major calculations. Brash, silly things held no allure for him. He possessed a subtly developed sense of beauty, a feeling for the discreet transitions from the real to the unreal. The proof is in the few paintings he bought. Or the suits he got made out of fabulous fabrics, which showed off their colours almost as ably as butterfly wings.

The perfection in Zurich was partly down to the miracle of the shoes. Without having asked for it, I found my shoes outside the door in the morning, wrapped in rustling tissue paper, each package closed with a golden paper seal. I don't know what fairy-tale pots the shoe polish came from that the employees rubbed on their cloths, or whether the staff were trained in the Swiss military and finished off the polish with a good dollop of spit. The shoes shone as if for a parade, and on top of that they smelt good—leathery-spicy with a slight after-scent of almond oil.

In the evening we were entertained at two long tables reserved especially for us. To begin with, Tabakoff's speech embarrassed us, but it only took a few minutes for our host to grow jolly, and his mood soon infected us. The Swabian Bulgarians were in the best of moods, as no one had anticipated that Tabakoff's generosity would turn out to be so spectacular. A familiar atmosphere wafted over from the days of childhood, a festival atmosphere that we knew from when the Bulgarians met up once a year for their Christmas celebration.

Orthodox Christmas took place according to the Julian calendar, in the night of the 6th to the 7th of January. In Stuttgart, where very few of the Bulgarians were religious, the festival was rather like a huge family get-together complete with dancing. There was a pole attached to a cardboard crown decorated with a golden paper star, to remind us of the religious background. The celebration was held in a restaurant at the centre of town owned by a Bulgarian. It goes without saying that only Bulgarian dishes were served. Golden pita bread with a lucky silver coin in it. *Shopska salad*, *banitsa*, stuffed peppers, stuffed aubergines, sour stuffed vine leaves, a strange red puree with a difficult name and dried fruit compote. The room was decorated with a plethora of flowers. It was a boisterous night, with us children dancing or running around the tables in a pack. Good-natured adults asked us to dance just for fun. The celebration went on almost all night, and by the end we dizzy daisies stumbled around in circles, falling asleep on the backseat, overheated and happy on our way home.

The real charm of the event was that everyone who had anything to do with Bulgaria, regardless of their social standing and their jobs, was there. The men sat on the benches along the walls in their dark suits, as if they perched there every evening, still sitting together outside their front doors in their provincial Bulgarian towns for a while. The electrical-goods salesman alongside the import–export man, the hosiery rep alongside the car dealer, the proud owner of a greengrocery stall in the covered market alongside the doctor, and he in turn alongside the rose-grower. The blonde, permed wives exchanged the latest Stuttgart gossip, when they weren't dancing that is, and the landlord watched over us all, making sure the party went on and the glasses were topped up with his French wine—not Bulgarian wine; that was too bad even for the Bulgarian patriots.

Doncho Gitsin. The rose-grower! I'd forgotten all about him. He was still alive and his wife was too, it seemed. They were seated across the way at the other table.

So Tabakoff wasn't the only one of the old club to survive after all. It was typical of the rose-grower that I would assume he'd long since gone to his grave, while he headed for his seat with tip-tapping footsteps, hunched over, having stood up with some effort to whisper something in Tabakoff's ear, cautious because he was so fragile, unfamiliar with the luxury all round him, gripping the back of his chair with fumbling hands before he sat down again.

The rose-grower had been the odd one out in the club. A thin, unprepossessing little man, wilted even in the days when he must have been quite young. He worked for the Stuttgart city council and was responsible for putting up and maintaining municipal wastebaskets. But his passion was rose-growing, and he practised it on an allotment above the Fellbach vineyards. He specialized in old English roses, strongly scented, full-bloomed types with resounding names, which he pronounced in a strangely tender tone with a rolling *r*: *Cottage Rrrrose, Morrtimerr Sacklerr, Sisterr Charrrity*. The sound of his voice as he recited his beloved rose names is pretty much all I've retained of him. The rose-grower's main trait was that he was almost always silent, only opening his mouth in extreme cases, if there was absolutely no alternative. His leporine eyes roamed desperately as if looking for something, one heard a weak sighing, and then he said something, or rather he said as good as nothing. Malicious gossip had it that he hadn't spoken to his wife for a full eight years, prompted by some kind of petty irritation on her part. His wife gave little cause for trouble. She was the most loveable of all the Bulgarians' wives, not in the slightest bit argumentative. And she was by no means an empty vessel; on the contrary, she was surprisingly clever and hard-working too. She worked as a draughtswoman in an architectural office and took care of three children.

The Gitsins brought up a professor of solid-state physics—the red-headed Iris flown in from Cincinnati—and Stefan and Alexander, the founders and owners of an exhibition-stand construction company in the Allgäu, who flanked their parents like twin pillars that evening. Tabakoff had invited the Gitsins along even though they had no corpse to transport, and the whole family had turned up.

Why had Tabakoff chosen the complicated route via Zurich, Milan and across the sea to Greece rather than the simple way via Belgrade? He loved the sea. The hotels he favoured were along the route he chose. And he couldn't stand the Serbs.

Perhaps his mother's Greek roots played their part as well, a mother originating from the legendary line of the Phanariotes, who had held sway over the Black Sea for many years and were by no means wiped out under Ottoman rule but advanced to important positions. Tabakoff's mother was said to have been related to the Kantakouzenos clan—probably rather distantly.

It's hardly conceivable that his mother, if a direct descendant of this powerful house, would not have smelt the communist rat and jumped ship in good time.

Stories fluttered right out of Tabakoff's sleeves, about Abdul Hamid II for instance, the last absolute ruler of the Ottoman Empire, known as Abdul the Damned or as Abdul the Fearful or Abdul the Distrustful. Our businessman, grown rich in Florida, did not baulk at giving advice beyond the grave to this pointy-bearded and permanently broke ruler, on how he could have rescued his ailing finances.

The Baghdad Railway! Tabakoff ejaculated, amazed that we knew so little.

The Phanariotes had held the Black Sea in their grip—Tabakoff positively shouted out his historical abbreviations, one fist aloft.

I had changed seats over dessert and was now sitting close to him. Having calmed down somewhat, he described his mother to us as a tall, proud woman (I heard the rattle of headgear although Tabakoff never mentioned any), and another image forced itself into my mind—Tabakoff's mother holding up the Black Sea like a sponge and squeezing it, water running down her arms. The words *mother* and *sea* generated such a fiery exhilaration in Tabakoff that he had to grasp at his bald head now and then to calm down.

We were allowed to share in Tabakoff's thalassophilia. But that time hadn't quite come yet. The next day, the limousines glided out of the garage in impeccable synchronization, as if they'd been practising. The chauffeurs in peaked caps stowed our suitcases, and on we went to Milan. It's a mystery how Tabakoff managed to get the black worm of our parade over the border to Italy unobstructed. We caused a sensation everywhere we went. People leant out of passenger-seat windows on the motorway—their amazement as we passed them by at a leisurely pace imprinted itself on my mind as if I'd photographed them with camera eyes—children waved like crazy and held up cuddly toys, people stopped at the side of the road and watched us disappearing into the horizon.

Not even the most spoilt individuals in our party had anticipated that anything could top our wonder-hotel in Zurich.

The Principe di Savoia. Jesus, what a name!

Jesus will strike me with a migraine of steel if I keep on using his name in vain.

We stood around in the entrance area, embarrassed. A good number of us looked nervously down at ourselves, plucking at our clothing here and there, gazing shyly around as we entered, doubting we were the right people for this palace. Not Marco and Wolfi, particularly not the manager in the energy sector, who strolled under the spectacular art nouveau dome as if he were a fat cat from a folktale, taking possession of his house as naturally as can be. Stares from the hooded eyes of other guests didn't bother him in the slightest. Quite the contrary; it was as if these stares flew straight back to his assailants and did them the damage.

My sister and I ran into the twins again only a few minutes later, when we tried out the swimming pool that belonged to the presidential suite. Tabakoff had hired the suite for himself but invited us all to swim. When we knocked at the door he was on the telephone in a bathrobe and gave a generous wave towards the pool at the two of us, standing there as if we didn't know quite where to go with our swimming kits.

Two rows of windows offered a view too overpowering for our cowed hearts. Involuntarily, I grabbed my sister by the arm. Mild, slightly reddened evening light flooded in, making the pool shine like a huge turquoise jewel. Two dolphins swam motionlessly on its floor, head to tail, tail to head, enclosed into a circle of black and white stones. The thoughts came like falling stars the instant we lowered ourselves into the water. But the twins were there before us. Marco slapped his hands against the surface, occupied with some kind of jumping exercises, with plenty of water splashing and surging and spuming around his torso. Wolfi swam lengths as staunchly as a record-breaker, delicate goggles strapped around his head on black rubber ties. Stroke for stroke, his head turned to the left and the right. Once again, I admired my sister for her gift of swift composure as she simply swam off and found her way, neither fast nor slow, while I, forever inhibited, swallowing water and zig-zagging between the brothers, could hardly propel myself forward in the Savoyan princely waters.

The next morning, over breakfast in the winter garden (O gliding serving trolleys, so deliciously laden, who shall compose an adequate anthem to your silently raising silver lids?), we experienced a completely different Tabakoff. Paying no heed to anyone's coming or going, he had immersed himself in his newspaper. Morning greetings were not returned. He seemed no longer to know his guests.

Wolfi, who had pretended not to know us in the pool, pretended not to know us over breakfast as well and entrenched himself behind a newspaper of his own. I'd had more than enough of all this twin drama, and sat down with the Gitsins with the intention of contriving an exchange of places in the limousines.

Rumen is anticipating the evening with some concern.

Some days ago, he called a former school friend of his who lives in Varna. As expected, the result was an invitation to visit. The school friend is no ordinary Bulgarian. He may have been ordinary in school, perhaps affable, perhaps a bundle of laughs. But not any more. Sashko Trendafilov has graduated into a local Mafia boss, having won his stake in tough territorial battles over the coveted stretches of the local beach. These battles were anything but harmless. The knife-and-gun fights cost more than a hundred lives. Now that the ground has been distributed, the battles have died down but they might break out again at any moment, should someone want to break into the business or put up a fight. Sashko Trendafilov has grown into a dangerous man. And to make matters all the more interesting, he has married the wife of his former boss, whom he is said to have wiped out with his own hands. But that's just a rumour.

Rumen was by no means eager to make contact with him. He told us about poor little Sashko more in the manner of *isn't life strange*—the pitiable lad who had to get the answers to the maths tests thrown to him on crumpled scraps of paper. We were curious about the spheres of power and drew Rumen out on the subject. And now there's no going back. Now that we've forced his hand we've begun to realize what a complicated position we've put Rumen in. I won't be able to cry off with an approaching migraine.

He's more nervous than usual, smoking and laughing for no reason and wiping the sweat from his forehead with his sleeve, stabbing about so hectically with the gear stick that I feel nauseous. We drive up a freshly tarred road that encircles a hill slightly north of the town. For a while we drive alongside a high wall, freshly plastered and painted brick-red, then we stop outside a gate.

We'd reckoned with a gate, and that it would be guarded. With cameras too. What we hadn't reckoned with is a solid metal construction over four metres high, double-sided and imitating a fortress gate with exaggerated crossbeams and protruding nails.

I've been here since biblical times, says the gate, though it can only be three years old at most.

Rumen gets out of the car and speaks into a machine, and then the gates swing aside and two guards present themselves, electronic equipment around their heads, guns at the ready. We don't quite know what to do, and Rumen is confused too because the two men just stand there so stiffly. He gets back in the car and cuts the engine. Then one of the guards waves us through. At a snail's pace, Rumen drives along the road to the house. The driveway looks less fortress-like and more reminiscent of a palace, with two pavilions flanking the road, albeit not of the permeable, delicate French kind, but block-like constructions distantly recalling Prussian guardhouses, which have been contorted into octagonal shapes for no clear reason. At every turn are wild displays of blossoms, as if the flowerbeds had been watered with champagne. The building is extremely long, with a stone base topped with areas marked out in brown and dark blue, and bay windows protruding from the second floor.

Dressed in white, taking measured steps, a man strides towards us—the man of the house, as it turns out. He starts fumbling at Rumen the moment he gets out of the car, kissing him and pinching his cheeks. Guaranteed genuine Bulgarian gestures. Hirsute chests rub together, hands slap against shoulder blades, there is thudding, sighing and exulting as the drama of hearts reuniting is played out using every trick in the book.

I say to my sister, thank goodness for the English, who only extend their hands with the greatest of reluctance.

Trendafilov gives us both a courteous kiss on the hand and announces in a rattle of English—Frriends of Rumen, my frriends.

We've picked up his scent. There's something fascinating about interpreting a man who's killed other men and won battles.

He smells like someone who thinks he's the bee's knees. Not a primaeval beast but still primitive enough not to shy from the scent of his own private parts. Amazingly for a Bulgarian, he's not wandering around in a cloud of aftershaves. He wears his slightly long, shiny black hair smoothed back, and his loosely flowing shirt, were it black, could belong to a man of the cloth. He is neither fat nor thin, neither tall nor short; not one feature stands out, his long glued-back hair seemingly his only flourish. But wait, there is something. Sashko has a slight overbite, pretty much the least dangerous dental position a man can have. If you knew nothing about him you might mistake him for a nice guy, all things considered.

Our host leads us into a low-ceilinged but incredibly wide hall, with stone floors topped with Persian rugs, certainly not cheap ones. Strange things are on display at the sides, partly in glass cabinets, partly planted freely and lit up by spotlights like in an ethnological museum, all sorts of things brought forth by the different peoples in the course of their battles and then sunk back into the earth—pieces of armour, weapons, harnesses.

We're instructed to look about in peace while Sashko explains each and every object to Rumen, and after that Rumen passes on the explanations on Greco-Thracian-Roman cavalry battles and their remains now torn from the Bulgarian earth.

A scene of a lion rending a stag on a stone pillar. A stone horse's head, the mane standing up like a brush, its jaws opened wide as if for a horrified scream, a subtle play of nerves around its muzzle. Pot-bellied amphorae wait in their stands for the answer to why they were made so large but can't stand up on their own. A stone fish with dragon's feet, as low as a bench. Sword handles ending in bent ram's heads. Poles with attachments in the shape of stag's heads. The upper part of a bronze helmet with a head seam and a ducktail at the back, slightly too small for modern-day Bulgarian heads. A silver plateleg riddled with holes hovers above its black pillar, transported into the class of a magical object with which one might heal sore limbs.

Crossed swords on the walls but also a black felt coat covered in tiny plates of gold. A collection of arrowheads is spread out in the cabinets, sewn on a cloth in a fan shape by tidy hands, along with lancet-like gold sheets in the shape of fish and many, many decorative elements from bridles and saddles. All manner of coins, spurs, bridle bits. Then comes the pride of the collection—a delightful golden rider with a fluttering cloak, whipping away at something that's broken off.

They probably dug up entire kurgans especially for Sashko, presenting him with the treasures on bended knee.

According to Rumen, Sashko's father had an affair with Zhivkov's eccentric daughter Lyudmila. Lyudmila, a skinny matron with a tremulous voice, believed in the holy powers of magical stones, in the magic of holy Bulgarian treasures and above all in the prophetic powers of her own good self. She made sure everything unearthed by archaeological excavations in the 1970s and 80s was presented to her personally, and read it all as symbols and signs. She was convinced that a miraculous thousand-year Bulgarian realm was nigh. Following an accident, she wore a turban draped around her head in public, perhaps to hide the fact that there was something not quite right about that very head. There were rumours that she'd had a silver plate implanted in her skull. A Tatar-silver plate myth just like the one about Joseph Beuys. Lyudmila's head found no rest until it had come up with a genealogy for Lyudmila going back to the year 324 BC. She procured imposing roots for the Zhivkov family, with one of her ancestors being an outstanding warrior under Alexander the Great, an exemplary Thracian warrior who won his bride at a mass wedding of ten thousand soldiers to ten thousand Persian brides, that highly symbolic Eurasian melding of the peoples instituted by Alexander.

On we go, our host striding ahead in his white outfit; and, oh yes, *he* hasn't made his presence felt at all so far, lying absolutely calmly in a corner—a grey molosser dog, probably a Neapolitan mastiff, who gets to his feet, and having shaken a wedge of saliva out of his wrinkles as he stood up, trots after his master. A placid dog, hard to rile. I'm instantly fascinated and ask Trendafilov his name: Roxy—so she's a lady, and she obediently stops and looks when I call her name.

The next room is just as low and wide but this time a slight dome crowns the ceiling, decorated with a wooden sun surrounded by wooden stars on a dark blue background.

Rather chilly in here.

The style varies between an Oriental reception room, the living room of a rich farmer and a bear-hunter's cabin. Were hordes of guests to come dashing in, they'd soon be sitting on the divans around the walls, stretching their legs out beneath the low tables. The room has something of a temple about it too. Two temple steps lead to the sepa-rated-off arcades in front of the windows. Wooden carv-ings around the raised seats there. Furry, chunky items on the walls, bearskins, woven things with tassels, in between them folkloric belts with heavy hangings.

We walk down a couple of steps. After the next door-way, the floor is tiled in peachy tones, the walls smooth and just as peachy, and we cross a modern room complete with cantilever chairs, racing-green club chairs and a huge bar equipped with hundreds of bottles, lined up neatly between red and golden semi-pillars. In front of it a counter with squares of gold leaf. If it weren't for all the bottles, we might mistake it for the spacious anteroom of a celebrity hairdresser, what with all the glossy magazines lying around in piles. Not a book to be seen.

And—no, I don't believe it: on the opposite wall is—Jackie! It really is her! Jackie from Warhol's Jackie series. I head straight for her, it looks like an early series, *Andy Warhol, Sixteen Jackies, 1964*, announces the proud post-card-sized label alongside her: six smiling Jackies with a white pillbox hat, ten Jackies as a widow, even more gor-geous than the smiling version—black, upright and softly blurred and absent around the mouth. *Holy Jackie, Holy Time in Eternity, Holy Eternity in Time*, as Allen Ginsberg once psalmodized in the good old days of LSD.

In a museum, I'd walk on after a brief glance, but here I sense my excitement rousing my headache and I feel dizzy for a moment. There's no way to talk to my sister right now; although she's surprised by the change in the rooms, she hasn't yet read the passages from the diary. Rumen understands. Sashko gives a greasy smile, saying nothing, savouring the general amazement and walking outside ahead of us as soon as he's had his fill.

And another old familiar sight—a second swimming pool. This time it's a large one. A shimmering, glimmering, magnificent giant pool, lined with palm trees in huge pots. A woman is sitting under a sunshade and a Chihuahua leaps off her lap, one of those awful yap-yap-yappers, hoarse and neurotic, and it won't stop its yapping, acting like it's about to let loose on Rumen's trouser legs. With every forward step Rumen takes, the dog absconds backwards with more shrill yaps, eventually jumping back onto the lap and grumbling and growling on from there. Meanwhile the mastiff stands as motionless as a sculpture, gazing out to sea.

The building, a straight bar to the front, opens up in a semi-oval to the rear, with a balustrade facing spacious grounds. I whisper *national revival at the front, Washington round the back* to my sister, but that's not quite right. The pool is the eye-catcher in the middle. The lawn is greener than green, probably refreshed with tinted lotion every three hours. Further to the right, behind the oleander bushes, the quartered rectangle with the chain-link fence around it is no doubt a tennis court.

We are introduced to Sashko's wife. She holds out a casual hand without getting up, which agitates the

Chihuahua all over again. Chairs are pushed to and fro. A servant comes bustling over with a tray loaded with aperitifs.

Down there, rather a long way away, is the mass of the sea, rigid and grey.

She speaks much better English than her husband, and fluent French too. She's not necessarily pleased to have us. At a brief glance from several metres' distance she's a piece of bric-a-brac, framed by dark brown curls. But not so. Her eyes are extraordinary, deep, intense blue in colour, not watery or blurry eyes but with something terribly precise about them. Most surprisingly of all, she's a good bit older than Sashko, perhaps even as much as ten years. A dreadful age difference for the Bulgarians as we know them. A well-kept woman over fifty, or at least that's what she looks like, and Sashko is Rumen's age, in his mid-forties at most. There's even a trace of puppy fat on his eyelids.

There's an art to making such little use of the facial muscles while talking.

Would we care for a swim before dinner? There are swimsuits and towels over there in the cabins. My sister and I gratefully decline but there's no escape for Rumen. Sashko grabs him by the arm and drags him off to the cabins. A little later they emerge again, our host in a long burgundy bathrobe with a crest at chest level, Rumen in the uncrested blue and white of a sailor. Their robes fall onto deckchairs and whoosh, the boys flop into the water bottoms first with their knees pulled up.

Roxy lies down. Time for a little chat from woman to woman. We're asked how we like Bulgaria and the answer is supplied for us—beautiful land, very hearty people, strangers are welcome everywhere. Just the kind of conversation during which lice begin to creep over my body. I circle the ice cubes in my glass and take a swig of Campari. The wrong drink, as I notice instantly. Not what this frightened stomach needs right now at ten past seven in the evening.

I leave it to my sister to start the conversation, although that's a mistake. In a matter of minutes it's clear that the lady of the house can't abide my sister, although she can put up with me. An all too familiar experience. Difficult women get on better with me than with my sister. They see my sister as competition, a slave to Eros who speaks in her sleep and can be woken easily by any man; they don't take me seriously in that respect. And that's just the case here. It's I who reap the tiny amount of affection our hostess can possibly spare for another woman.

I hope to get us out of this spot with a bit of canine chatter, even managing to find words of praise for the flimsy pooch on her lap. It's trembling and trembling. She assumes a thin line of a smile—Roxy and Kato are very good friends. I can't quite see why a mastiff, one metre forty or fifty shoulder height, might be friends with this hysterical rat, but of course I don't contradict her—I find it just too cute.

Kato glares at me from eyes screwed out of his head.

I do a bit of haha-ing, not always at the correct moments. She's a bombshell of a woman, I think, the personal trainer round here on matters of cruelty and business. A half-baked husband with an overbite and a wife as tough as an old boot. Roxy! I whisper. Kato responds with a yap. Roxy leaves her muzzle on the ground, only raising the wrinkles on her forehead, and yes, for a moment her soft red-brown eyes meet mine.

My sister is chattering away, babbling into vagueness; I can't possibly concentrate on what she's saying. *No books in the house.* Isn't today the 24th of May? The festival of Bulgarian writing, the festival of Bulgarian education and culture, the festival of Constantine Cyril the philosopher and his brother Methodius? Of the alphabet the two of them invented? Ancient Bulgarian scriptures and so on? (The Bulgarians tend to forget that the famous brothers never set foot in the country and it was their students who developed the alphabet.)

Gracious goodness, there probably isn't a single book in this house. That's a declaration of war, that's a refusal to learn from the dead.

And you? Learnt what? Learnt how? What do you want anyway? What? Layers of mist above the sea, layer upon layer, veiling. The sun low. Stinging. Learnt what? From whom? All wrong. We're children of a homunculus. The plural of homunculus—homunculi?

Here comes the hammering, the migraine hammering it in—wrong. All wrong. We had the right parents, we're just the wrong children. Absolutely wrong children. Idiotic children. Goody-two-shoes, scaredy-cat, idiotic children. Dis-gust-ing children.

For all my not knowing how to escape from this hammering, I take another swig of Campari, a big one, and some of it sloshes over and runs out of the corners of my mouth. Roxy casts me a glance, a kindly one—what would I do without you, Roxy? Galloping greengages, absolutely wrong children, God-fearing, stupid children, our parents would have needed terrorists, not these stupid God-fearing children they had, we ought not to have let them have a moment's peace, we ought to have infuriated them, rubbed them up the wrong way, niggled at them, by the age of four at the latest we ought to have behaved like Stalinists, Maoists, fascists, *empo-rio*—no, *empi-ri-ocriticism*, twelve, fourteen, sixteen letters, *What Is To Be Done*, nice short words, *Over The Line*, another short one, *Getting Down To The Root of Matters*, too long to count, but instead we placated and pacified, we were such good girls it almost makes me vomit, enough of this, but no, Roxy's a good girl too, oh yes, Roxy's a good girl and a gorgeous girl, so gorgeous she gives you wrinkles, and grey too, no, not smoky grey—glossy grey, a spe-he-cial glossy coat for extra God-fearing characters, who—who—shine li-hike—

Straight to the loo. (Three letters.) My time's up in one damn minute. My sister asks the way on my behalf. The last thing I notice is Roxy getting up and accompanying me to the doorway, the servant showing me the way. There's no use walking at a strict pace any more. Now's the time for inconspicuous acceleration. Still walking but not quite running. There's the door, close it, shut it. Up with the toilet seat and out with it.

There's a hammering, a whistling, I stagger and lurch, but still I feel lighter and, of course, I clean up like a good girl with moistened toilet paper, even though I feel nauseous again the instant I bend over. The after-bang comes as I stand up, as if my skull were exploding. Splash water on my face. Rinse out my mouth. Why didn't I just vomit right there on the table, I ask myself on the way back. Why did I only go wild at the age of twelve and try to drive our mother crazy? Our mother who lived absolutely averted in her own grief, obstinately obsessed with earning money, getting into the VW at seven every morning with a rep's case of medication samples and too tired in the evenings to be interested in systematic provocation with the aid of Mao Zedong, only interested in maps, how to get from Weilimdorf to Tuttlingen, from Doctor Wilfried Pfleiderer to Doctor Achim Metzger— for which I certainly can't blame her any more.

I missed that one. On the left, half vanished in the bushes at the edge of the embankment, is something in the nature of an Easter Island-ish cranial, looking out towards the sea. Made of wood. Presumably a modern Bulgarian sculpture, a giant club chewed by Roxy, who knows. I'd even put it up in my garden for Roxy's sake. The dog's been waiting for me at the door to the patio and now walks me back to the others, dropping to the stone flags next to me with a deep, devoted sigh, almost a grunt, the kind only those experienced in melancholy can muster.

The men are still in the water but now telephones ring, two in a row, and it's only now that I spot a small telephone station set up on the edge of the pool, with holders for six telephones—honestly, six! Sashko takes one call, says something, puts one phone down and picks the other one up, talks here, talks there, as I admire his multi-conversationalism with various devices. Modern-day speaking in tongues, as speedy as a lizard. Not one of my talents.

Rumen is seeking the silence of the water, head over heels. Have I mentioned that our Rumen's not bad-looking, despite a huge pair of baggy trunks with a buttercup pattern? A bit chunky perhaps, those peasant ancestors haven't been bred out quite yet, and a bit of a rug on his chest, which doesn't exactly raise my enthusiasm, but just strictly in the Kristoline sense—this man is acting as if he wanted, in a modest manner but definitely decidedly in some way, to imitate our father visually. It's rather nice the way he raises his head and the water whips out of his hair as he shakes it, just like it once whipped out of our father's hair.

There's no need to worry about Christian blessings in this house either, as Sashko's wife informs us. They've had a private chapel built, and inside it lives a valuable icon that we simply have to take a look at later, and yes, the metropolitan of Varna dashed over in person to consecrate the chapel. I bet every time Sashko cut off a rival's testicles he devoutly kissed his Hodigitria—holy mother of testicles, says my migraine, which is nonsense of course—no, he kissed an austere wavy-cloaked leader of the way with babe in arms, dabbed onto wood by the brush of Luke the Evangelist with unearthly care.

The men swim side by side in harmony, more electronic applause swelling for the killer from his devices, all of which ring simultaneously in a tinny crescendo.

Slowly, dusk has spread over the land from the direction of the sea. We make a break for it. Rumen steers the small car out of the gate like a learner driver. We can't just go to our beds with our muddled heads; we drive to the busy part of town but can't find the right kind of place. Rumen stops suddenly in the middle of the road, gets out of the car and walks over to a woman hunched outside a doorway, then gives her something, probably alms. He closes the car door behind him with emphasis and drives on.

We wander along the beach in the hope of a restaurant with a terrace looking out to sea. I've never seen such an ugly beach. At every turn are rancid bars with music blaring, the kind of music with which to start civil wars.

I walk a few steps behind the others and vomit on the ground, shovelling sand over the mucous with one foot.

Rumen is agitated; he keeps talking and talking, digging his shoes into the sand and wanting my sister to understand everything. I still feel nauseous. I want to go back. I can find my way to the hotel but my sister has to convince Rumen that I really will find it and that I'd rather be alone in my state. We wave and I move off.

I wander along the ragged palm trees to the hotel. A good deal of traffic but barely any people on the streets. Here and there, the odd splash of stomach fluid wants out, less and less each time, almost incidentally, perhaps a canine compulsion to mark the streets of Varna with the last remains of my contempt.

In the hotel I feel exhausted. But I can't bear it when one leg ends up on top of the other. Nor can I bear it when my ankles press into the mattress in parallel. It's as if my ankles were capable of a repulsive connection to my brain, generating flashes of lightning and psychedelic waves behind my closed eyelids. Tabakoff flashes in, good old Tabakoff with his braggadocio bald pate, and then I myself rattle through my brain, not as sharp-focus as Tabakoff—one's mind's-eye images of oneself are always rather vague but it's still definitely me, with my illness theories so quick to trip off my tongue, self-hate theories—bursitis, Alexander Gitsin had said, he suffered from an inflammation of the bursa.

Faster than I was able, my sister took action and found herself a new seat. To my surprise, Marco too had said adieu to our car. Only Wolfi was left. In the place of the escapees, Alexander and Iris had embarked.

Bursitis, said Alexander. What kind of nonsense is that? I asked gruffly.

Alexander pointed at his left elbow.

You ought to keep away from sick people, I said. Like it or not, you catch their sicknesses, and behind the sick person rises an ocean of men in white coats, reaching out their arms for him. A sick person never gets well if you give him sympathy. You have to patronize sick people, then they struggle out of their misery because there's no way out other than death or life.

Iris laughed, Alexander was slightly offended, and goodness me, a weak smile crept over Wolfi's face. I had found an unexpected ally on matters of repugnance for sickness.

The theory's rubbish, of course. I'm living proof of its falsehood. According to my contempt for sickness, I ought to be absolutely hale and hearty. But it always finds me, that rotten migraine, it doesn't care what I think, just to spite me it flashes, presses and squeezes and stabs behind my eyes. How terribly embarrassing. I've taken on this theatrical ailment from my father, he was another of those migrainous wet blankets. Its vengeful drives behind it, beating me with steel rods, creating a perverse orgasm of the soul, and wham, it's rammed down my throat what a lying piece of work I am, and bam, how wretched this perpetual revelling in me-me-me, and thank you ma'am, open up the grave in my head to put an end to this pathetic grousing existence that tosses and turns in bed and gurns and grinds its teeth.

I beg your pardon?

Ever felt pity? Do tell.

Not a jot. Not for my dying mother, not ever for any human being, at most for neglected street mongrels and shaggy cats. I couldn't even touch my mother for all my horror. Who was it that cut her toenails? Not me, it was my sister, and that's why she's never troubled by headaches, the big sister I hate with her glowing head of health, her head of care, her head that has everything I don't have.

Iris Sinclair, who's married to an American, and Alexander Gitsin—they're the kind of children parents wish for. Fun-filled, gentle children always prepared for whatever life throws at them. Everyone likes Iris; a vivid sense of intelligence veritably leaps out of her button-holes. Her strawberry-blonde curls are statically charged. Iris wants to know everything, studies everything; she has tiny, wrinkled fingers that won't stay still and she brought a delightful upheaval into our limousine with those fingers, making me so jolly that I no longer felt the slightest yearning for a private slumber trip. Even Wolfi thawed out and started a conversation with Alexander about trade-fair construction, which gave Alexander an opportunity to tell us about his company. He was proud of his success, that's for sure, but without a hint of brag-ging. Firmly soldered to the everyday, Alexander seemed like the prototype of a Swabian, albeit with skin and hair melted into a darker tone than is customary for Swabians. I built up such trust in him that I felt like asking him to deal with my finances, redecorate my apartment and make me a plan of when to work, when to eat, when to go for a walk, when to watch TV and when to read. Had I met Alexander earlier, he'd have advised me on how a sensible person treats their parents. It might even have taken effect while our mother was still alive.

Mind you—I'm starting to doubt that. Amicable words were of no use at all. It's less than likely that the honourable Alexander could have dealt with our ruthless mother, a mother who did not simply die in her armchair with a cigarette clamped between her lips, as I'd always though she would, but after a temper tantrum.

She too roused herself for a huge scene of Christly indignation on her deathbed. Actually at the end of her strength, barely able to raise her head, her eyes wandering restlessly, studying the ceiling rather incredulously with slightly squinting and almost cheeky girlish eyes, her rodent mouth gnawingly repeating its mutters of *so, what comes now* or *so, look where we've got to*, her haggard arms as thin as sticks, she suddenly reared up, grabbed whatever was on her bedside table, threw all the stuff, plates, cups, pills, spoons, boxes, at a crucifix on the wall— aimed and hit it. The wall dripping with fluids, the remains on the floor. Our mother wiped out.

No, at that moment she didn't mean the redeemer hanging on the cross. She meant the unworthy bearer of his name she'd married. Not a word of hate, no defamation, no curse had ever crossed her lips, not even harmless accusations that might have bought her some breathing space and reduced her resentment, or at least never in our presence. She wouldn't tolerate the remaining family horde taking revenge in words. She of all people, the mistress of sharp words and unfounded gestures of profligacy, acted tame. She had never rid herself of her husband. Her husband had to stay intact with a nice tie

around his neck. And even though he tortured her down
to the bone, scraped her emotions down to the bone, she
still had nightmares till a late age, dreaming of slittings
and hangings, hangings and slittings, ineffectively com-
bated with far too many sleeping pills. She lived in cold-
ness, tidiness, cleanliness, with eighty cigarettes a day
(always airing properly, butts thrown away immediately),
impeccable bookkeeping and an untamed rage at Jesus
Christ.

A gloomy still life appears—our mother shortly
before her death, looking out of a high, lit window, night
after night, over the patchwork of Degerloch, the unat-
tractive roofs of Degerloch. Bloodstained clouds above
the roofs of Degerloch. Cold 1980s concrete. A brittle
moon above the neon lamps. Gas-station air. Architectural mincemeat. Neighbours told us she'd stand at the
window, motionless, for an eternity—the very idea of it
always grips me. Our father was another of those terrible
standers at the window, his shoulders in a deep shrug,
deaf to all words and appalling his hosts. In a friend's
house on Killesberg hill with a view of the city from the
living room, he stood in a dark mood, stood there forever
and was not to be removed from the window—Stuttgart,
city of hills and lights, sinister city of assiduous citizens,
oh yes, he was capable of earnest offerings—whilst the
puzzled company, not quite knowing how to do without
him, dragged their laborious conversations out with shy
glances in his direction. Pictures as if etched into my
brain of these lonely parental standers at windows,
hooked to the night with the eyes of junkies.

Our mother, a nicotine-addicted canaille preserved in alcohol. I mean that in the most respectful way. She did have one thing after all—she had her eccentricities, and she lived them to the full, not caring what the rest of the world was ever concerned with. Television was absolutely irrelevant to her. She never possessed a television, never ogled at the box, not even during the moon landing. She didn't even consider it worth the effort rejecting television, she simply sat uncaringly alongside while her friends were fascinated, and smoked away in silence. The most important medium of her times didn't exist for her, not even in old age. By that time she restricted herself to reading the local broadsheet, taking the dog for walks in the Weidach valley—not the dachshund, of course, he was long dead and gone, but a large, placid Bernese mountain dog, with whom she went to the pub, smoked, drank white wine spritzers, ate a little and read books. Apart from that she wrote rather well; the surviving letters have a smart and jaunty tone to them. And then she had that obsession of hers with fingers. Her hands were the most important element of her personality. She consciously placed them or set them in scene so that one couldn't help noticing them. Painted, slim fingers that held each cigarette a tad casually but at the same time with marked elegance.

Our mother was a digit philosopher, drawing her knowledge of human nature from fingers. My sister's hands were *too petite*. She seemed to think mine were *all right*, although she never usually had a good word to say for me. At least I inherited her steel-hard fingernails, while my sister has soft ones. Our father had *creative yet muscular fingers*, with no hairs growing on them thank goodness, I hasten to add. The deeply odd thing about her finger obsession is, aside from lying around in a decorative manner, our mother's hands were rather good for nothing, at least not for fine motor skills. Our mother's fingers got nervous when it came to aiming the end of a thread at the eye of a needle.

And beseethed by these hyper-nervous fingers, while grains of rice rain down from my frontal lobes and the flames in the background flicker ever smaller, I gradually succumb to sleep.

Despite the warm weather announcing itself through the open windows, I awaken as joyful as a child on a snowy morning. My head is light, filled with a euphoria-inducing gas. My high spirits make it grow higher and higher out of my neck. As long as my head's a head of pain, it's pressed into a bowl, perpetually just about to burst. Now there's space and air everywhere, for my head, for my arms and my legs, air, air, air. The sudden absence of pain makes my body walk out of the room in guileless expectation of the world—no, not walk but stroll. Oh, no matter that the breakfast nook looks grubby. Joyfully, I whiz out of the door ahead of my fellow travellers to look for a cafe. It's not as warm outside as I thought.

And something else is different. As I watch my companions sitting at the table in such blushing embarrassment, I entertain a certain suspicion.

Feeling better?

Feeling marvellous.

Jesus, I'm glad to hear that, says my sister, and sighs as fervently as if Jesus had just performed the miracle of Lazarus upon me. She's besieged by a guilty conscience, her usual morning calm all awry, her slim fingers twirling a coffee spoon in mid-air. When the two of them chorus simultaneously, then stop and giggle, the matter's as clear as day.

Rumen now declares unctuously that we are to obey the diktat of my wishes all day today. Embarrassment forces him to leap from one stepping stone of monstrously bureaucratic language to the next; he substantiates the dictatorship of my wishes, indeed, the dictate of my wishes shall be his command.

I laugh out loud, which has a rather unsettling effect on my two turtle doves, who can't possibly imagine how quickly their cover has been blown. My sister looks beautiful. Her melting charm, rather chipped at the edges over the past ten years, holds her face smooth again; immersed in a rosy glow, she bites into something too rubbery for a croissant and too soft for a roll (as I just noticed as I bit into a similarly ominous something). But the incompetence of Bulgarian bakers shan't rob us of our jollity.

Your wish dictator thinks we should drive along the coast and see where we end up, I say.

Good, very good, says Rumen, we'll drive and see.

How right you are as usual, says my sister. Varna has nothing to offer. Let's get out of here.

Half an hour later we're ready to go. My sister virtually begs me to sit at the front and enjoy the coastline, but no, I don't want to, not now by any means.

As we drive out of Varna I consider the new situation. I haven't seen my sister in love for a long time now. I like her in this shimmering state. And Rumen, looking beyond my own erotic idiosyncrasies, is not a bad choice.

I don't begrudge my sister this romance one bit. It's about time too. The only thing is, it puts me in a difficult situation. I can't sneak off and not bother the two of them. They'd get a shock if I wanted to take the train to Sofia from Burgas. They wouldn't allow it at all, Rumen would insist on driving me, and I'd only have truncated the time they have together in Bulgaria. My sister is now veritably clinging to me, constantly worrying about maintaining our merry band of three because the tenderly woven band of two is still fluttering too excitedly in the wind for them to cope without me.

To make matters much more complicated, my sister and I never talk about men. We talk about books and all kinds of other things, but never do we touch upon men we are seeing, other than in formulaic phrases. A touchy subject. Although I generally tend to fire my comments straight out, here I'm trapped in a complicated entrenchment. There's lots of not mentioning, the occasional sweet nothing, hellos to be said to this man or that, inconsequential and insincere, and there are obedient pretences that the recipient of the hellos has returned them in kind. No word even close to the truth has ever slipped out of me concerning my sister's men.

Whenever we're infatuated, we err our separate ways. The difference could hardly have been greater, even in our school days. I loved the high-octane speedsters or the very opposite dry bone-creakers. And nothing in between. My sister, meanwhile, oh boy, my sister let herself in for the suave mother-in-law-charmers, for notorious flower-and-chocolate-givers, to our mother's guaranteed delight. While I brought home chaps guaranteed to make her hair stand on end—a Rasputin, a politico all dressed in leather and a Finnish Afghanistan tripper who had rather a high dose of LSD in his bloodstream when he refused to shake hands with my mother and steered past her with a slight lurch to slouch all over the red sofa.

The Persian my sister married and had two children with is another of those mother-in-law-charmers. On the outside a Sky du Mont dragged through olive oil, only more petite, more Persian. Not a bearded Ayatollah. More of a Shah fan. Although it's hard to imagine him beating up dissident demonstrators. He got a holder mounted in his Mercedes for his Kleenex box because he always has something to wipe up. It's not so bad that the man's unfaithful. Faithfulness is incredibly overrated. What's bad is his saccharine, wimpish, faux-gentle, manipulative, utterly phoney egomania. *I thought of you as the sun rose this morning, Cherie.*

If we were ever to talk about men, I'd have to ask my sister how she takes a little statement like that. Why the reading matter that accompanies her so intimately has rubbed off so little on her love life. And we'd have to talk about why she clings so terribly stubbornly to her miniature editions of our father. Her husband, you see, is also the kind of doctor who mainly deals with women. He's a plastic surgeon, however, perfect typecasting for a soap-opera plastic surgeon.

If we were to grill each other by turns, I'd have to provide information too. What on earth is so great about the blond skeletons you're so infatuated with? My sister would have every right to ask. What idiotic deviations does your avoidance of our father lead to? At least in my case the books I like reading and the men I like wooing are more compatible, I could state in my own defence.

It would be touchy, more than touchy, if we got onto the topic of children. My sister's spoilt, deeply unhappy children. My radical lack of interest in children.

Actually, I'm feeling light and free enough to think differently for once—it ought to be possible to see my sister's family in an easy-going light, as if they were curious lilies, Frankfurt lilies, lovely and sweet in their own way as they flourish so perkily on Beethovenstrasse, but as soon as I lose hold of the lily image, I can't find any good alternative.

When I think of those children in Frankfurt, I think of the hellishly overstuffed toy cupboards they have just grown out of. How they were dragged off to remote corners of the globe four times a year, thus losing all interest in the world. They're semi-adults by now. The chatterbox son, a terrible braggart, has crashed and ruined his seventeenth racing bike and now drives a convertible (at least he's interested in money; that's a clear enough passion, albeit a cold one). And then the portly, depressive daughter, who gives no sign of ever being enthusiastic about anything, let alone ever being capable of anything.

Why for God's sake has my sister, this loveable bookworm, awakened so little delicacy and curiosity in her children? For the first time, I feel pity for them. They seem like they've been condemned to stumble about an even worse as-if-world than we ever had to deal with. They're not even granted a little tragedy.

Despite all that, regardless of all tragedy, I'm taking everything lightly today. I'm pleased the two of them are so busily occupied with pointing and showing—look over here, look over there—discovering everything anew with borrowed eyes. They're working as accomplices—my sister knows where Rumen keeps his cigarettes, takes out the pack and lights one up for him. How quickly my sister adjusts. I've always found that amazing. In Beethovenstrasse guests have to go out on the patio if they want to smoke; the Persian can't abide ash on or smoke around his Memphis designer furnishings and cowhide loungers.

Our father veered between excess and asceticism, smoking, drinking, gorging and then giving up. He was a great covered-market shopper, loved meeting his Bulgarian buddies there. And he knew all the Greeks, Italian and Yugoslavians who had stalls there too, joked and joshed with them, felt up the fruit like a connoisseur, handed out medical advice, brought along medicine. On the few occasions I went shopping with him, my father revealed himself to be the most popular person in the world. He was greeted with two-handed handshakes, people embraced him, patted him on the back and paid reverence to the munchkin at his side as if to a visiting dignitary. When he came home from the market loaded with rustling paper bags he was in the best of moods. He proudly spread out his wares in the kitchen, praised by our grandmother, who was an excellent cook. They put their heads together to plan and banter, the leaping dachshund running tail-wagging rings around them and receiving half a sausage from our father.

We drive and drive, drive along the eyesore of a coast. At every turn are building sites, piles of refuse, the earth broken open, columns of trucks, and in the midst of it all, although not as often here as on the inland roads, are donkey carts. The Stalinesque blocks and their successor buildings in the gentler brutalization style have now been encircled by Disneyland architecture. Rounded, puerile forms reminiscent of pink marzipan cakes. Inflatable plastic monsters grinning an evil welcome down from the sky. The most popular colour after pink is ice-cream yellow.

I notice our father has cast an eye upon us. How, I don't know. But it's definitely open, the paternal eye. Half-asleep, half-awake, our father rests on the horizon. The eye watches the coast along with us, his beloved Black Sea coast, which he always spoke of in glowing tones.

As if my sister had guessed my thoughts, she turns around to me. Do you remember what Papa always said about fishermen?

Oh yes, I remember, and how! There was nothing and no one to top the strength, the courage, the skill of Bulgarian fishermen. The fishermen were his heroes. Before sunrise even, they went out to the treacherous sea lying smooth in the golden-red morning light. A smiling, beguilingly obedient sea. But then—darkness! Our father made the Black Sea surge mightily, boiling and spraying, men went overboard and were rescued by brave comrades, the skin rubbed off their hands as they reached for the ropes, which contorted like snakes, blinking bodies of fish seethed in the boats—but thank goodness, the enraged sea calmed down again at some point, the men returned home and were rewarded. By the women who waited yearningly for them, by the marvellous fruits and fishes they ate, and by the wild beauty of a coast that out-land-scaped all others. And when he switched out the light for us to sleep, he talked on about the legendary underwater world of the sea, about luminous fishes that moved through the night-black waters, tiny lanterns suspended in front of their heads, about shimmering plankton that slipped away between your hands in glittering veils when you swam in the sea by night. He talked about electrically charged fish that lay in wait in caves and could give terrible shocks, or about jellyfish that were only ugly when they lay gloopily on the sand, but in the sea, oh, in the sea, they were more beautiful than mermaids and they veiled through their habitat with inimitable elegance.

I don't know whether our father really was familiar with the Black Sea fauna. Probably not. He tended to exaggerate when he was on a roll. For instance, he was absolutely insistent that fishermen were the only true philosophers. Anyone who didn't spend hours staring at the sea and learning patience by patching up fishing nets was not a philosopher at all.

As I only realized later, naturally enough, this theory was an odd contrast to the fact that our father probably never read any philosophers other than Nietzsche and Schopenhauer. Perhaps a little Plato at his Bulgarian grammar school. Nevertheless, the philosophers, even more than the poets, enjoyed his greatest reverence. Even before I could spell the word, I knew that philosophers were the most splendid individuals that could ever exist. They were above all others, possibly even vastly superior to our father. When I heard years later that Hegel was allegedly a world-famous philosopher, and a Swabian to boot, I refused to believe it. Hegel didn't have the sea. So how could he have been a philosopher?

Degerloch is a particularly boring place, I sometimes thought by night. The occasional hill, the dull, canalized Neckar that you couldn't even see from our house, no luminous fish, no sea as a school for philosophers, no Red Indians, not a single man with a dangerous profession far and wide.

Papa, would you ever have thought your coast would one day be so ugly?

It looks different from a distance.

Aha, that must be a very long way off then. From high up, the Black Sea might be no more than a bruise. Incidentally, it's neither blue nor black, but grey. A completely undistinguished, if not dreary sea. There's no sign at the moment of either its beauty or its treachery.

I wish I knew how Degerloch seemed to our father back then. As dreary as the Black Sea seems to me now?

I don't know, says our father, too long ago. And I don't care either.

Perhaps the dead have even worse memory loss than we do. Perhaps they're so weak that they can't conjure up anything at all that they once hated or loved. The dead have less strength than a wrinkled old pile of skin. You have to be full of the joys of youth for hate or love.

Our father won't have hated Degerloch. But loved it? Degerloch after the war was hardly damaged, a rather sleepy suburb split into two halves—the richer part with stately houses towards the forest and a petty bourgeois part on the wrong side of Epplestrasse towards the sauerkraut fields. Then they built an autobahn across it, mutilating the old heart of the village. Within a few years, the petty bourgeois part of Degerloch looked the same as all the horribly samey suburbs of Stuttgart, their squalid architecture cut through by broad streets, the miniature plots of land each with their own miniature wood-trimmed house and garage, the concrete hut hiding the refuse bin, with pebbles pressed into it for decorative purposes.

Degerloch never recovered from the butcher's blow of the autobahn. It would cause me bodily pain to live there today. It didn't look as bad when our father was alive.

Or did it? Was it awful back then too?

No comment from our father. If his eye is still open, it's looking at the sea. Perhaps he's turned into one of those ubiquitous Swabian-haters by now. Even though it all started out so cosily between him and the Swabians.

The main legend of his glorious arrival in Swabia related that when he came to Tübingen to visit a fellow student in 1943, he handed in his winter coat at the station cloakroom. It had got warm and the coat was a heavy load. When he returned, the stationmaster asked him for a moment's patience. It turned out his wife had taken command of the coat, sewed on a loose button and repaired a damaged spot. Our father was said to have been terribly impressed and decided to continue his studies in Tübingen.

He soon found a similarly caring individual, the mother of his future wife.

Did our father marry our mother just because of our grandmother? I ask my sister.

Where do you get such ridiculous ideas?

After a short period of gazing at the surroundings with brisk head movements to and fro, she gives in. It may have played a supporting role in his marriage plans. She must have been an ideal mother-in-law for starving young men during and after the war, as ingenious and generous as she was.

I see my grandmother, as clearly as rarely before. Her grey hair in a bun. A black dress with cloth-covered buttons, white lace collar, held together in the middle by a brooch.

It was she who held everything together.

My sister and I are too tall to find space on her lap. Our grandmother wants to get us used to the fact that our father's gone. Your father's gone up to heaven. Things are good for him up there.

I've forgotten how she explained his ascension. Cataplexy—I was lamed by the shock. In a disturbed state everything contracts, nothing can make its way in. Anyone can come along, anything can be said. As accustomed to my grandmother as I was, I obeyed automatically, received her consoling words automatically, let the gentle palms of her hands do whatever they did, breathed in the pure smell I usually loved. But still, heaven convinced me. Not immediately, but over the subsequent days and months. My sister was too old for that kind of fairy tale. She stared at the ground in concentration.

There was one thing though that our grandmother hadn't reckoned with—knowing our father was in heaven rather than a decomposing pile of bones in his grave was consoling, but it had the disadvantage that I felt I was being watched. That was fine as long as our grandmother was alive. She was the guarantor of heaven, keeping the sinister at bay with hymns and prayer books. She knew whereabouts Moses sat in heaven, where the apostles were and where Jesus was. Our father was slightly further away, cramming up on Jesus. He was a newcomer to heaven, after all, and had to wait and learn. Our grandmother couldn't say how long this waiting status would last, but it wouldn't be too long considering his diligence and good background. After this waiting time, he'd be free and he'd come and protect us whenever we needed him.

Our grandmother died a few months after our father. From then on there was no heavenly intermediary far and wide. I read the *Odyssey*, where the heavens were a very different place, read books in which the heavens were mere colour or were criss-crossed by bomber planes. My sister had her first boyfriend, and turned away. I was left with the dachshund. Since then, only animals have had the power to distract me in times of dire sorrow.

It was not a calm, benevolent father slumbering in heaven above Degerloch and waking in times of need to rescue me. He had cast an evil, swollen eye upon me, opening and closing it according to his own rules. A punishing eye that pursued me. At fourteen, I tried LSD for the first time; and the bloodshot punishing eye lay spread over all of Stuttgart, chasing me down Killesberg hill in long leaps. Trembling, I sat on the number 6 tram up to Degerloch and saw my father's gaze boring through the metal roof. Not even a bombproof ideology, the cast concrete of Leninism with all its aggressive force, which barricaded my thinking for years on end, could compete. People rotted away in their graves. Once and for all. Revolutionary heroes lived on but only in people's memories. Religion was the opium of the people.

But all I needed was to smoke a bit of hash or take LSD and a Christian thunderstorm instantly erupted above my head. Jacob's ladders, fluttering fathers, heavenly choirs, pointing fingers of judgement, words like *blood sausage business* and over and over the smell of my grandmother, who was cleaning the chaotic heavens up there with a sponge. She closed my father's eye, ensuring order and moments of bright delight and delicious nonsense.

You're blind, my dear God, and I'm rid of you.

I felt the urgent need to use the words that came to me in these moments of tumult, in a novel. A manhole cover opened up and out came a Jesus figure with glowing poppy-red eyes, who travelled to South America. Not in the classic Jesus manner with a fishing boat and apostles and walking on water; more like a vampire. Wherever he set foot came revolution and carnage. In Ecuador, in San Salvador, in—I can't remember where else. He used the pseudonym *Müller Mayer M.*

Our mother came across the papers and was alarmed, or worse; she not only confronted me with them but secretly passed Müller Mayer M. on to one of her friends, who had once worked for the Birkhäuser publishing house. A well-read old gay who adorned himself with a garland of female admirers, whom he would wittily inform that they knew nothing. He sitting, me standing. He sat haughtily in an armchair, gestured me over and instructed me that writing was an art form. He quoted some of the particularly silly parts back at me with relish, from then on calling me Revolver Emma. It wasn't difficult to incite me to hatred for my mother at that time. And this man had found a sure-fire way to do so.

This unpleasant memory prompts much hilarity today. *Revolver Emma* hit the nail on the head—it was just the wrong point in time.

The finger performance!

I remember that the man had the same finger tic as my mother. His fingers were slim too, his nails carefully manicured although not actually varnished, and he wore an eye-catching signet ring. While he spoke to me from the depths of his chair, a magnificent performance of fingers and cigarettes was put on, a fleeting play of swathes in motion, exaggerated blowing away and effortful musing. What a shame humour comes late in life. I'd put up with such insolence today if only it were performed with so much opulence. Back then I was an unpleasant teenager full of lust for revenge and rage.

Not one disruption on the drive, although the surroundings certainly don't get any more attractive. Quite the opposite—the land seems to contract, crowded with buildings. There are miniature casinos everywhere, more like concrete sheds canvassing trade with neon playing cards and tipped top hats. The only thing that's smoother is Rumen's driving. No truck can upset him, he lets other drivers pull into our lane with a shrug, brakes with measured care and accelerates gently.

Nessebar. The famous fishing village where I'm said to have been with Lilo and her daughter. I don't recognize anything, not even the windmill at the entrance to the peninsula, which doesn't mean much because my memory for places is not particularly well developed. I remember a wooden ship with a skull and crossbones, an old, tall ship on which a young donkey had to hold his woolly head upright for stroking hands in order to attract tourists.

We park outside a small building with a front garden near the beach. Rumen has probably realized that all their loving tiffs have not gone unnoticed, and perhaps he's surprised by my goodwill. Waves of love, obligations of love, breakdown of love—it all comes and goes; all you have to do is wait. He opens the door with a flourish and stretches out a gallant hand to help me disembark. Frowning dramatically and attempting a Swabian singsong, he says cheerfully, now we shall all observe the misery of the Bulgarian hotel trade.

The hotel is owned by a Greek family. The landlady gives off an aura of relaxed efficiency. Portly but not fat. Strong but not rough. The rooms are large, done up in the spartan Greek style, but it's by far the best hotel we've found on the three-man leg of our tour. There's a terrace with a view of the sea, the little garden below winding downward in steps and obviously tended to with a great deal of love. Weak plants are tied to sticks, the stronger ones have pebble ornaments piled up around them. We praise the facilities in various languages, thus winning over the landlady. She serves us a welcome coffee.

As we book the rooms, I think, why all this nonsense, they should just take a double room, but I don't say so. One mustn't intervene in matters of other people's hearts.

We go for a walk, not on the seaside but along winding paths to the fishing village, on a catwalk connecting the island to the mainland. Above the old city walls, on the rocky side, are intricate wooden houses with terraces. They could be landing and nesting places for large sea birds, albatrosses for instance, although there probably aren't any albatrosses on the Black Sea.

One of the oldest settlements in Europe, founded by the Thracians, a Greek colony with a temple to Apollo and stone fortifications, churches, churches and more churches, constant ups and downs between a flourishing trading port and a fishing village—Rumen tells us fiery stories; he has slipped back into his old tour-guide skin. He even draws a crowd of German tourists who form a circle around us.

Suddenly, he puts a finger on his nose, gives the new arrivals a strict look and says sharply, they want to take it off the UNESCO cultural heritage list because of dumb construction projects but it's already chock-full of dumb constructions! And with that he scatters his little group of onlookers.

He winks at me—the misery of Bulgaria, in the flesh.

Let's head upwards, says my sister, to get an overview.

She leaps ahead, taking two steps at a time, her suppleness signalling high spirits. She was always the more agile one, even when we were little. She ran fast, liked swimming and gymnastics; while I was a loser at sports, preferring to sit around, and could only be brought out of my reserve with ping pong. At that, however, I was better than my sister—perhaps because I liked hitting things.

English tourists block our way on the stone steps. It's hard to get an undisturbed view. The houses at the top are typical Black Sea buildings with stone ground floors and dark wooden top halves, with plenty of flourishes and figurines, all kinds of alcoves, balconies and cornices of impressive sizes. Everywhere are restaurants and cafes with terraces and balconies, red tablecloths, decorative jugs, wineskins nailed to the outside walls; barrels, old wagon wheels and bright red geraniums flank the entrances.

We find some space on one of the wooden balconies and look out to sea. It's actually a wonderful place for a sit-down, with a calming view. But the music is so loud there can be no way of enjoying food and drink. Rumen tries to negotiate with a waiter over turning the volume down but the waiter doesn't understand him. I'm not up for loud music even in the most composed of moods. My sister is the first to take flight. We try the next place and the one after that. It's the same every time. One cafe seems slightly quieter. We inspect the balcony and there's a long discussion over which of the two free tables is furthest away from the speakers.

We place our orders. The minute the waitress leaves us the volume is turned up. And now Rumen and I experience an astounding performance—my sister's features twist. Her head descends between her shoulders in wrath. Suddenly, she hammers both fists against the wood (how slim her wrists are, not made for punching at all), the ashtray—peacock-eye design!—flies up in the air and smashes on the floor. She bellows. Really, my sister goes right ahead and bellows. And that's not all. The bellowing is just the beginning—she grabs a chair and fires it in the direction of the speaker but misses. The chair, a chunky imitation peasant affair, is obviously stable. It doesn't break. My sister stands there, her head lowered, taunted by a hysterical pop singer squealing down at her.

Rumen and I sit motionlessly beside each other. My first ever role-reversal. Usually, I'm the one in charge of creating chaos, not her. My sister stares at the ground, her fists clenched again. She turns around, marches past a few tables in a stiff-legged gait—everyone on the crowded benches has long since turned around to gape at what happens next. And really, something does happen next. She positions herself in front of the swinging door to the restaurant and bellows. Her exact words? I'm not sure. All I know is that the words *assholes* and *shitty* are said, several times over, which I find hardly less astounding than the stunt with the chair. Like her haircut, like her handbag, like her delicate wristwatch—a characteristic of my sister is that she strictly refuses to utter profanities.

Pandemonium. Waitresses, the landlord, they all come running, guests standing up or rubbernecking. My sister turns around and walks, strangely stiff, her fists still clenched, slowly down the steps to the lower terrace, still complaining under her breath which, from a distance, sounds like *harrrrr, harrrrr*, interrupted by sibilants.

She's left her jacket and handbag behind. I have to take care of them while Rumen negotiates with the landlord, but that seems to have escalated too, agitated shouts from all sides. I tweak at Rumen's jacket to hold him back but that's not enough, I have to drag him away backwards, which he doesn't want to put up with (like the dachshund, I think, growling and snapping when you hold him down in the heat of the moment), but then we're on the stairs and Rumen has to turn around just to keep his balance, and is thus rescued from the threat of fisticuffs.

Not victorious nor defeated, we vacate the scene. My sister is already a good way ahead, down the hill towards the sea. We find her leaning at ease against a wall. She's looking up at the sky. A dense grey film is suspended above land and sea.

So, says my sister, are you two feeling better now?

She turns her head and looks at us with a strange expression. That's how people look when they've just woken up from a faint, I think, despite never having seen anyone wake up from a faint. There's something fresh and at the same time remote about that look, backlit from mysterious sources. It's not possible to ask a face like that what on earth was the matter.

Shall we tackle the inner village? My sister peels herself off the wall. Her rage is completely extinguished. I hand her the jacket and bag. Goodness me, she says, that had to be done, and she takes a confiding hold of my arm.

Everyone's allowed to explode once a year. Rumen rather likes his own words, in the tone of an academic statement—I explode twice a year.

Who explodes when and how and how often is a great subject, and we draw it out in all directions as we meander around Nessebar. Our conversation soon breaks off though. Too many tourists pushing through the narrow streets. It's noisy. The houses are doubtlessly beautiful, or rather they used to be. If you were only to look at the wooden parts at the top, you might well fall in love with the sight of them. Yet, at the level our heads are on, they're a nightmare.

Every ground floor, every basement has been rejigged into a souvenir shop. They used to be cool rooms for storing goods, perhaps a few vats by the entrance or water troughs with googly-eyed fish swimming in them. Now, the ground floors are spilling over, spilling out of the entrances, with unspeakable trash, the stuff piled higher than a man's head; and above it all, every shop-keeper plays music at an absolutely insane volume. An aural hell. A burst gall bladder exuding noise. It has nothing in common with the clamorous conditions in Italy, Brazil or Egypt. Life doesn't simply throb with sound here; it's caught up in a maelstrom. Contorted, smashed, booming, jangling out of shape; screamloads of international hysteria have tipped over into the street and there's no getting away from it. A sluggish, samey stream of mushy people, people with behinds a metre wide, prevents all escape.

For all the churches, the art treasures, the artifice and beauty—

It's difficult to see when your ears are worn down. The church of St Stephen, the church of the holy archangels, that one over there seems to be the church of Christ Pantocrator, it's famous, probably for good reason, and certainly exciting with its slim, almost invisibly slim strips of alternating bricks and stones. I'd have liked to have looked at the ceramic bowls set into it, *ceramic bowls* sounds good, they were mentioned in a guidebook but, by now, I'm so disturbed that I have neither the will nor the way to look at anything.

Unfortunately, we're hungry. We end up in a dark room rather a long way out of town. Poor lighting does have its advantages; it means you can't study the grub all too closely. Reddish mash with a good glug of engine oil. We turn our backs on Nessebar and wander back to the hotel along the seaside.

It's not warm enough to swim yet. Only the head of the occasional swimming pioneer here and there in the distance and their abandoned towels on the sand. I feel the time has come to bow out tactfully and leave the two of them alone. An excuse about walking back to look at Nessebar from below is quickly invented, and my turtle doves withdraw.

I take a few hundred dawdling steps back for form's sake until the other two are only inches high, then I find a rusty old chair half-buried in the sand, sit myself down and stretch out my legs.

The grey veil on the horizon is dissolving into strands. The late afternoon sun is coming slowly through, pleasantly warm. I'm perfectly comfortable on my semi-submerged seat, watching tourists trudge across the sand, luckily on the very edge of the sea and, hence, not casting shadows across my knees. Above me, seagulls lurch and saw at the horizon with their screeches. The water is calm, running against the beach in thin folds that barely break.

How different it was only a few days ago! The Adriatic worked itself up into a rage as we crossed it on the ferry. It began harmlessly. A well-behaved, obedient evening sea greeted us. The limousines made a huge impression on the other passengers as they drove over the extended metal planks into the belly of the ship. We had disembarked beforehand. Two elderly couples were standing together, voicing their conjectures that a president must be travelling with them. Out of vanity, I raised a finger and claimed to be travelling in the car with the decorated roof. Suspicious amazement and looks that spoke of disappointment, which made me shrink down to the botched-up thing I once was, the shadow of the shadow of our begetter.

We gathered on deck once we'd inspected our cabins. White-and-yellow-striped curtains with a border of anchors and leaping fish. White-and-yellow-striped bedspreads. Everything laid out genteelly for a quiet night. Chocolates wrapped in metallic paper, with a hint of navy medals about them, as a bedtime treat. From the belly of the ship came the confidence-inspiring sound of the engines. The ferry glided slowly away from the shore, her speed not initially recognizable, partly due to the fact that the engines were relatively quiet.

We enjoyed a bountiful evening meal, and even as we ate we felt things stirring below us. Iris leapt up with a cheerful Oh deary me, I think I feel sick and was not seen again for the duration. The first jokes were cracked about seasickness, then more and more people retired to their cabins. My sister also took her leave early on. Only our unshakeable chief sat at the table with a hardy rump of diners, his arm spread along the back of the rose-grower's chair. No matter how large and stable the ferry seemed, it went up and down most heartily, with a particularly unpleasant tremble as it oscillated back into position sideways. Although I usually feel nauseous everywhere, I do have good sea legs. And as there was a decent storm blowing outside, I didn't want to miss a chance to view the tumbling waves.

We were warned not to go outside but it wasn't directly forbidden. And it was hardly possible to fall overboard. Closely fitted railings would have caught anyone who lost their balance. But you could easily slip or hurt yourself staggering to and fro. Really, it wasn't a good idea to walk about on deck without a firm grip, especially not wearing leather soles.

At the prow, not at the outermost point but slightly towards the rear, in the protection of the structure at the top, was a screwed-down bench, damp and sprayed with water, nevertheless a safer place from which to stare out at the impassioned night. From above, the tumbled-up waves looked different, foaming and boiling and splashing black with pale tips, not quite all the way to the bench but as far as the ship's rail.

The moon was concealed and revealed at close intervals, the clouds darkening it entirely over and over again. The few stars visible for brief moments trembled like needles. I revelled in the way the ship fell, its saturated splash as it landed, the gurgling and the subsequent snow of foam.

It wasn't long before I had a guest by my side—Wolfi, who had been ejected from the dining room with his cigar and wanted to smoke it out here. At the first moment, any one staking a claim to my bench was unwelcome. But the sea's churning had such strength and force that a new relationship came to play between us.

Mind if I join you? asked Wolfi, sitting down as he said it.

You've got good sea legs; we've got that in common.

He said that after a long drag on his cigar, its smoke instantly blown away behind us.

I was too surprised by this opening gambit to find a suitable reply. Wolfi bailed us out by announcing he'd get us something to drink. He jammed the cigar between his teeth and careened off. Some time later he returned without his cigar, pressing a glass of beer and a glass of cola carefully against his chest so that he could hold onto the railing with his other hand. Wolfi had remembered I didn't drink alcohol. There was a quarter of a slice of lemon floating in the cola. I thanked him, rather touched.

There's plenty to see here, we've got the best viewing point.

So we have, said Wolfi. I've been wishing for a night like this.

And apart from that? How are you liking the trip?

My brother's an idiot, said Wolfi, practically unbearable. We only see each other every few years when there's no avoiding it.

He's a prize idiot, I said maliciously, but whatever happened to brotherly love? Twin brotherly love? He's fat, you're thin, how come?

Wolfi laughed, this time less staccato than usual. He launched into longer sentences, the longest I'd heard from him so far.

I was fat, too, as a teenager. But my brother abandoned all moderation after that. He's been annoying me with his little mouse nonsense since the age of fifteen. My brother and his little mice! And then his awful kids. Children, family, the whole kit and caboodle straight out of a soap opera. He refused to understand it left me cold, I—he made a conciliatory gesture in my direction—I wasn't interested then and I'm not now. Nothing doing. The idiot refuses to believe it. Your sister's an idiot too, by the way, a pretty version of an idiot, who just doesn't get it.

That's not true, I said, you're way off the mark there.

I used to envy you two as a child, I thought you had it better. Your mother had something about her.

I noticed my defence of my sister had been pretty tame. She's, well, she has something hyper-hyper-hyper-responsible about her and she's sometimes rather saccharine when she's embarrassed, but don't get her wrong, my sister's brain works very well, thanks.

Wolfi raised his golden glass to toast the moon, its disc revealed for a moment and shining full above us. We talked and talked, giving our siblings a verbal drubbing, and the entire Bulgarian and Swabian club along with them. Whereby Wolfi tended to view the Bulgarians a tad more mildly, and I was easier on the Swabians. We were having a ball and grew obnoxious, as vicious as can be. Wolfi was the more unabashed of us. He set up the chamber of his family's horrors down to the eczema-riddled folds in their fat and their corroding hair. And—something I'd never have expected—he had a gift for imitation. Herta,

Lilo, our mother—he could imitate them all perfectly, with a particularly good ear for Lilo, her plunging and rising, drawn-out *Lilo Taba-ko-off* when she answered the telephone with its palindrome of *O*s and *A*s.

Why did you give up teaching?

That's none of your business, he answered brusquely. After a while he added in a milder tone, I fell in love with a seventeen-year-old, and he fell in love with me. Happy now?

I am. And anyway, if the ages are true I don't think there's anything wrong with it. Maybe I don't even think there's anything wrong with it if the ages aren't true.

How nice for you. Let's leave it at that.

There he was again, the aggressive little blighter who was hard to get along with. The moon was still blazing, clouds ragging and veiling blackly past it. We fell silent for a while.

Did you know our fathers were in jail together?

What? Where?

In Sofia, of course, where else? You didn't know?

No, not at all.

You didn't know he went to Bulgaria to see his family in '46, and disappeared for a while?

I vaguely remember the story.

They put him away. And my father, too, as it happens, but for different reasons. Black market, who knows?

Wolfi told the story obligingly. Although he didn't know much, even the little information he had made my heart skip a beat. According to Wolfi, our father hadn't stayed with his parents in Sofia but with his aunts, who shared a larger apartment in the city centre (that must have been Mila and Zveta). The aunts were hiding a young German soldier in a cupboard after finding him injured in the hallway when the Russians arrived. The hiding place was discovered and all the apartment's inhabitants were arrested. The aunts vanished into a camp and our father, having spent the past few years in Germany, was suspected of espionage and put in prison.

Apparently, Wolfi's father made friends with our father in jail and pulled a few strings for him; Zankoff obviously had better connections. The two of them were released a year later, once they'd signed a paper obliging them to work for the secret service. They returned to Stuttgart together, or rather our father was the returner; Zankoff had never been to Germany before. Escape or legal exit? How they got across the borders and what papers they had, Wolfi didn't know, and nor did he know whether the secret service had followed up on it, whether and how the Bulgarian families had been punished for the runaways.

I asked Tabakoff about it, Wolfi said. He must know something but he's keeping his cards close to his chest.

My mind conjured up the ugly word denunciator.

Your father was a nice guy, said Wolfi, but a bit of a softie.

We sat on the bench for a long time until we started juddering with the cold. For the rest of the journey, we treated each other in a friendly but superficial manner. We never conspired again like that night. It was advisable to be careful with Wolfi; he wasn't one for friendships. I didn't tell my sister anything about it, perhaps because I was ashamed of having been so obnoxious about her.

It's getting chilly here as evening approaches. I'm starting to feel as if the rust on the chair had migrated into my bones. There are only a few people left walking along the beach. Plastic bottles are strewn around, rubber items, children's spades, sandals, beached jellyfish, a dead seagull with a sand-encrusted head. The sea is calm, not bringing anything onto land at this hour and taking nothing away. Not one alluring shell to pick up. The perfectly clean, raked and just watered little garden of the hotel is a lovely sight. I meet the landlord and the landlady out on the terrace and they ply me with cheese and bread. We have a bit of a chat in English and then I take my leave.

I fancy a book night tonight. The balcony door open, I lie in bed and read the Stalin book. Read Martin Amis venting his spleen about the British communists, his father among them, believing in Stalin for so long, read myself into the high-level psychosis that must have dominated the February/March sitting of the Central Committee in 1937, where every single speaker threw about the familiar vocabulary of the Trotskyist conspiracy digging away with its grubby paws at the ground beneath their feet. Shouting down, swinging of fists, interrupting, hectic applauding. All with feverish eyes; only Stalin's close-drawn eyes remain clear. The most adventurous specifications of the enemy vermin emerged, words that might come across as funny if one didn't know the consequences they had for those to whom they were applied. The Russian word *dvurushnik* means double-dealers but is actually a rather pretty idea, double-tongued creatures conjuring up images of adders undulating and lisping their way through the world. Yet, under this description alone, hundreds if not thousands of party cadre are thought to have been tortured and killed. For the millions of others who perished, there were other words. In the skilled way in which Amis compiles it all, the words summon up hot and cold shivers. The comrades must have succumbed to a severe case of collective paranoia with a subsequent killing frenzy, not hot but cold-blooded. A pseudo-rational frenzy, in which every man betrayed his friends and neighbours and every betrayal had murderous consequences. The psychosis of the country's entire leadership is beyond comprehension, seeming more and more strange the deeper one immerses oneself in the subject and the more details one unearths.

Deep sea. For a moment I think of the pale creatures that robot cameras recently discovered in the gaps and fissures of the Mariana Trench in the Pacific. They seem more plausible than the Soviet comrades of 1937, and certainly more likeable.

Relishing my dread, I read on and on, perhaps because the book reinforces my aversion to the Slavic languages, by the by. *Fiskulturniki*—are there any words sillier than those invented in the Soviet Union under

Lenin and Stalin? On the other hand, I myself believed in Lenin, Trotsky and Mao for at least four years of my life. I can no longer make contact with that part of the past—that member of the Spartacus Bolshevik-Leninists was a complete stranger. It can't be because I was young—thirteen when it began. That same year, I was enchanted by James Ensor's pictures—bright, flaming, jubilant enchantment—which has lasted and lasted and leads to an overflow of happiness whenever I come across his scurrying Christs or astounded masks in a museum. And Bob Dylan's voice has resided in my ear since then too; the boy can sing what he likes, there's no getting rid of him. These two passions, and perhaps two or three more, have melded into my mental DNA.

But a glance at Lenin's head ought to have sufficed to be certain—for God's sake, leave well enough alone. How can I possibly have fallen for Brechtian theatre with its odious types? What was the point of those flowery, absolutely idiotic Mao texts? And why on earth Trotsky? Because of the ice pick? As Stalin's antagonist? Or because I, like most impassioned leftists at the time, was searching for a Jewish adoptive father and didn't understand Adorno?

ONWARD!

Breakfast on the patio with better coffee than usual.

For once, no plastic tables but a whitely weathered wooden table with softened edges, its grain inviting me to follow it with a finger. My fellow travellers appear neatly combed and as if scrubbed with brushes. I note a trace of irritation in their expressions. Perhaps they've had a bit of a tiff. Perhaps I'm mistaken and they're already living together as routinely as if they were married. The thin canvas jacket my sister is wearing this morning looks slightly childish.

Cold today.

Rumen's looking forward to winter, says my sister, because then it'll get bitterly cold and he can prove his worth as a winter hero.

Rumen doesn't quite know what to reply. He seems rather frozen already, at least more of a summer hero. He lowers his eyelids and strokes a cat that rubs its head against his calves.

We take our leave from our hosts with sincerely felt gratitude.

My sister gnaws at an apple. I doze on the backseat, having read for too long yesterday, my memory of the book floating in vagueness. A quote appears out of context—*contradictory traditions of permissiveness and sans-culottes Puritanism*—we pass flower salesmen who try to pass their wares in through the window. It's a dank day now. Neither hot nor cool. From a hiding place, the sun illuminates the grey spread far and wide.

The horrific pressure of the past.

Perhaps the Soviets failed so miserably because they spurned help from the realm of the extra-mundane civil servants, demolished churches, melted down bells, killed priests. Behind every natural civil servant there must be an angelic helper, otherwise the state degenerates, I think, but I don't have any arguments at hand to defend this hypothesis if push comes to shove. I believe that no fish gets cooked and no schnitzel gets fried without the secret support of an angel. And, at the same time, perhaps with the quiet tremble of their wings, they teach us to respect the secret melancholy of all living creatures; there's no use in killing anyone, the angels teach us, as no one is happy.

This dismal, angel-free monotony drags itself out along the coast. No point in looking out of the window. I nod off and see white-dusted bodies before me, squirming on the floor, but lo and behold, they unfurl wings from beneath their bellies. I receive the information that they're Bulgarian wings; they are smoothed out and general shy attempts are made at flying. Then I see square slices of bread popping out of a toaster, while in the next room someone in a doctor's coat cleans a lavabo.

Burgas. I must have been asleep for ever. There are red marks on my head. A crunching in my neck. Pathetic casinos wherever I look. We park outside a low building with a flashing roulette wheel and stumble listlessly out of the car. Tourists are wandering around, merged into search parties. Perhaps they don't know what they're searching for. We don't know either, and we decide to keep driving, onwards to Plovdiv.

A black jeep with tinted windows has parked next to our Daihatsu. The bonnet is open, someone's head hidden beneath it. A boy stands next to him, tugging at the cord of his anorak. A series of deer trot across his chest. Rumen addresses him but doesn't get an answer.

All this driving is getting too much for me today, but every mile that brings me closer to Sofia and thus to Berlin is a welcome relief. Only two days before I'm home. What's the point of the sea, if the sea's uglier than Berlin? Not for the first time, but this time more seriously than usual, I decide never to travel again. What's the point of travelling, if all the world descends sullenly into sleep and rises ill-humoured in the morning? What to do in an adverse situation to make time pass faster? Doze off and wake up again after a while. We treat ourselves to a snack at a place near the motorway. If I had the courage to simply wander off across the fields, my possessions tied in a handkerchief over my shoulder, hunter's hat on my head, up hill and down vale with a staff, marching for Berlin, I wouldn't need to worry any more about what was and what will be; a fundamental meaning would have settled within me, which I could draw upon for the rest of my life.

Do something right away that no one ever does.

Despite sore feet, I'd be saved by liberal floating above the forests and fields. I might even learn to sing. But it's not advisable to start a discussion about it. My fellow travellers seem to be undecided on how to behave, far from wanting to sing; they seem rather odd, as if they've been rendered silent. Perhaps we're a three-person tableau, with them embodying female boredom through opening and closing of make-up mirror, and male boredom through pressing of cigarette and disappearance behind map. I've been chosen to listen in to the creating and extinguishing of emotions, so I fold myself huge ears out of paper napkins.

A pack of dogs helps us get over our embarrassment. Young, old, all ugly, all swinish. One with more fur stands to the side, instantly bitten away by the others if he approaches the guests. I throw something in his direction but he doesn't have the guts to keep it. The others tear the chunk away from him and he shrinks further back with his tail between his legs.

A Trotskyite deviant, I say to Rumen, but he has no ear for my jokes and doesn't seem to want to come out of his map ever again.

Before we get back in the car, I ask my sister to let me sit at the front, just this once, until Plovdiv.

Of course, you're very welcome! She eagerly digs out her two or three possessions from the glove compartment and makes herself comfortable at the back.

Rumen's mood lifts and he fastens my seatbelt, like one does with children or helpless old fogies. The co-pilot's seat, he assures me, is a serious responsibility.

Trotskyite deviants will not be tolerated. There's to be no grabbing of the steering wheel. Nor am I allowed to wave the map around in front of his face. And he's quite capable of finding the way on his own.

The basic idea of driving is onwards and onwards and ever onwards, Rumen lectures, rather like five-year plans. Even in Bulgaria. With the difference that the driver here has to struggle with five different speeds and the complete absence of traffic rules.

There's no need to struggle right now; there's little traffic on the freshly tarmacked road. There are as good as no road signs. Instead, though, large signs showing impressive coats of arms have been planted along the side of the road. One might think Bulgaria was an offshoot of the Saxe-Coburgs. The ads are for a company founded by Simeon II Sakskoburggotski, the re-found tsar the desperate Bulgarians fetched back to the country as prime minister and quickly voted out again. Rumen hates Simeon. He considers him a bankrupt, lazy gambler and cheat, who only let himself in for the Bulgarian adventure for the purpose of reclaiming his estates. It's probably better not to ask him what the advertisements are all about.

Have you noticed, chirps my sister from the back, how dauntlessly our good man holds the steering wheel with both hands? He's a determined Bulgarian driver.

He's a determined fighter too. He very nearly had fisticuffs with the landlord yesterday, because of you.

Rumen giggles, only too pleased that we're paying him so much attention. Waves of jollity, balm to the soul, smooth, pliant tarmac.

There are good reasons why you two aren't allowed behind the wheel in Bulgaria. You're welcome to chauffeur me around in Germany.

A pause, during which a rusty van loaded with cement mixers is overtaken. The pause lasts more or less all the way till Plovdiv.

The modern city in the valley is ugly. The usual decayed pomp. I almost want to suggest we simply keep on driving; the motorway's much nicer. But then there's a steep hill, and lo and behold, a completely different city comes into view. We get stuck in a narrow road, no going forward or backward, and Rumen allows us to get out while he drives haltingly, at walking pace, behind a small three-wheeled vehicle weighed down with paint pots.

Now, what do you say? My sister is standing in a courtyard entrance, her arms folded, and marvelling.

Great balls of fire!

Courtyard gates of impressive stateliness, strongly hewn, solid stone bases, and bulging on top of them the wooden upper storeys. One magnificent beauty next to another.

Up on the hill is a parking space.

Really a joy to behold at every turn. The buildings look surprisingly different than the ones we know from well-preserved Western-European cities. The clever wooden upper floors with their bay windows, medallions and decorative ribbons, houses arranged into quads, the range of colours—wood-dark decorated in rusty-red at the top, sand-pale at the bottom, between them a strong blue—all a sight for sore eyes. And just so that we can enjoy Plovdiv to the utmost, the evening sky glows reddish bright, only a few tiny clouds around the edges like puffs of smoke. Opposite us, an arrow points to a cafe with a roofed garden at the back. Rumen knows the place. There's a view of the whole valley from the garden, he tells us.

The basic economic principle here is improvisation, a patchwork that seems rather familiar from our student days. A random collection of chairs, wobbly tables, crates, candles, bearded men holding long discussions, women in long skirts with Indian knick-knacks and many, many bangles. The hookah pipes are a new addition. The people who meet here have probably rescued quite a lot of the old Plovdiv.

A falcon takes flight from a nearby tower. A swarm of tiny birds dot nervous patterns upon the sky.

A slight turmoil is trembling within Rumen. While my sister heads to the bathroom, he turns quietly to me and says, I'm not an idiot. I know the differences between our lives, and the consequences.

Oh, dear me, this calls for a pacification specialist. I assure him that no one considers him an idiot. My sister doesn't and I certainly don't. Why should we? But there's no point in detailed comparisons between the borough of Mladost and good old Beethovenstrasse. Some things deal with themselves, under a mantle of discreet silence.

On our search for a hotel, we stumble into a rather pompous place, its entrance lit up by huge candles in huge glass jars. Inside, the kitsch is of such flaming insanity that it's hard to keep our laughter under control. We've obviously ended up in Plovdiv's First Mafia Place. There couldn't be a better film set for, let's say, the boss marries off his daughter, a severed head is thrown at the wedding cake, a huge shooting match ensues with an orgy of red on the walls and a red-spattered wedding dress. I bet it would be incredible fun to tart up a hotel like this. They probably handed over a huge pile of money to a bunch of children and told them to garnish the place. Gold, gold, gold, flourishes upon flourishes, trim upon trim, carpet upon carpet, murals in hissing colours, Herculean bouquets of monster gladioli—except if you touch anything with a fingertip it wobbles. (I take a look around one of the bathrooms, tap at the taps and nozzles, everything's a-wobbling and a-crumbling.) I bet, at night, golden cockroaches come squishing out from beneath the wainscots, and rats with gilded tails chase across the kitchen.

We get lucky at the next hotel. The rooms are delightful. Large, with beautiful wooden floors, delicate nineteenth-century furniture against wallpapered walls—desk, table, chairs reminiscent of German Biedermeier, crossed with Napoleonic influences. I open the window and look out over an idyllic courtyard just as my sister walks in, allegedly to take a look at my room. She shows me a piece of coral branching out like a tree, which Rumen has given her.

I shower it with the requisite praise. Since we arrived in Plovdiv, my sister's facial expressions have assumed dimensions of minor tragedy. I expect she'll keep it up for at least ten days even back home in Beethovenstrasse.

She's just about to make a confession. There's a quaking, a knocking; something wants out that can only be prevented by determined changing of the subject. I'm very old-fashioned about that kind of thing. You can be as unfaithful as you like, but do please hold your tongue. I praise the room, praise the corridor, praise the bathroom, lean out of the window once again and suggest we absolutely have to try out the restaurant down in the courtyard this evening.

And now, my dear sister, I need to go to the bathroom in peace.

The courtyard lives up to its promises. No music, comfortable seats, decent lighting, immaculate food, good wine. We've probably come across the only perfectly acceptable hotel in the entire country. We chit and chat, revitalizing the old, entrenched Dostoevsky versus Tolstoy war, with Rumen bravely defending the Dostoevsky fortress all alone while we sisters combine our firepower beneath the flag of Tolstoy. We chat about the Molotov–Ribbentrop Pact, about Auntie Luise, about jumping beans and the *Vampyrotheutis infernalis*, the most blood-curdling of all blood-curdling deep-sea squids.

In other words, we have a fine time of it.

On a midnight stroll, a bar beckons my two turtle doves and I leave them to it. This is the last evening they have; I'm only in their way.

Bookless to bed. Sleep creeps up unnoticed, and before there can be too much thinking and tossing and turning I'm off.

This morning, we just have time to visit one of those famous Plovdiv houses. How annoying that we didn't make it here earlier. They are small palaces of ingenious design. Even the courtyards with their magnificent displays of stone invite us to stay a while, tubs of flowers blossoming with a desperation as if all our days were numbered. The transfer from outside to inside, from the protected space of the courtyard to the private sphere of the house, takes place as if in a sleepwalk. What subtlety. What harmony between nourished nature and architecture. Did the builders sing as they put up the beams? Did the wood-carvers envisage paradise as they guided their chisels and knives? Beauty escapes all description, living only in context.

All the Bulgarian angels must have helped in the building. Some of them stayed behind and still breathe warmth into visitors' hearts.

The house's interior structure corresponds to a complex family cosmos with significant representative tasks. Cupboards that plausibly suggest there is such a thing as domestic bliss and good order. Delightful salons, painted with frescoes telling of a longing for Versailles and French customs. The *hortus conclusus* is pure French. The merchants, rich yet banned to the provinces, wished for a synthesis of Paris, Vienna and the Golden Horn, and lo and behold, a Bulgarian beauty was born, determined to live on its own strength and with its own grace. It must have been a happy moment in Bulgarian history. What an upright and honest country this could have been. I wish I knew more about the melting pot of many cultures that once settled in Plovdiv.

It's no use though; we have to leave.

En piste! On the old Dacian road to Sofia. The familiar seating plan is restored, so in that sense everything is back to usual, except that our souls are soft and sensitive, even mine, and a gentle suffering lies in the eyes of my fellow travellers.

We first arrived in Sofia only a few days ago, approaching from Greece that time around, my sister in a robust state of mind and I tired. Our first stop on Bulgarian soil was Melnik. Up to Melnik, I slept wrapped up in the Escher curtain of my limousine, not having found a moment's peace on the ferry overnight.

It was in Melnik that Tabakoff's mood first darkened on home ground. Melnik refused to be what Tabakoff had expected of the place. Admittedly, the town had a picturesque location in the midst of excitingly jagged cliffs, and one or other of the houses built between the steep stones made an impression due to the splendid balconies and the way they stood adhered to the rock, but the wines and the food that came to our table in Melnik angered

Tabakoff. We held back politely. We weren't paying the bill, after all. In the wake of all the luxury we'd enjoyed so far, we were perfectly jolly about the Bulgarian landlords giving us a bit of a beating. Tabakoff, however, was upset. He had prepared everything so well, and been prepared to dig so deep into his own pockets. We had to placate a rumbling, grumbling chief, watched his wrinkled throat fighting back untoward swallows, sending one bottle after another back to the kitchen.

We lowered our eyes in modesty and smiled our cryptic Bulgarian children's smiles.

We didn't stay long in Melnik, soon heading off for Sofia. I fell asleep again. I woke up because the volume of the conversation around me rose suddenly. By now, the rose-grower and his wife and Kolyo Vuteff's son were in my limousine.

Pernik had shaken them up.

We were driving past giant industrial ruins. Mile after mile stretched a catastrophic landscape of semi-collapsed buildings, smashed windows, dug earth, rubbish tips, rusted cranes, pointlessly raised digger shovels, abandoned mechanical components. That's no exaggeration; it really was miles long. An out-of-order industrial intestine, the like of which none of us had seen before, where lonely and god-forsaken individuals appeared every now and then like in a bad dream, a security guard with a dog for instance, or a man digging through the rubbish.

The rose-grower's laugh sounded like snapping toothpicks. He was inconsolable; he'd known the area as a child.

No comparison to the industrial landscape of the Ruhr Valley, its mines, its monumental structures from the turn of the previous century that possess a Titan beauty. Pernik is evil and empty, lost in a dream that knows no mercy, an industrial combine plague of junk dotted with light-metal structures of a more recent date, all battered and tattered. Impossible to philosophize about the passing of time with sighs and frowns, about the work of human hands descending to the bosom of nature—no pioneering plants have yet broken up the terrain, no tender birch trunks yet flag the roofs.

Oppressed and mute, we drove into Sofia.

Our star limousines, with the decorative lids on top, soon veered off to deposit the dead for further treatment in a suburb, while we drove to the centre and were delivered to the door of the hotel.

The Grand Hotel Sofia, a shiny new box with a glass top half, Bulgaria's premier five-star hotel, welcomes us as if we were the first truly serious guests, for whom it had been waiting since its opening. Dark wooden panelling. Delicate palm trees in tubs. Words of welcome in various languages. Tabakoff had, of course, arranged everything in advance but unlike in Melnik they obeyed his every word here. We didn't even have to give our names at the reception; a secret hotel agent had already seen to that. We weren't allowed to touch our suitcases. Young men in smart uniforms accompanied us to our rooms and I was given a large one, a huge one in fact. I stood rather embarrassed on the green carpet while the

page looked at me in expectation. Unfortunately, I had to
let him go unrewarded, having no money on me apart
from fifty-euro notes.

A green sea of carpet dotted with golden plankton.
The pile was still upright from being vacuumed. Someone with a symmetrical conscience must have been at
work, for the vacuum stripes were astoundingly parallel.
There were ladylike bedside lamps, something I rather
liked, for a change. The back wall of the bed was magnificent, above all thickly padded, as every splendid bed ought
to be; the buttons made the upholstery splurge out in
lozenge-shaped bulges. A beige counterpane was spread
over the bed, turned back coquettishly at one corner, as if
drenched in iridescent liquid silver. A fifties Hollywood
beauty could have lounged there, flicking through a magazine, lying on her stomach, dressed in a dusky pink suit, her
calves upright and pumps dangling from her toes.

And goodness me, next to the bed was a long-missed
item of furniture from my childhood—a leather pouf. In
this case, however, a brand new one made of pale leather
(Doris Day would have loved it), while the pouf from my
childhood was a Red-Indian-like ragged thing patterned
in red, green and brown, on which I had jumped around
with the dachshund and scratched and scraped to encourage him to bite into the leather.

I drew back the curtains—no, there was no need to
pull or even tug at them, the slightest touch sent them
gliding to and fro in the tracks. I played curtains open,
curtains closed a few times over, amazed that there were

tracks in Bulgaria on which wheels ran immaculately, which made me ponder whether I might have formed the wrong impression of the country.

The view of the city from the ninth-floor window was pleasant, the yellow-plastered square below not bad at all.

I unpacked my case and created military order in the bathroom. All very practical, very generous. Lots of free space. Clean. The blinding white oval of the basin was set into a dark, grey-green sheet of marble. Apart from that there was a wall-mounted toilet and a wall-mounted bidet, very popular lately and, in my expert experience, very practical for cleaning purposes.

We had the evening and the next two days free, as most of us wanted to meet relatives. My sister and I went out visiting our cousins. That was where we met Rumen, whom Atanasia had already recommended as a guide. We adventured away linguistically, in an excited mishmash of German, English and French. Rumen spoke fabulous German and seemed to know his way around both Western and Eastern Europe. My sister, who has a tendency for carefully dosed acts of theatre, stood up especially to make a small speech, polite but cordial. How glad we were, she announced, that he had declared himself willing to sacrifice so much of his valuable time for us!

We had no idea *how* wonderfully you speak German, of course, said my sister, placing her fingertips together and then opening them again to hint at applause. Now we're all the more ashamed that we don't speak Bulgarian, she added in her most saccharine hypocrisy. Even back then I noticed Rumen following her every move with his eyes alight. He entered our service that very night by driving us back to the hotel. And yes, we were satisfied with him and quickly switched to first-name terms.

That was last Wednesday. And now? Now, melancholy reigns supreme. My turtle doves are sitting at the front like wistful corpses, silent, not even smoking, my sister merely placing her hand on Rumen's knee very gently now and then. Rumen has never driven so slowly. It's practically a snail's pace.

I'm condemned to silence too. It would be more than tactless of me to exude jollity from the backseat, wittering on about how I can hardly wait to get back to Berlin.

And it all began so cheerfully between the three of us. Rumen had turned up in the hotel lobby the next morning to chauffeur us to the borough of Bojana at the foot of the Vitosha. He was wearing a dark grey suit, and a brown-and-green silk scarf fluttered around his neck, patterned with lilies—really very smart.

Our first trip was to the National History Museum, to the golden treasures of the Thracian princess. The mood between Rumen and me was soon screwed up, as I started complaining loudly about the building. It was one of Zhivkov's many former residences that are now museums. Flat as a square pancake, very broad, very ugly and with an endless staircase up to it. A pompous, extremely run-down building constructed like a divan, influenced by Mussolini's marching style.

Even the staircase! It would have been the perfect place for a legion of blackshirts to practise their braked assaults (if there is such a thing). I pictured myself yelling orders—Run! Climb! Run! Climb! Quick-sharp!

Perhaps I'm drawn to the ugly because I'm permanently looking for proof of how rotten and depraved the world is. The ugly drew me first to the left and then drew the others in behind me. There were tons of blocks standing around inside, unpleasantly white marble blocks, dozens of newly made heroic monuments that had not yet found a suitable graveyard, as Rumen informed us. Every marble block was a gravestone for a Bulgarian hero, whereby these stones were more suitable for ridicule than reverence, as roughly as the blocks were hewn, as amateurishly as the hollow letters were cut into them. The patchily applied gold of the lettering looked shockingly ridiculous.

The low-ceilinged entrance hall was a place to learn what fear feels like. I felt as though my head had been placed in a crusher. It would have fitted the building to see slogans emblazoned across the walls—*The Bulgarian people need the friendship of the Soviet Union like living organisms need light and sun*—but that type of slogan art had gone out of fashion. There was at least John Heartfield's famous poster showing a giant, googly-eyed Dimitroff leaning over a tiny Göring in jodhpurs.

But the Thracian treasures were a delight. I'd never seen such finely worked gold. The word *work* is misleading—the cabinets contained items of astounding fragility, more delicate than wafers, miracle upon miracle, which one might believe had been created by a puff of breath and not with the aid of tools.

Leaving by the rear exit, we arrived in a terraced garden with various pools of water. The water in these pools may once have gurgled or sprayed skywards in bubbling fountains, but now rusty, bent pipes emerged from the mouldy bases. The plants cowering on the ground gave the impression they were disabled—a dust-coated army of crippled pines, tatty hedges, faded grasses, everything taller than two feet drooping in tiredness. Two lonesome plastic tables and three plastic chairs on the patio announced that if one absolutely had to, one was allowed to sit. Rumen tracked down a waitress in a remote corner of the building and ordered tea. She came drudging along half an hour later, bringing lukewarm water and three mummified communist teabags on a greasy saucer.

Late that night, we met an astonishing number of our fellow travellers in the hotel's cigar bar. Dark wood, dark-brown leather sofas, a number of armchairs reminiscent of soft animals. There was a high-octane atmosphere. We bitched about Bulgaria, in the best of moods. Everyone had brought along a sack full of Mafia stories from their relatives. Even considering the lively Bulgarian imagination and subtracting fifty per cent, there were plenty of terrible things left. Law and order? Laughable. Members of parliament beat up other drivers who got in their way, in broad daylight. It was fine to announce on television that Jews and Gypsies were good for making soap. Ophthalmologists forgot to remove the stitches after eye operations and no one held them accountable. Avarice, shoddiness and sloppiness at every turn.

Not wanting to anger the chief, my sister and I held back. But Tabakoff himself was firing off complaints. He'd never seen Sofia this rotten; it was a scandal. The rose-grower cursed the crumbling pavements, there was cursing of the cars parked all the way up to the houses, cursing of the subways where the ceiling panels were dangling down or had fallen off, cursing of the terrible monuments and the gruesome Palace of Culture, cursing of the dirt and grime—you name it, we cursed it.

Kolyo Vuteff's son added a shy objection that he'd passed a market and seen some nice fruit.

Drenched in pesticides, Stefan Gitsin dismissed him. No one checks it at all.

My sister suddenly grew animated. She might not have had a cigar between her teeth but she swayed her cognac wildly in its glass and veritably knocked it back. Her face flushed red. She claimed to be in possession of a medication immunizing her against all the Bulgarian impositions. A thick American novel. Balloonists above the slaughterhouses of Chicago. Dogs that read books. A talking ball of lightning. Balkanesque entanglements of the most amusing kind.

There's no such thing as balls of lightning, the manager in the energy sector declared categorically. His face, also reddened by alcohol, rested on his chest like an udder.

Oh yes there is! said Tabakoff. The whole of Florida's full of the things. I've seen one myself on the beach. Great stuff!

It works, said my sister. It works, because the ball of lightning's called Skip. I can't remember the name of the guy who talks to him.

She took a good glug of cognac and beamed, although no one wanted to follow her into the world of American novels.

Wolfi told us he'd seen plenty of balls of lightning in the National Painting Gallery. As long as the Bulgarians had been content with copying the French Impressionists everything had been fine, but then!

Exploding strawberry jam above wheat fields. Iris stirred the air with both hands as she described a picture.

The rose-grower's terribly sensible wife butted in to express her pity for all the poor people on the streets. We shouldn't talk so much, she implored, we should do something about it.

This put Tabakoff into a rage, reminded of the Red dictatorship by even the most harmless welfare-tinged comment—I've been trying to teach my countrymen how to do business all my life, he crowed, I've dedicated the best years of my life to these idiots! And all for nothing. Isn't that a service to society? Or what?

Alexander steered the conversation back to the less objectionable waters of art. These Bulgarian artists have a sinister obsession with auroras, red and yellow auroras. I don't know where they got if from. Maybe the Futurists?

Stefan suggested confiscating the Bulgarians' paints and brushes. For at least a hundred years.

Wait, said Wolfi, commanding silence with a raised hand. The eighteenth-century portraits, still executed according to the laws of icon-painting and yet completely new and different, are absolutely charming, he continued.

He leant forward and put his glass down gingerly. He didn't have the words to describe precisely what was different about them, he told us, but he was certain they were well-painted, beguilingly beautiful pieces (he really did say *beguilingly beautiful*, astonishing me not for the first time).

They say they have an amazing painting in their depot, my sister announced. *One hundred Bulgarian wet-nurses suckling Stalin*. That was after her third cognac.

Let's not be too quick to pass judgement, Wolfi warned us, thereby successfully defending the honour of the National Painting Gallery.

I turned back my bedcover just before two. In the beatific glow of the bedside lamp, I gazed for a while at the dark windowed facade. A patient silence. Provided you don't enjoy it every day, there's something incredibly calming about luxury.

I was woken early in the morning by rain blown against the windowpanes. I felt a slight irritation in my throat, and since I'm a dyed-in-the-wool hypochondriac who welcomes any excuse to stay in bed, especially in an extremely comfortable, exemplary bed, I decided to spend the day right there. What's the point in walking around a city you can't stand? Perhaps the tickle in my throat was due to the approach of the day on which our father's remains were to be put to rest.

I want to become a blank page, said our father, I want to stop hiding behind curtains and clouds.

We shall see, I thought. I'd be happy enough if you'd just give up the stupid rope trick.

I liked the hotel slippers on my feet. The Do-Not-Disturb sign was soon suspended from the doorknob. I decided to be out of the question for anything else, and went back to sleep under the warm cover as soon as possible.

That Friday was a glorious sunny day. The rain had washed the dirt from the panes. Everything shone outside as if newly cleaned. Having spent so long in bed, I felt as if I'd turned to wood.

Most of us appeared at the breakfast table in dark clothing. We were restless and at the same time inhibited, trying to master the fermentation of our tempers through frivolous comments, but the fussy way we requested tiny portions of scrambled egg from the waiters and fell into pointless laughter revealed that something sinister had us in its grip.

A whip-cracking tablecloth flew through the air at the next table. We could veritably hear the burst starch particles raining down. New guests took their seats, not part of our party.

Stefan Gitsin told a story about the legendary funeral of a Gypsy baron that took place more than thirty years ago in Bulgaria. The baron had had a huge burial chamber built in the Egyptian style, kitted out with furniture and curtains and even a colour television.

Stefan forked up a piece of scrambled egg, which slipped off again. The Gypsy baron had him firmly in his grip. He'd been laid out on a magnificent bed, he told us, wearing his sleeping cap. Slippers, housecoat, cigarettes, whisky—nothing had been forgotten.

And? asked the manager in the energy sector. Weren't there any girls?

Oh yes, there were. Twenty or thirty of them, probably all poisoned or strangled.

We put on our multi-purpose smiles and changed the subject.

With the exception of Tabakoff, who had been busy during the past few days with his new Bulgarian burial business, none of us had taken care of the remains of the dead. He didn't go into detail, merely assuring us everything was absolutely fine.

Necrologies? the rose-grower allowed himself to ask. Yes, obituary notices had been printed and pinned up everywhere, on trees, in the tower blocks where relatives were still living and in the places where it had become a custom to display the black-framed death notices complete with photos.

Tabakoff had chosen Sveta Nedelya for the Mass, a church about a ten-minute walk from the hotel. In bed the day before, I'd had enough time to read up on the building. I was all the more amazed by Tabakoff's choice, and not because the church was any kind of remarkable architectural monument. What remained of it now was based on a mediaeval construction, but Sveta Nedelya had been rebuilt at the end of the nineteenth century.

The church had a sinister side because of 16 April 1925—a day of great horror. Prominent representatives of the government, the military and the royal court had appeared in large numbers for a funeral service. They were expecting the tsar. And then a bomb went off. Screams, ragged flesh; the middle dome collapsed. Rubble, dust, blood, bones—about a hundred and fifty people were killed instantly, a hundred injured, many of them only surviving with severe mutilations.

It had been an assassination attempt on Boris III, who had gone unharmed because he had not taken part in the service. Even then, the detonation fanatics were far from squeamish, in this case communists, as it soon emerged. The church was entirely renovated in 1931. When the communists came to power they planned to demolish Sveta Nedelya to make way for a huge Lenin monument. Perhaps the new rulers were secretly embarrassed by the thought of the brutal bombing that killed and injured so many. But the preservationists protested and the church was rescued from demolition.

Sveta Nedelya is moored on an island in the midst of traffic. When we set off on our march from the hotel, stepping onto Sofia's famed yellow cobbles, I realized I'd forgotten my glasses but didn't dare to leave the group to fetch them.

Everything had been refreshed by the night's rain. The sun had sucked up the puddles, only occasional damp spots to be seen here and there. We'd been warned that the yellow cobbles were extremely slippery when wet. But they were dry by that point. We walked past the tsar's palace and around the back of the Archaeological Museum.

I felt like an object mechanically lifting its legs, and I admired my sister's smooth elegance. She was wearing a dark grey suit with a black trim, black stockings patterned with sophisticated vertical stripes and black patent shoes. The open-backed black gloves and the handbag repeating the motif in leather mesh were perhaps a touch over the top, but I thought they were delightful. I trotted along behind her in my usual black uniform.

Left, right, left, right, leg up, leg down—really, I was walking like the Golem in person.

Gypsy women swarmed around the entrance to the church, offering palm readings. Beggars stretched their caps out to us. We kept close behind Tabakoff, a small glued-together group from which no one broke ranks to dig a coin out of a pocket. Instead of the raised coffin lids customary at funerals, there were black-varnished boards on each side of the entrance, listing the names of the dead. In my stiff state of mind and body I failed to see our father's name.

Tabakoff and old Mrs Gitsin made the sign of the cross three times as they entered the church. The rest of us lowered our heads slightly to hint at a salute.

Inside it was both dark and light, hundreds of candles burning at the front while barely any light fell through the windows. The room wore a hood of night. Tabakoff handed out candles, lit them all and led us to the front. Framed by a sea of candles, black-varnished crates stood on a pedestal.

The crates were only slightly larger than shoeboxes. They could have had expensive boots packed in them;

golden lettering protruded slightly from the black varnish. That much I could make out from a distance. There must have been nineteen crates, seventeen men's crates and two women's crates, accurately aligned on black velvet in three rows of five and one row of three, at a slight slant, probably equipped with stoppers so they didn't slip down.

The church filled up fast, and not only with relatives. More and more curious onlookers crushed in, presumably having heard about the unusual journey of the dead. As I stood around somewhat awkwardly with my candle, fearing it might get too crowded, the choir raised their voices out of the invisible darkness.

I felt as if life were flooding into my every follicle.

I could only vaguely follow what went on during the Mass, what with not having my glasses with me. Much waving and swaying, rather a lot of opening and closing, plenty of to and fro and in and out.

The doors of the iconostasis opened and closed, magnificently dressed priests came and went, sang, read, swayed the frankincense burners, things were carried in and then out again, the holy objects were blessed, the crates were blessed, and singing sounded out over and over again. Speaking and singing, singing and speaking, perfectly interwoven; the speaking (I didn't understand the meaning) drew something like a rock beneath the singing, from which it released itself, while the singing raised the speaking to heights to which reason was unable to follow it. The acoustics were unique. The singing never droned, never grew piercing, swelling at the subtle moments and then withdrawing to silence again, only to collect itself again, resembling the ebb and flow of a calm sea.

Shhh, Father's asleep. Don't be afraid.

Although I usually have problems standing still, am quick to collapse or start wriggling, this singing must have possessed a revitalizing force for the muscles and bones, for I stood still all the way through the Mass.

Tabakoff gave us a wave—the time had come to file past the crates.

Ah, yes indeed, stoppers. Tiny slats of wood nailed onto the velvet.

But I must have been jinxed. I couldn't find our father's name. Was it because I didn't have my glasses? I ought to have recognized it, even in Cyrillic letters. Instead, Lilo's crate leapt out at me, perhaps because her name was given in both alphabets: *Lieselotte Amalie Tabakoff* it said, *née Wehrle, 1921–1981*. Her crate was in a prominent position, in the middle of the row of three at the front.

An elegant shoebox was certainly the right container for Lilo, although perhaps red would have been more suitable, I thought, a boastful shiny red in the midst of the black boxes. I was overcome with a brief tide of woe. It was so unlikely that Lilo wasn't her same old self any more; I wanted to press my childish cheek against her warm neck like I used to.

We went out along a corridor that opened in the middle of the crowd. Outside in the sun things relaxed.

Relieved faces all round. Cigarettes were smoked and jokes told. The traffic roared around us. We were glad the first part had been so uplifting.

Tabakoff hadn't told us how we'd be getting out to the central cemetery. Our limousines were waiting to the left, with only the decorative-lidded cars missing. In their place a funeral scaffold on wheels waited by the side of the road, with a black canopy covered over and over with tassels, a canopy held up by four flower-twined pillars.

We saw our gloved chauffeurs emerge from a side exit of the church, all in a row headed by a priest; they carried the crates with the appropriate care and set them down on the funeral carriage. Once they had delivered their valuable burden they returned the same way to fetch a new one.

Then came the first calamity. Tabakoff blanched at the sight of the horses. They weren't right! Tabakoff had ordered black horses. He'd wanted shiny black exemplary beauties of horses, but what he'd got was one thin brown nag with three tail hairs and one small grey horse.

In a public place, surrounded by curious locals who had come to see the great American Bulgarian, Tabakoff couldn't afford to lose his temper. But he was beside himself, we could tell.

I thought the grey horse was rather pretty. I admit it was rather on the short side, but there was no criticizing its proportions. It shook its head in jolly expectation. I had to stop praising the little grey horse mid-sentence. Tabakoff gave me a piercing look and turned away. The funny thing about the horses was their feather head-dresses. They looked like vegetable garnishes dipped in black varnish.

We got into the limousines. Tabakoff occupied the first one along with three priests, who had trouble finding space for their voluminous robes. The original composition was restored to our car—my sister and I and the Zankoff brothers were reunited. We did have a new guest in our midst though—Rumen. The column moved off at walking pace, following the horse-drawn canopy carriage.

We drove out of town, out to the central cemetery on the Boulevard Maria Luisa, along the tram route. We drove on the tracks themselves. The horses weren't the only reason we made slow progress. Traffic jams kept forming as pedestrians crossed the road in swarms and peered in at the windows, unable to make anything out. It certainly wasn't the triumphal procession Tabakoff had imagined; it was chaos. Our progress was so slow that some of us got out of the cars and walked alongside. For a while there was a tram ahead of the horses, which resulted in an interesting new column of vehicles. We picked up speed on the Lions' Bridge, everyone got back in the cars and the horses switched up a gear. Then we turned off to the left and the road from there to the cemetery was free.

Marco, submerged in a huge suit that made him look like a business magnate fattened by a bevy of man-servants, lowered the window and waved at the people on the street. Summer air mingled with exhaust fumes wafted in.

What a lovely day, he murmured. If only Mummy was here to see it!

Wolfi didn't bat an eyelid as usual, merely pouring himself a whisky and removing an ice cube from the cooling urn, making perfect use of the tongs hanging from the container's handle.

Anyone else want one?

I could do with one too, said my sister, and Wolfi served her.

I watched a film about leafy sea dragons recently, said Wolfi. They looked like they had holes all through them and were kind of crumbling away. And all the way through the Mass I kept thinking, they're full of leafy sea dragons.

I love leafy sea dragons, I said.

My sister laughed so hard she almost spat her whisky. I found it hard to think about anything at all during the Mass, she said once she'd regained control. Least of all leafy sea dragons.

Rumen gave an embarrassed smile.

And then we arrived and the conversation had to stop.

The air was like glass—blue, liquid glass. First-class cemetery weather. The horses brought the canopied carriage safely through the gate, its mounted structure swaying dangerously on the uneven path as the little grey horse nodded its head in a cheerful manner. Part of its headdress had come loose, however, and dangled on the right-hand side.

Green, green, green, wherever the eye could see. The graveyard was apparently a jungle, an exuberant growth of all manner of things. Stalks shot upwards, trees and bushes seemed to be bearing double the usual burden of leaves. Only the main paths and the very fresh graves were free from vegetation.

The priests strolled behind the carriage, constantly swinging the incense burners. Tabakoff handed out more candles and lit them. Most of the burial sites looked smaller than the graves in our cemeteries. There were tin Christs under weather-beaten iron rooflets, angels holding strange tubes—perhaps writing angels?—angels with their hands pressed together, oil lamps everywhere, and we saw old women topping them up from bottles of oil.

Beyond the main path the graves were even closer together. They say a man was buried in his Porsche in one of Sofia's graveyards; there was no room for a Porsche in the rows we passed. Further back, in the Catholic section of the cemetery, there were quads of old mausoleums not laid out from East to West like the Orthodox graves.

Enamelled photos here and there recalled the deceased. I saw a small stone medallion bearing a man's profile and was reminded of the round seal on our grandfather's philatelist-Esperantist folder. A terrible fashion had caught on recently—computer-manipulated photos applied directly onto the polished stone using a black-and-white linear technique.

Even the angels had turned state-of-the-art.

And then it came into sight, the monument to a recently deceased gangster. He was depicted life-sized on a polished pillar, complete with monobrow and cell phone raised to his right ear. The front of a Mercedes peeped out behind him with the registration plate *SIMO*, no doubt his nickname, for the young man who had bitten the dust at the age of thirty-three was called Simeon Valentinov Angelov. (Rumen helped me decipher it, although, with a little patience, I'd have managed on my own.)

Angelov—a common angelic name in Bulgaria. We had three of them among our ranks, one in a crate and two alive and well, albeit with a smart *ff* at the end, the old-fashioned transcription that lends the name a greater dynamic. An angel with a *v* at the end comes across as rather limp, not capable of flying; he's hardly lifted off from the ground before he lands softly and clumsily in the mud.

He's got very feminine little breasts under his sweater, I said to my sister, don't you think?

He has, said my sister. And what a darling splayed energetic hand with the Rolex round it. I wonder if it's still ticking?

The gravestone was shaped like a sinus curve at the top, with two slightly back-set extensions on either side, rather like a long pair of ears, the left one bearing a black cross on a white background.

Simo and his telephone had, of course, captured all our attention; many of us had stopped to look and now we had to catch up with our carriage at a natty pace. The horses lollopped past modern but thoroughly battered walls of caskets, dusty plastic decorations in the niches. There followed a group of graves without crosses, deliberately simple. Rumen whispered in my ear that they were the graves of former Politburo members. Crosses were not the done thing for them.

Rumen and I wandered along side by side for a while, abandoning the subject of the Politburo in favour of our families, and I realized that he had known my sister and me from stories since he was in short trousers, perhaps not always correct stories. We had even met on my first trip to Sofia, which I couldn't remember at all, embarrassingly enough.

Tabakoff's monument helped us out of our tight spot.

Is that what I think it is? asked my sister, rather superfluously.

Addio for ever, I said. That's where they're going to go.

It was big, white and either silly or impressive, depending on the eye of the beholder. It had an almost three-metre, rather broad base with the names of the Stuttgart Bulgarians chiselled into it, and above that the grave niches rose in offset composition, leaping forwards and backwards. Like in the church earlier, the order consisted of three rows of five at the top and one row of three niches at the bottom. Beneath each cavity the name of the future inhabitant must have been engraved again in smaller writing, although I could only assume so.

If the whole structure had been made of adobe, one might have thought of a miniature pueblo, set up for display purposes in the courtyard of an Indio museum. What didn't go with a pueblo, however, was the little brass doors in a woven waffle pattern attached to each grave niche. They stood invitingly open.

They won't survive three days here, said Rumen. Who won't? asked my sister.

The brass things. Much too expensive. They'll be dismantled any minute.

And then the chauffeurs stepped into action again, having stood discreetly aside up to that point. They fetched ladders from behind the monument and set them up, the most agile of them climbing to mid-height and their colleagues passing them one crate at a time. The chauffeurs must have been practising, for they were as slick as a ballet, and even a small obese one who broke out in something of a sweat completed his task with grace. The most surprising thing for me was that they managed to stow the correct crate in the correct home without hesitation, starting with the top row, left to right. Once the crate was inside, the key-holder climbed the ladder—he was one of the drivers of the star limousines, a sedate older gentleman—closed the brass doors and locked them. He did so carefully, gave the knob of each now locked door a test shake and then stroked it gently with his gloved hand. Next came the oil-lamp man, another of the chauffeurs, placing a lamp before each niche and lighting it.

To accompany all this, the incense burner was swung and the priests prayed and sang by turns. Then a trembling Tabakoff handed his candle to the rose-grower and read out a speech, planned in two languages, part-German, part-Bulgarian. He got his tongue so twisted over something along the lines of *eternally our territory* that he simply skipped all the rest of the German section and sought refuge in his native language.

Was I surprised that no father put in an appearance? Not behind the green bushes, not in the sky's brightness and nor in the distance on the peak of the Vitosha.

It must have been one of those days when nothing, nothing at all could tempt my miracle-addicted tendencies. The sky is formed out of many millions of fathers, I thought, their mucus, their tears, their semen, so it's foolish to try and make out your own father among them. Although the idea went against everything I was accustomed to—from our father up to then—my thoughts were locked and I couldn't occupy my mind with the matter any longer.

There's no hassle when you've turned into wood.

I hadn't even noticed which niche our father was put into, I was so distracted by the climbing chauffeurs' performance. He had to go into his hutch without flowers. Some of us had the chauffeurs place blood-wet roses or lilies on the base. Not we Kristo daughters.

My sister didn't exactly attract attention through her pious behaviour; at most because of her nervous digging through her bag and multiple handing out and taking back of candles from Rumen. I managed to stand still, clutching my light without attracting attention.

Not a single butterfly landed on my finger and lisped, it's me.

You can all get stuffed, said our absent father. No, it wasn't him, of course, it was me on his behalf, soundlessly as ever. Someone had to pretend on this important occasion that there was a father, and say something fatherly, whereby the getting stuffed was malicious invention, as our father was always—how do they say?—averse to such words.

Perhaps, I thought, perhaps everything will go smoothly for me, wheels under Tabakoff, wheels under the chauffeurs, wheels under all of us, because—yes, why exactly?—because less than little is left of him, or nothing to be precise. Perhaps the jar full of paternal crumbs is just a trick of my mind. The crate might contain dirt or the cryotechnically shaken tibia of the inhabitant of the neighbouring grave, shovelled up accidentally.

Tears?

Nope.

A bit of handkerchief snivelling?

No.

Two or three balmic sentences?

None.

That's that then, I said to my sister, and she echoed, that's that.

She really is my sister, I thought, she thinks the same way as I do when it comes to the crunch.

Something took flight—a hat. But no, it was just the hat of a funeral party gatecrasher, who had joined us in the hope of a decent lunch.

There was a funeral party, of course, with many, many guests, and it was as lavish as we had come to expect of Tabakoff.

Ought we to eat together before our flight? Although I do feel a slight pang of hunger, I don't say anything.

Such a banal thought might seem out of place, now that my turtle doves' sorrow could easily fill the Sofia airfield, including all the take-off and landing runways. It's up to the two of them how they want to spend their last couple of short hours.

And now we're already on the edge of town in the middle of tower blocks, at the sight of which I close my eyes in piety, not wanting to take this hideous image of Sofia onto the plane with me. We turn left and have reached the road to the airport.

Now my eyes are open again, and lo and behold, a black jeep approaches in the overtaking lane and stays alongside us. As if by magic, the tinted windows turn transparent. Our father is behind the wheel and our mother beside him, both staring stubbornly straight ahead, him wearing his driving cap as always, we daughters perched motionless on the backseat as if painted on.

The dead bide their time, they come in person and not only in the inky slough of the night. I, however, keep up a cool courage. I have at least managed to live longer than our father and to lead a more friendly life than our mother. It's not love that keeps the dead in check, I think, only good-naturedly indulged hate.